Leslie C. Youngblood

Praise for *Love Like Sky*

"Brims with charm and compassion. Readers will immediately be rooting for G-Baby, a girl with the biggest heart, trying her hardest to help everyone around her."
—Vashti Harrison, *New York Times* bestselling author of *Little Leaders*

★"An openhearted, endearing, and unforgettable debut about the challenges of friendship, growing up, and the boundless love of family." —*Kirkus Reviews*, starred review

Praise for *Forever This Summer*

"A glorious, bighearted, and joyful novel!"
—Jewell Parker Rhodes, *New York Times* bestselling author of *Ghost Boys* and *Black Brother, Black Brother*

"The characters and setting in *Forever This Summer* are depicted with such clear-eyed tenderness that I felt like I was visiting with them—on their front porches or in the diner booth. Youngblood's writing sings: I would follow her stories anywhere." —Linda Sue Park, Newbery Medal winner

★"Packed with important life lessons, this story is also a captivating tale of summer adventure and mystery."
—*School Library Journal*, starred review

FOREVER THIS SUMMER

LESLIE C. YOUNGBLOOD

LITTLE, BROWN AND COMPANY

New York   Boston

Little, Brown and Company
Hachette Book Group
1290 Avenue of the Americas, New York, NY 10104
Visit us at LBYR.com

Originally published in hardcover and ebook by Little, Brown and Company in July 2021
First Trade Paperback Edition: June 2022

Little, Brown and Company is a division of Hachette Book Group, Inc.
The Little, Brown name and logo are trademarks of Hachette Book Group, Inc.

The publisher is not responsible for websites (or their content)
that are not owned by the publisher.

The Library of Congress cataloged the hardcover edition as follows:
Names: Youngblood, Leslie C., author.
Title: Forever this summer / Leslie C. Youngblood.
Description: First edition. | New York : Little, Brown and Company, 2021. | Audience:
Ages 8–12. | Summary: When eleven-year-old Georgie and her sister Peaches relocate
to Bogalusa, Louisiana, with their mother to help their Great Aunt Vie, Georgie
becomes involved in the search for the truth about her new friend Markie's mother.
Identifiers: LCCN 2020036750 | ISBN 9780759555204 (hardcover) |
ISBN 9780759555228 (ebook) | ISBN 9780759555211 (ebook other)
Subjects: CYAC: African Americans—Fiction. | Friendship—Fiction. | Family
life—Louisiana—Fiction. | Louisiana—Fiction.
Classification: LCC PZ7.1.Y8 Fo 2021 | DDC [Fic]—dc23
LC record available at https://lccn.loc.gov/2020036750

ISBNs: 978-0-316-10321-3 (pb.), 978-0-7595-5522-8 (ebook)

Printed in the United States of America

LSC-C

Printing 1, 2022

To my parents, Winston and Daisy M. Raby,
who welcomed me home when I needed it most.
I'm forever grateful.

1

BABY

When Mama told me that we were going to Bogalusa, Louisiana, for the summer, I should have said, "Even if dollar bills grew on oak trees there, I'm not leaving Atlanta." Of course, I hadn't had the nerve to say that, but it didn't cost a thing to imagine. Now I'm stuck here. And to be honest, it stinks. Not the people but the factory that runs twenty-four hours a day—the paper mill. The funk smells like that time my best friend, Nikki, left her egg salad sandwich in her locker over a three-day weekend—pew-ew.

"Georgie, did you run that vacuum like I asked you to?" Mama yelled from the top of the stairs. "I'm expecting company a little later."

"'Bout to do it now, Mama," I called.

My summer had come to this: daily vacuuming instead of creating dance routines with Nikki—but with no homework to worry about. Free*dom.*

Mama was upstairs taking salmon croquettes to my great-aunt Vie, who taught Mama to make them while other kids were making mud pies, Mama told me.

Aunt Vie was seventy-six and the main reason why I didn't pack a bag and start walking all four hundred and thirty-five miles back to Atlanta. She founded our family diner, Sweetings, and ran it for nearly fifty years. I even heard that Aunt Vie knew every customer by name, but now she doesn't even recognize her sisters—my great-aunt Essie, Grandma Sugar—Mama, or me these days. Mama said I'd been in this house before, but I don't remember. Even when I squeeze my eyes real tight and concentrate, I can barely recall the time I met Aunt Vie at the family reunion. Aunt Vie didn't want to forget stuff. It was because of the Alzheimer's, which is like a big bully that takes stuff that doesn't belong to them and won't give it back.

I went to the hall closet and pulled out the vacuum cleaner. The top shelf was stacked with three versions of Scrabble, other board games, and tons of books. I yanked the vacuum out of the closet, and its cord was a tangled mess like a garden hose.

While I worked to straighten it, Mama eased downstairs and eyed me like she'd found me lounging by the pool drinking a slushie, another thing I missed about Atlanta. Well, Snellville, Georgia, actually. Snellville is where Mama, my baby sister, Peaches, and I live with my stepdaddy and fifteen-year-old stepsister, Tangie. Frank couldn't get the time off work, and Tangie stayed with him. I tried to get out of coming when I realized she wasn't. No go. Daddy lives in College Park, which is close to downtown Atlanta, with his new wife. "Snellville after Splitsville" is how Nikki summed it up. Even when I say it now, it sorta makes me smile. "Splitsville" sounds better than "divorce."

While I was thinking about what I was missing in Atlanta, Mama surveyed the living room. It had a green velvet couch with wooden feet. Two cream-colored high-back chairs. And all the lamps had shades as fancy as Aunt Vie's hats.

"I thought I'd asked you to vacuum earlier."

"You told me to wait, remember? You didn't want to wake Aunt Vie."

She walked over to the curtains and parted them. The sun flooded in. Mama poked her finger in the pot of one of the plants. "Water this one. The rest should be okay."

"Yes, ma'am." I took a breath to get my nerve up to ask the question that she'd said no to two times before. "Once I finish, you think I can work at the diner today? Grandma Sugar said there's a girl who works there named Markie Jean and…"

"She wants you to meet her?"

"Grandma said that we're about the same age." Grandma Sugar lived in Atlanta. She arrived in Bogalusa days before we did. For a week or two during each summer, she comes and works at the diner. In the past I've heard Mama and Grandma arguing about Mama not letting Peaches and me tag along.

"Your grandma mentioned Markie. I met her briefly. She's a bit older than you."

"What does that matter? Tangie's older, too," I said.

"Neither of them nor Aunt Essie have time to train you. There's lots to do there and, right now, you'd be in the way."

"But you said—"

"Not the time, G-baby."

"*Georgie*, Mama. You said you'd call me Georgie from now on."

This time her sigh was so deep her hair rippled like one of those inflatable Air Dancers Daddy had advertising a car sale at one of his dealerships. But she managed, "Sorry. Just a lot on my mind. Everyone is getting used to Aunt Vie never running the diner again. Her health declined quicker than we expected." Mama looked up to the ceiling like it was the sky, then shook her head. "The diner is out today. There's too much I need help with."

"I don't even get to help with Aunt Vie. You do everything."

Mama rarely let me sit with Aunt Vie when she wasn't around. Even when Grandma Sugar said she'd stay at the house and let Mama go to the diner, Mama chose to stay.

"Everything you do around here is helping. Maybe you can go up to the diner tomorrow."

"That's what you said yesterday. Today is *tomorrow*," I said.

"For you, tomorrow is whenever I say it is," Mama snapped. She was going into Mama mode, and I'd never win. Mama wasn't listening to Grandma Sugar or my great-aunt

Essie. She sure as heck wouldn't listen to me. I squeezed the handle of the vacuum like it was one of those stress balls the school counselor gave me when I was "adjusting" to our parents' divorce. I squeezed the handle so tight my knuckles burned. Truth was that I only needed to make the strokes with the vacuum cleaner. The carpet wasn't dirty. The entire house was spotless.

Mama grabbed a bottle of water from the fridge and headed back upstairs. I lugged the vacuum cleaner to the center of the living room and plugged it in. Once it sounded like a herd of cattle were stampeding through, I left the vacuum running and slipped into the kitchen to call the one person who might be able to rescue me.

I ducked in a connecting hallway between the dining room and kitchen. The walls were lined with wallpaper. I ran my fingertips along the floral print and it was tissue soft to the touch. My cell phone felt heavier than usual in my hand while I waited.

"Hey, baby girl," Daddy said. "How are you?"

"Not that great, Daddy." Soon as he asked what was wrong, I said, "Mama barely lets me leave the house. I can't even help out with Aunt Vie. Only thing she wants me to do is stay inside and do chores." One of Daddy's sports shows was loud in the background. Someone was going on about LeBron James.

"Is it really that bad, G...Georgie?" I wanted to thank him for calling me Georgie, but I didn't want to get off-track.

"It is. I can't even walk to the store alone. Mama and I were in the one not too far from here and six-year-olds were in there by themselves, Daddy, Peaches's age. Mama's over-doing it. Can you please, *please* talk to her?"

There was a sound like a ticking clock, and I knew Daddy was tapping his pen on his desk as he thought.

"I really don't want to step in without being there. You know your mama and I have been through a lot to get to—"

"I know. I know, Daddy. 'A good place.' I want to be in a good place, too. And this isn't it."

Daddy's seconds of decision felt like hours. The upstairs floor creaked. Mama was on the move. Finally, he said, "I'll see what I can do, baby. No promises, though."

"Thank you. Thank you, Daddy."

The closing credits to *SportsCenter* echoed, then Daddy started channel surfing, which Mama hated. Frank doesn't even have a TV in his den. He and Mama spend hours together reading the same paper sometimes.

"Hey—" he said.

"I know. . .no promises."

"Long as we're clear."

I nodded like he could see me. "How is Peaches?"

Daddy laughed. "She and Milly are cooking breakfast. Think I smell the burned bacon now."

Peaches didn't travel with us. She was recovering from meningitis, even though the doctor gave her the "all clear." Daddy convinced Mama to let Peaches stay with him and Millicent until he traveled to Texas for business. After a few doctor follow-ups and Daddy reminding Mama that Milli-cent was a nurse, Mama agreed. Daddy might have been

teasing about the burned bacon but I doubt it. The last dish
Millicent cooked for us was some sort of Tater Tot casserole
that I was sure made Peaches nauseous until we found out it
was more serious than a stomachache.

"Tell Peaches I'll talk to her tonight, Daddy. Please call
Mama soon. And...and..."

"And what?"

"Don't let her know I called you?" He was quiet again.
"I'm not playing you against each other."

"What do you call it?"

"She's stressing. Maybe it's taking care of Auntie. I don't
know. I don't want things to get worse."

Tap. Tap. Tap. "You know what would make things way
worse for all of us?"

My shoulders drooped. "What?"

"Your mama and me not being honest. You know how
much it took for her to let Peaches stay behind. After all
that, you think this is the best way for me to communicate
with her?"

"No," I admitted.

I loved the way Daddy reasoned with me. "I'll call her,
but I'm going to tell her that we talked. Not being honest isn't
the way to get what you want," Daddy warned. "Got it?"

"Yes, sir," I said.

"Love you."

Guilt threatened to suck me into the Hoover. "I love
you, too."

After I vacuumed and put it away, not even bothering
to wrap the cord properly around the hooks, I watered the

plant, and was on to do the breakfast dishes by hand, even though there was a dishwasher just sitting there taunting me. Then I thought the doorbell rang, but it was Mama's phone. I could hear it all the way upstairs.

Our science teacher told us that there are over thirty-seven trillion cells in our body. Every one of mine was on edge, wondering if that was Daddy.

"So instead of talking to me, you go and get your daddy involved." Mama stood in the doorway while I finished up the breakfast dishes.

"I tried to talk to you. You're not listening to me."

"Then you try again. What we aren't going to have is you calling your daddy behind my back," she said.

"It wasn't behind your back. He said I could call him anytime. It was one of those times."

"Georgiana Elizabeth Matthews. You know what I'm talking about. You called him to 'talk' to me about you not traipsing up and down these Bogalusa streets?"

"I don't want to traipse, Mama. You said that I could work at the diner. You said you'd stop treating me like I was a toddler. We've been here for more than a week and I've done nothing but clean up and sit on the porch."

"We drove to Covington to go to the movies just the other day."

"Yeah, just you and me. Fun times." I wanted to take it back because it really was kinda fun, but not the same fun I'd have with Nikki, or even my stepsister, Tangie, who went to the movies with her boyfriend most of the time.

"You supervise my every move. I can't even sit with Aunt Vie alone. Feels like I've been grounded without doing anything wrong."

I bit my tongue because my voice was going to crack. I was not, no way, going to stand there with my hands in dishwater and bawl like a baby. Mama walked over to the refrigerator and ran her hand along the piece of masking tape that read *fridge*, then another that said *cabinet*. Most of the appliances were labeled. The words were used to help Aunt Vie remember. Mama said they weren't helpful anymore, but no one had the heart to remove them. Mama stared at me as if there was a label on my head, too—*BABY*.

"Go on up and get dressed. As soon as Auntie's company comes, we'll go."

"I know the way to the diner from here. It's about five blocks and you make a right at that stop sign."

"No. It's a left. That's Columbia and Fifth. But I said that I'll take you. Everyone isn't always friendly when they know you're not from around here. Don't ask me how they know, but they do. I don't want any problems."

I took quick breaths until it felt like my insides were twirling around like a cyclone.

"You've let me walk farther than that at home," I said. "And when we used to live in College Park, Nikki and I walked everywhere. I know how to mind my business. Not talk to strangers."

"Correction, you didn't walk *everywhere*. You never have. And that was a neighborhood that you grew up in.

People knew you and you knew them. You've never been by yourself here before. It's not all as calm as you see from the porch."

Tangie and I read all about the history of the town, everything from it once being called Klanstown, USA, to the establishment of a group of men who helped the town fight back, the Deacons for Defense. We even watched a movie about it.

"Tangie and I read all the bad stuff. It was a long time ago, right?"

"Not even all about that. Kids bound to single you out. It was like that when I was a kid when someone wasn't from around here. You're not used to that."

"I'm not a baby. I've dealt with bullies before. And I change schools this year. I have a lot of new kids to meet."

Mama folded her arms. "Okay, okay. You can walk up there by yourself."

"Thank you," I said.

"You're eleven, Georgie. Eleven isn't thirteen. It isn't fifteen. And it's certainly not sixteen. Out of the two of us, I'm the only one who's been all those ages and then some. Your daddy did make me see that I'm being a bit overprotective. I do trust you when you're not in my sight, remember that, okay?"

"I will, Mama!"

"You'll meet a lot of people at the diner—not everyone has your same values or upbringing."

"Sorta like school. Everyone is different there, too." She did that stare-into-your-eyes thing that mamas do when they're deciding if what they said was enough.

"The diner and straight back home. You hear me? Straight back," she added.

"Yes, ma'am."

She pulled me in for a hug. I savored it for a moment, but as soon as she released me, I tore up the stairs to go freshen up. I couldn't wait to get out of the house, alone.

2

THE SUMMER ME

As soon as I left the gate, I glanced back and was happy to not see Mama waving me off like I was on my way to sleepaway camp. Aunt Vie's house had a wraparound porch with ivory wicker rocking chairs with comfy cushions, a porch swing, and plants drooping with pinkish blooms. The porch was like an outdoor living room. Mama said my great-grandfather built it with money he earned working at the Great Southern Lumber Company. Grandma said that he built it with bricks so it would be harder to burn down if any of the white men in town thought he was getting "too uppity."

The other houses on the street weren't as big and were close together. Only a few of them had trees so big they blocked the sun. Most sat behind link fences burrowed into red dirt. A couple homes had netless basketball hoops at the end of driveways. Kids pulled them into the street when traffic was slow. At night I'd hear the bounce of a ball, the rattle of the rim, and that's what I'd fall asleep to.

Aunt Essie said that during Hurricane Katrina, trees fell on houses and churches. And that some neighbors cut down trees on their property scared it would happen again. But Grandma said my great-granddad planted that oak tree in the front yard and if Katrina didn't uproot it nobody was about to cut it down. Even the thought of Hurricane Katrina made me glance up to the sky and wonder why something so scary had to happen. I was a baby when Katrina hit. The only thing I knew about it at first was that it had the same name as Mama. Then I saw pictures of all the damage it had done and cried for people I didn't even know. Mama said that's okay.

As I walked, the scent of the paper mill reduced from old egg salad to a sweaty sock. But for the first time, it didn't bother me one bit. I got to take in the town on my own, and if that stench was a part of it, bring on the funk. Odder than a paper mill that stunk up the town was the fact that Bogalusa, the entire state of Louisiana for that matter, doesn't have counties like all the other states, it has parishes. The reason was complicated and had some-thing to do with different sections of the town belonging to the same church and having the same priest, like a huge congregation.

My definition of parishes was fuzzy, but I loved the fancy-sounding name better than "counties." I knew for sure that Louisiana had sixty-four of them, and I was smack-dab in the middle of Washington Parish for the first time on my own.

Everyone I walked past spoke or nodded. Nothing like Mama said at all. One lady stopped and said, "Now, just one second." She carried a covered dish with a seafood aroma so strong it cut through the odor of the paper mill.

"You must be Elvie's grandniece, G-baby."

I wanted to say Georgie, but I said, "Yes, ma'am."

"I'm Mrs. Corine. One of Vie's longtime friends. I'm on my way there now. Girl, you couldn't look more like your mama if you tried." Mrs. Corine managed to fold her arm around the dish and grab my hand and twirled me like she wanted to dance. Everything my training bra held jiggled and the twisting turned my shorts to the most awkward angle. Then she lobster-clawed my cheek and pulled a hunk of it between her fingers.

"It's good to meet you, ma'am. My mama is expecting you."

"Call me Mrs. C, G-baby. You're just as pretty as your mama was at your age. Would you look at this hair? As thick as Vie's bowl of gumbo."

I tugged at one of my twists. "Thank you."

"What a dutiful daughter you are to come help your mama see after Vie." I thought back to the way Mama monopolized Aunt Vie's care, but I didn't say that, of course. "I hope you're having some fun, too, in ole' Bogalusa."

The way Bogalusa flowed from Mrs. C's lips was completely different from the way I stressed each syllable—Boh-guh-loo-suh. Mrs. C's way had a rhythm that sounded like some kinda dance they did in the old days. Let's do the Bogalusa Boogaloo!

"Look at me, just holding you up." Right after she pinched my cheek again, she waved to another lady across the street and I was on my way.

With each step, I wondered what task I'd do first at Sweetings. I bet the neighborhood kids stopped by for cake or a soda, or as Aunt Essie called sodas, a "cold drink." Maybe I'd serve them. Maybe Aunt Essie would let me run the register. I'd tell her about my A in math and how I usually handle the money at all the bake sales for the step team Nikki and I belonged to, the Georgia Peach Jam Steppers.

I'm glad Mama mentioned the street name, because I was so lost in my thoughts that I almost walked clean past it. The stop sign was at the corner of our street, Fifth Street, and Columbia next to a fire hydrant. Then I remembered Mama saying, "It's a left." My stomach roller-coastered thinking of the possibility of getting lost. I could hang up the idea of even walking out on the porch alone. My nerves settled when I saw the sign that said *Boga-Littles Day Care.* And remembered that name from when Mama and I drove by the diner on our way to Covington. *Thank you, Boga-Littles.*

I walked like I was in the Olympic trials for racewalking, which Nikki and I couldn't believe was a *real* sport. And it's not as easy as it looked. Within a couple minutes, the diner was in sight. I stopped and wiped my forehead.

The standalone building had an emerald-colored awning with scalloped white edges. The front of the building held a huge window, but SWEETINGS FAMILY DINER written in block letters and a picture of a barrel of gumbo teeming with loads of shrimp and crab legs obscured most of the view inside the restaurant. Right outside the door, an A-shaped chalkboard listed the breakfast special: *Fried Catfish or Whiting, Grits, Toast, Home Fries, Coffee, and Orange Juice.* Grandma Sugar's fancy cursive writing floated on the board like skywriting.

Even though I thought I'd given myself a minute to be what Daddy called the three Cs—"Cool, Calm, and Collected"—I opened the door with such force I almost fell in. Sweetings was like a classroom-sized gallery with pictures of ole-timey singers and musicians on the wall. They were all framed and had signatures scrawled across the bottom. And just like Otis Redding, whose "The Dock of the Bay" rang out, I'd heard of most of them from Grandma Sugar or Daddy. "This here is Bluesman food," B. B. King wrote on his picture. He had his eyes closed, clutching his guitar, Lucille, with sweat rolling down his face.

Grandma Sugar and Aunt Essie were busy with customers. There was a small podium where guests stood who were waiting to be seated.

I waved to Grandma Sugar. She blew me a kiss back. "Be right there," she said. I eased over to the side and continued looking at all the pictures of singers, musicians, and even some local activists. And the one Grandma Sugar called "The Queen of Soul," Aretha Franklin, wrote, "Food for the Soul. Thank you, Ms. Vie," her hair as high as Mama's wedding cake.

Then someone said, "Are you here to pick up an order?"

When I turned to face the voice, my tongue flapped, but I couldn't spit out words.

Her voice wasn't high or squeaky but a little on the alto side, and her words were clear and pronounced like she was a teacher's aide. I tried hard not to stare at her, not to notice what I couldn't help but notice.

"Uhm. Uhm. I'm not a customer. I mean not a regular one. You're Markie Jean?" The cowbell above the door dinged and two ladies walked in wearing scrubs. I hadn't paid attention to the bell when I entered.

"Yep. Let me know if you need anything," she said and moved on to the ladies. "Got your to-go orders coming right up," she said and headed to the back.

Grandma Sugar sidled up and kissed my cheek. Aunt Essie caught a quick breather and waved.

"What took your mama so long? I've been telling her to let you come down here and work for a few days now," she said and called for Markie Jean to join us.

"One oyster po'boy, one catfish, two orders Cajun-fried pickles. One slice of chocolate cake and one lemon. Thank you," Markie Jean said and sat the order on the counter as Aunt Essie rung them up. Markie Jean hustled over, stuffing a tip in her apron pocket.

"Markie Jean, this here is my oldest granddaughter, G-baby. You two about the same age, right?"

"Georgie, Grandma."

"Sorry, honey. I remember you telling your mama and me that. But wasn't it Gigi for a minute or two?"

"Yes, ma'am. But it's just Georgie now," I said, feeling my feet start to sweat.

"I'm right about y'all being around the same age?"

"Not so much. I'm twelve and a half," Markie Jean said.

I stuck out my hand to shake hers. Markie Jean stared at it like I was holding a flopping fish. If it wasn't for Grandma Sugar, I bet Markie Jean would have left me hanging. Finally, she shook it and I felt like the dorkiest girl in all of Bogalusa.

Unlike the Costco three-for-twenty short set I wore, Markie wore her apron over a T-shirt that had a faux bow tie and jean shorts that had a satin stripe down the sides like tuxedo pants. Tangie and Nikki would greenlight her outfit, even with the apron. Her skin was the color of those brown eggs that Mama bought from the farmers market. Her hair was thick like mine but in neat cornrows that let out into an Afro puff. It glistened like she'd just sprayed it with oil sheen. Her legs were sort of like mine. She'd seen action: scrapes, scratches, and cuts. Way more than the one bruise that I had on my knee from a run that went wrong.

But even though I tried to stop it, my eyes returned to her arms. One was long like mine, but the other didn't come down all the way. When one of Aunt Vie's friends who had a folded-up pant leg and empty space where a leg should have been had stopped by the house, I didn't stare. I'd met older people without a leg before, but never a girl, especially a girl around my age, with a halfway arm.

"I'm almost twelve," I said. When she caught me looking, I made eye contact with her and was pretty much too embarrassed to blink. She squinted, which said to me, "I saw you staring—don't try to play it off."

"Georgie started saying 'almost twelve' a month after she'd turned eleven," Grandma Sugar said.

"I didn't, Grandma."

The cowbell rang, and three new customers entered.

"Pardon me, please," Markie Jean said. She went over and escorted them to a booth. "Welcome to Sweetings Diner." She wiped down the tabletop and seated the customers. Then she bustled back with water, complete with lemon wedges on the side, and took their orders, all like she was a *real* teenager with a *real* job.

There she was, not much older than me, dashing around the diner like she ran the place. I had to plot, plan, and unleash Daddy as my secret weapon to get out from under Mama's thumb. As I stood there eyeing Markie doing the job that I thought I'd have this summer, I didn't want to acknowledge the twinge of jealousy that made my skin tingle. Why was she allowed to work in the family diner and I wasn't? For all the reasons I thought Mama wanted me to stay close to her since we'd been in Bogalusa, something told me the biggest reason wasn't that big at all. She was strutting around with her Afro puffs and freedom, taking orders, collecting tips, and all with a triple scoop of confidence and attitude. Pretty much everything I thought I'd do at the diner. The person occupying my spot was Markie Jean: the summer me.

3

WHAT'S YOUR DEAL?

When the diner wasn't as crowded, Grandma Sugar cleared off a booth herself and summoned me from my stool, which I slid back underneath a counter against the back wall. At the top was a signed photo of Michael Jackson and the Jackson 5, next to that picture were the Supremes with Tracee Ellis Ross's mama, Diana Ross.

"Georgie, you and Markie Jean come on over here now and sit down for breakfast." She even went and brought us two glasses of water like real customers. She wiggled her fingers and Markie Jean took off her apron. Grandma Sugar flung it on her shoulder.

Since I was so upset with Mama, I'd picked over my breakfast at home, so I was hungry.

"Pancakes and sausage, okay?" Grandma said.

"Yes, ma'am," we replied.

Markie Jean yanked a sleek phone out of her pocket and scrolled. I didn't dare whip out my phone. It was so old that Nikki stamped its embarrassment level: Code Red. I busied myself reading the daily specials that were handwritten under the laminated tabletops.

"Your T-shirt is cool," I said.

"'Preciate it," she said and pretended to straighten her T-shirt's faux bow tie.

A young woman with long, blue braids and a baby straddling her narrow hip walked in and looked at the menu. "Let me have two orders of shrimp and grits."

"Toast or biscuit?" Grandma Sugar said. When it came time to pay, the girl was short and Grandma Sugar pulled out her coin purse and added what she needed. The emerald beads on the purse glistened.

Markie's chuckle diverted my attention.

"What's so funny?" I said.

She stared at her phone and chuckled again. "Nothing."

A few minutes later, Grandma Sugar called "Order up!" as she waltzed over to our table.

The tray was above her head and balanced on her fingertips. She slid plates of pancakes, sausages, and grits in front of us. "Enjoy, and there is plenty more where that came from," she said and strolled back toward the register.

After plopping her phone next to crawfish-shaped salt and pepper shakers, Markie took out a mini bottle of hand sanitizer and flipped the cap as she clicked her tongue. I didn't want to stare again, so I watched her from the corner of my eye. She squirted a bit of the sanitizer on her little arm and then used it to spread the sanitizer around in her palm.

"This stuff lasts me twice as long. You know, with the one hand and all," she said. "Want some?"

I pulled out the one attached to my purse strap. "Nah, I'm fine," I said, unsure if I should say something about her one-hand comment.

Markie Jean tilted her head over her plate and sniffed. Then she leaned back, closed her eyes, and inhaled the aroma the way someone would do after smelling a rose. A second later, she leaned in again.

"Mmm, Double D smoked sausages are the best in the whole wide world," she said, her nose almost touching them.

I sniffed but couldn't match her enthusiasm. "They're good."

"They're local. Made not even twenty miles from here. The plant cranks out about eighteen thousand pounds a day. Went there on a field trip last year."

"How was it?"

"Hog heaven."

She picked up the Double D and bit it like it was a carrot, then buttered her grits. Instead of holding the butter dish so it didn't move, she pushed it against her plate to secure it. I pretended not to be impressed with the way she did most tasks with one hand that I did with two.

As I was thinking of something interesting or cool to say, she said, "So, G-baby, what's your deal?"

"Georgie," I said.

"Sorry, *Georgie*. Short arm. Short memory," Markie Jean said and laughed.

"Forgetting stuff isn't funny."

"Who says it was?"

That ended our first attempt at conversation. I reread the menu a million times, people-watched, and she busied herself with her phone. As we were clearing off the table, Grandma Sugar said, "Let me get those," and loaded the dishes on her tray.

"Thanks," we said.

"What you want me to do first?" I said to either of them. Grandma Sugar scanned the diner. "It's not that busy in here now. Why don't you and Markie Jean go enjoy yourselves awhile..." She probably could see alarm in my eyes. I told Mama that I felt like I was grounded, but that wasn't the same as really being grounded, which is where I was heading. "Don't you worry. Leave your mama to me. You've been cooped up in the house enough."

She reapplied her ruby lipstick and blew me a kiss and winked. Unlike Mama, she let me try on lipsticks so I could "find my color" when I was ready.

"Thank you, Grandma," I said and would have hugged her neck if I wasn't clenching on to a few cool points.

"Stop back later. If not, we can certainly put you to work tomorrow."

Markie Jean checked her phone. "Well, in that case, *laissez les bons temps rouler.*" She strolled toward the door.

Grandma Sugar placed fresh napkins on the table. "You behave yourself, Markie Jean."

"See you later, Grandma," I said, and she winked. I didn't repeat Markie's phrase, but I'd been in Louisiana long enough to know what it meant: let the good times roll. I didn't know what Markie had in store, but I didn't care. This was the most freedom I'd had since I *rolled* into Bogalusa.

"Glad that the good aromas coming from the diner knocked out some of that paper-mill smell," I said and tooted up my nose. We had to agree on that.

Standing outside under the awning, Markie Jean put her balled fist on her hip and puffed out her chest. As she took a deep breath, she lifted her chin to the sky.

"For me, there's nothing like filling my lungs with the sulfuric fumes of our paper mill. Lets us know we're home. Fresh air is overrated," she said.

I tried not to breathe in through my nose. "I just know it stinks."

"You haven't been here long enough to appreciate it. Most Bogalusians know it's the smell of moola. Keeps this town percolating."

"Still stinks," I said.

"Enough relaxing. I have business to take care of. You coming?" she said, already walking.

I didn't bother asking where we were going. My only criteria was that it was not back to the porch. That meant the opposite direction of the stop sign at the corner of Fifth Street and Columbia. And away from my landmark of Boga-Littles. It was time to see more of the town. Neither of us spoke for a couple of minutes. I tried to not act like the open ditches on the side of some parts of the sidewalk weren't a little scary. I could see the huge exposed pipes mixed with debris. What I knew for sure was that I didn't want to topple over. I walked in a straight line like a tightrope.

"Guessing they don't have gullies in Atlanta," Markie Jean said.

"Probably, just not where we live," I said.

"Bet it's all fancy schmancy."

"A few areas."

It was more than a few. Daddy used to drive us to gawk at the mansions behind pointed iron gates in Buckhead's Tuxedo Park, and then onto his favorite neighborhood in Southwest Atlanta, Cascade Heights, which he called the "Black Beverly Hills of the South." I put that out of my mind and tried to think of something interesting to talk about. But it seemed like she already knew what she wanted to say to me before we even met.

"You don't really act like I thought," Markie Jean said.

"What does that mean?"

"Thought you be more conceited. You know, full of yourself."

"Why would you say something like that?"

"Everyone talks about you. You get good grades. But I remember hearing that you took your parents' divorce hard. Grades dipped a bit."

"Whose wouldn't?" I snapped.

"Just telling you what I heard. Not digging on you or nothing. Wasn't your sister sick recently?"

"Meningitis." I hated the word.

"Parents both remarried. And you have a stepsister, right?"

"Yeah, Tangie." Then I thought for a second. "What you know about me and what I know about you is lopsided, don't you think?"

"Nah, probably the way it should be. With two moms,

two dads, a baby sister, and a stepsister? That's family galore. Lots to talk about."

If she only knew that not so long ago the thought of all those changes made me cry and my grades more than "dip." I wanted our lives back the way they used to be until I realized that wasn't going to happen, *ever.* I held up my hand to block the glare from a car window.

"Doubt I have more to talk about than you. You're working and handling things. Bet no one treats you like you're in kindergarten. You have freedom."

"That's true. More than I can handle sometimes."

In an open yard, a few kids splashed around in an inflatable pool. Two women sat on the porch. One was peeling potatoes and the other reading the *Bogalusa Daily News.* Whenever I saw that paper, I remembered Grandma Sugar saying how the paper was shut down for a while after Katrina and still only ran three to four times a week years later, but they still called it the "Daily News."

"Staying cool this morning?" one lady said.

"As a fan on turbo," Markie Jean replied, which drowned out my "Yes, ma'am."

The lady's chest heaved in laughter. "I know that's right."

A splash from the kiddie pool hit me warm as raindrops.

After we walked a few more steps, it was time for me to speak up, flip the script. "Ahem, haven't said much about yourself. What's your deal, Markie Jean?" I liked the sound of two first names. But if she were at Sweet Apple Elementary, someone would have nicknamed her MJ by now for sure.

"Just Markie. Only adults like to say your whole name."

"Don't I know it. And they love to use your nickname even when you've outgrown it."

"Oh, the G-baby? What's that short for?"

"Grandma Sugar says it means Grandma's baby. And Daddy says it stands for George's baby."

She chuckled and laughed into her fist the way some kids do when something is extra funny. And when I realized she was laughing at me, I had a quick urge to yank that puff of hair.

"Of all the things to hate in the world, that's one of yours? What a life."

"It's not that I hate it, but I'm not a baby. That just helps them treat me like one."

"I'm just saying: as far as nicknames go, I've heard worse." She extended her stride. I skipped to keep up. "This way," she directed. Then she stopped. "Did you need to check in with your mom?"

I shrugged. "Why would I?"

"Just asking. Don't want you to get in any trouble."

"I'm good," I said, hearing Mama's voice telling me to come straight home from the diner. I blocked that out of my mind and kept moving.

4

AIDING AND ABETTING

We rounded the corner that took us off of Columbia onto
Lucy Burt Lane. The houses had more trees than Aunt
Vie's street, but only a few of them were towering and close
to homes. Two blocks down, we approached a house that
was various shades of brown with shrubs evenly cut, like
bangs. A big barrel brimming with peanuts sat next to the
door.

A man whose slender body swam inside a warmup suit
called out, "How y'all doing this morning?" and waved. His
foot was on a shovel and his other hand squeezed the handle of it.

"No complaints, Peanut Man," Markie said.

"Good morning, sir," I said.

His eyes locked on me. "You Mrs. Essie's people?" He applied his weight to the shovel. The dirt broke.

"Her grandniece. Yes, sir."

He leaned his shovel against the house, and we stopped along the middle of the gate.

As he strolled up to us, his toes curled over worn sandals and he cracked his knuckles. "Essie told me y'all was coming down. It's good to have you here in the Magic City."

"Magic City," I said. I thought about what Tangie and I had read up about Bogalusa. "That sounds familiar."

His fist opened and his eyes followed imaginary smoke into the air. "In the early 1900s it took less than a year to build Bogalusa to support the lumber company. Appeared just like magic," he said and gave us another helping of the imaginary smoke.

"By those tire people," Markie said.

"Yeah, the Goodyears, but we the ones made the wheels turn. Black people was only fit to clean the toilets at the mill to them but we didn't give up. Not in our nature." He stabbed his chest with his index finger—his thumb was missing.

"My grandmother said that my great-grandfather worked there. My uncles, too."

"Not too many lifelong Bogalusians don't have some ties to that mill. At times for Black folks it's been a blessing and a curse. Rather shoot a Black man and anybody who supports 'em than let 'em join the union." His voice softened. "Don't mind me none. This not the day to burn your ears with all that." Then his eye darted toward Markie like he'd pulled a penny from behind her ear. "You just tell Mrs. Essie that I'll have some peanut soup for her next week. Maybe even some goat."

"I'll get the message to her," Markie said. She ran her hand along the gold Christmas tree tinsel that weaved along the links of the fence and swirled at the top.

"Hope you get to taste some of my peanut butter soup before you leave, young lady. Got the recipe straight from my people in Ghana. Best you ever tasted. Peanuts are in my blood."

"He's a great-great-great-great-grandnephew of George Washington Carver."

"Two too many 'greats' in there, Markie Jean. But I sell the best boiled peanuts in town. I call them the Caviar of the South, trace the roots of 'em back to Africa, though you can do that with lots of southern delicacies."

As loud as a school bell, Peanut Man's house phone blared through his open window.

"Pardon me, please, young folks. I don't mess around with those cell phones, 'cept for emergencies. Don't forget to tell Mrs. Essie I'll be by," he said to Markie and leaped up the steps.

Once he was inside, Markie lifted the gate's latch and crept up the porch steps. She snatched a crumbled grocery bag out of her pocket and loaded it with peanuts.

"Come up. I have another bag," she whispered.

I thought I was speaking but it was just my head moving so hard I thought it was flinging words out. "No. I'm not stealing."

All I could see was Mr. Peanut rushing out of his door

and catching her. And here I was—an accomplice. When I told Daddy that I wanted to be a lawyer, then a judge, he let me watch *Law & Order* marathons as long as I didn't tell Mama. It was paying off now.

I kept my eye on the door. It made me think of how I scolded Nikki when she shoplifted some earrings on a dare. I didn't know if watching Markie steal from Mr. Peanut was any better. Just as I was about to decide to save myself and head back to the diner, Markie shouted, "Let's go!" and jetted off. I mean, flat out, Usain Bolt sprinting.

"You gotta pay for those. You'll get charged with stealing. And I'll get...aiding...aiding and abetting," I yelled to the back of her Afro puff. But I wasn't a tattletale, so I took off, too. The buckle of my left sandal dug into my skin.

"'Aiding and abetting.' Aren't you a smarty-pants? Might need to keep you around."

I hated that those words made me a little proud.

As we ran, the colors of trees, cars, houses swirled together like melted crayons. My legs were nothing but noodles, like when you ride your bike too long. And I couldn't help fearing I could get a bug stuck in my throat.

"Where are you going?" I forced out, feeling at any moment I was going to spontaneously combust.

Markie finally stopped at a clearing. I grabbed my knees, panting like I was in gym class doing laps. Markie hadn't even broken a sweat.

"So what was that all about?" I asked, still trying to catch my breath. "Why steal 'em? If you don't have the money, he probably would've let you pay later. Plus, I could have given you the money."

"First, where's the thrill in just paying for 'em? And two, I don't do charity."

"Oh, so you'd rather get in trouble, *literally*, for peanuts."

"You have a sense of humor." She held out the bag of peanuts to me. I shook my head. She shrugged. "Suit yourself."

Two minutes later, we stopped in front of a shotgun house with iron rods over the windows. Mama said some houses were called that because if you stood in the front door and shot a shotgun, the bullet would go out the back door without hitting a wall.

Markie strolled up and rattled the flimsy gate. "Yo, Scooter! Scoot!"

Seconds later, a boy scurried from around back with a wobbly baby stroller.

"Just cleaning it out for you," he said and paid me as much attention as he did the waist-high weeds surrounding his narrow frame.

Markie forked over two crumbled dollar bills.

"Bring it back this evening. My sister might need it tonight," Scooter said.

"I got you," Markie said and dropped the bag of peanuts in the stroller. He stuffed the money in a dingy fanny pack and disappeared around the rear of the house. Markie grabbed the handle in the center and started pushing. Then she stopped for a second to flatten the canopy.

"You can toss your purse in here if you want," she said.

"I'm good. Thanks, though," I said. "What do you need that for?"

"Are you hanging out with me or interrogating? Which one is it?"

I side-eyed her. Not sure if she was serious. "One doesn't negate the other."

"'Negate.' I like that word. Adding it to my negotiations repertoire." She then gave me a long look. "But I warn you, if you use 'negate' around here with other kids, you're going to really need some running shoes," she said and laughed.

"You haven't answered my question."

"I had a wagon. That went missing. So I rented this."

Guess she'd answer any question as long as it didn't really tell me a thing. For another three or four minutes, we ambled along Hopscotch-colored sidewalks, speaking to people and catching glimpses of others going about their daily business, which included everything from braiding hair on front porch steps or kitchen chairs planted in yards to "fixing" cars or frying fish in driveways. While Bogalusa was unfolding in front of me, I was taking it all in, with Markie leading the way.

If I had the idea of remembering landmarks and street names to make sure I knew where I was, I'd failed. I thought I would use the humongous stacks of the paper mill as a marker but the smoke blew up to the sky like streaming clouds and the distance seemed to change.

"What street are we on?" I said.

"Cumberland...Hold this," she said like she was handing me a dog on a leash. I stood there with the baby stroller, thinking at least it was much better than Great-aunt Vie's vacuum cleaner. "You want anything out of the store?"

"No thanks," I said. *Cumberland. Columbia. Fifth.*

The parking lot of the Food Depot was dotted with cars, one with music blaring so loud I could feel it in my chest.

They were lined up behind a concrete car wash. The banner said *Free Vacuum*, and my heart jumped, wondering if that was a sign I should head home.

For a second I considered it. But when Markie emerged out of Food Depot, with a buggy and two twenty-four packs of water and more peanuts, I needed to see where this was going. After transferring the goods into the stroller, we were on the move again. We stood at a crosswalk and Markie pressed the button to cross. As soon as the light changed, she jetted across the street. I could barely keep up. When we made it across, she said, "If you want to hang out with me, you might need to change those." She pointed to my sandals.

"These are okay," I said, though the buckle was still piercing my skin.

"Suit yourself," she said.

After about fifteen minutes of walking, all the residential buildings disappeared, and we were on a main street with a few fast-food places.

"This isn't downtown, is it?" I said.

"Nah, but if you keep walking straight, you'll run right into it."

I was used to seeing the skyline of Atlanta miles from downtown. "Oh," I said.

The tallest thing around was a mountainous water tower with the green picture of the state and *BOGALUSA* written in black letters. If it had swings hanging from it, it could be Nikki's favorite ride at Six Flags Over Georgia, Sky-Screamer. Last time we rode that, my voice was hoarse for hours.

When I stopped thinking about that, Markie and I were

on the graveled lot that led up to the paper mill. Up close, the paper mill was an iron dragon, resting in a spot, exhaling foul smoke. "This is the farthest we can go," she said.

There were two food carts near the entrance.

"We're gonna sell snacks?" Mama wouldn't approve, but Daddy would applaud Markie's entrepreneurial spirit.

"Correction. I'll be selling. Not to hurt your feelings or nothing, but you need to give me a little space. I need the money. You, not so much. And I know how to hustle. That's a win-win. Have a seat over there. This shouldn't take long."

"You don't know how many Sweet Apple Elementary bake sales I've worked. And one year I sold more chocolate bars than any of the other Brownies." I amped my voice above the traffic and puffed out my chest.

"Okay, Madam C. J. Walker, I get it. You think you can sell. Maybe later. But for now, have a seat over there, *please*. My regulars are used to seeing me alone. You'll cramp my style."

"Fine with me. Your loss." I marched over to the bench. As soon as I sat, I whipped out my phone and googled Madam C. J. Walker. After a million years, the information loaded: She was a salesperson. A millionaire. One of the first Black entrepreneurs. Markie's jab was there, but not as mean as it could have been. Actually, it was a compliment.

A deafening whistle rang out, and the gravel lot flooded with people lolling about and crowding the food trucks. Within seconds, Markie was surrounded. Men and women with jeans, T-shirts, others in uniforms with safety goggles atop their heads milled around. When they cleared, all Markie's peanuts were gone and only a few bottles of water remained.

She closed up shop and pushed the wobbly stroller over to me. I had out my notebook that was not a diary but where I recorded everyday things I imagined. Not personal, though. My daddy keeps a small notepad in his shirt pocket or glove compartment. Says it's better than a phone. I picked it up from him.

"Looka here." She held up a wad of dollar bills. "Not bad, huh? That's how you triple your tips within an hour." She smiled, pleased with herself. "I bet you would have taken your tips and put them in a piggy bank."

"No, I wouldn't."

She wasn't convinced. "Yeah, you got piggy bank written all over you," she said and laughed.

"I do not," I said, thankful she couldn't see the Volkswagen Bug bank that Daddy gave me for Christmas last year.

Markie stuffed the money in her pocket.

"Well, this is where we have to part. It's been real."

"What do you mean? It's still early."

"Yeah. I got a few more things to do. Best to go alone. They are a ways from here."

"I can come with you. Long as I'm home before dark, I'll be fine."

"See, I can't make that promise even. And I'm still getting to know you, feeling you out, sorta speak. Let's not overdo it the first go-round." Then she paused and tossed a peanut in her mouth. "Anyways, do you really want your mom upset with you already?"

I scraped my sandal along the pavement and looked down. "Definitely not."

"Well, there you go. She let you come down to the diner today. And your grandma let you go with me. You don't want either of them to regret that, right?"

"Nah, guess not."

"Go home early, so she'll let you come back tomorrow. That's the way you work it. Mess up now and your short leash is going to be that much shorter."

"Good point." Mama made it seem like hanging out with someone a little older would only get me in trouble, but here was Markie looking out for me. I couldn't tell Mama that because Grandma had already bent the rule for me, and I was the one going to snap it in two if not for Markie. *Cumberland, Cumberland, Cumberland.*

"Do you know how to get home from here?"

"Of course I do," I said with all the confidence I could summon while my eyes searched for a landmark.

"Are you sure? You look puzzled."

"Oh, no. Just thinking what I'm going to do for the rest of the day."

"Well, I'll be at the diner first thing tomorrow. Ms. Essie will call me if she needs me before then. If your mom lets you out again, guess I'll see you."

"I'll be there."

"And seriously, lose the sandals. If you want to keep up with me, you gotta be ready to jet in a sec. See ya." She saluted, then bent down and tightened a bolt on one of the wheels. "Oh, and if you have a few dollars, bring it."

"What do you think I'll need it for?"

"You just never know...incidentals," she said and laughed. After two steps she added, "Go straight home and don't take any candy from strangers. I don't want your face all up on that Walmart bulletin board."

I gave her a lame thumbs-up. I headed the way I hoped was home. When I turned around, expecting to see Markie strutting down the street with her stroller, she was gone. Every time I could, I remembered landmarks we had passed, including an abandoned Coca-Cola building, which was itsy bitsy compared to Atlanta's Coca-Cola world. I felt like I was on a scavenger hunt. Once I saw that beat-up-looking Food Depot sign my heart fluttered. From there I knew I could find my way back to the diner. I would just stop in to let Grandma and Aunt Essie know I was okay.

It didn't matter what it was Mama had for me to do tomorrow, whatever it was, I'd do it as my passport back to the diner.

5

GEORGIE ON MY MIND

The next day, when I readied to leave the house, Mama sat on the front porch like a gargoyle. On the positive side, Aunt Vie sat in a rocker next to her. Since I'd been in Bogalusa, it was the first time she'd sat on the porch.

"Good afternoon, Auntie."

Hugging her wasn't always the best move. Mama taught me to wait. See how she reacts. But this time her eyes widened, and her face lit up. She was like a butterfly. I barely budged, scared I'd do or say something and she would go away.

"How is your day, Aunt Vie?"

She reached out, grabbed my hand, and squeezed it. It was warm and smelled of that lotion Grandma Sugar kept in the bottom of her purse. When I thought she'd let my hand go, she pulled me closer. Mama stood up so I could sit next to her. The grip she had was tight like the way you hold a balloon when you're outside and afraid the wind will steal it.

There was a neighbor watering plants across from us who waved. Mama and I waved back. When Aunt Vie waved, too, Mama and I smiled at each other.

"It's good to see you," I said. "You look so pretty, Aunt Vie."

The wrinkles around her eyes looked like they'd even out with a light touch of your finger. Mama had braided her hair in six plaits and twirled them into Bantu Knots like she styled my hair for Cultural Appreciation Day at Sweet Apple. Aunt Vie didn't let either of her sisters touch her hair the first few days we were in Bogalusa, so I knew this was something special.

Aunt Vie studied me but didn't speak. Then she reached out and ran the tip of her finger along my eyebrow. I closed my eyes and the gentleness of the touch was like her saying "I love you."

" 'Bout time you come visit," she said.

I shot a glance up to Mama, who still had a light grip on Aunt Vie's arm.

"Why do you stay away so long?" She jerked her arm away from Mama and pulled me closer. "Why don't you come more often? I missed you so."

"I missed you, too, Aunt Vie," I said.

And that was so true. But it was also true that I wished that I could have known her better. That I wished I had more memories of us. I hated what was happening to her that made her world like a chalkboard someone had erased.

My heart ached thinking of Aunt Essie trying to label everything in the kitchen to help her remember. I'd give anything if Aunt Vie's memories were permanent, like markers.

We hugged and rocked back and forth. The scent of fresh-cut flowers sweetened the air.

I closed my eyes. "I miss you, too." I teared up. And that was really true. Even though I didn't have memories of her, I knew there were memories of me that were locked in her heart. She'd share them with me if she could. Mama dabbed at her eyes. Since I'd been in Bogalusa, this was the closest I'd been to her knowing me. *Remembering me.*

Mama said she used to sing verses of "Georgie on My Mind" to me. *"Georgie, oh Georgie. Georgie, a song of you comes as sweet and clear..."* Mama said when I visited as a baby that was my lullaby. Mama, Grandma Sugar, and even Daddy sang it to me, as well. But she was the first, and I wished that she could look at me and sing it. Just a verse. And I'd remember it forever.

Easing toward the screen door, Mama said, "Let me go get some lemonade." She held the door so it wouldn't slam behind her. Before she disappeared inside she said, "You okay, Georgie."

"I'm fine," I said. It was a chance to show Mama that I wouldn't do anything to upset Aunt Vie. I enjoyed sitting with her. And even though I hadn't worked with Aunt Essie at the diner, at night we played Scrabble. She said that it was Aunt Vie's favorite board game since they were kids because she loved to spell.

She would have been the spelling champion of not just her school, but the entire town. But the local championships were held at the Bogalusa Country Club and Black people couldn't attend events there. Black women could only cook and clean, and Black men could only be caddies.

"Aunt Vie would have dusted all those kids," Aunt Essie said and shook her head.

"When she stopped wanting to play as often these past few years, I didn't think anything of it at first," Aunt Essie said. "There were so many clues that she wasn't herself."

I didn't know if I liked Scrabble more or less after that moment. Our English teacher taught us about the first African American girl to reach the final five of National Spelling Bee, MacNolia Cox. I wrote a book report on her and didn't know that one of my great-aunts may have had a dream like MacNolia's.

Aunt Vie kicked her feet out a bit to rock. I did the same. I expected Mama to return any second, but her cell rang. Then I heard her talking on the phone to my stepdaddy, Frank. Through the open windows her laughter was soft and girlish like it used to be with Daddy.

I glanced over at Aunt Vie and the question I'd been wondering floated out in the humid air.

"Do you remember 'Georgie on My Mind,' Auntie?... Do you? Georgie, Georgie, such a sweet little girl, keeps Georgie on my mind."

My spirits lifted when she faced me. Mama said that it's possible that sometimes what the doctor called "moments of clarity" come. My knees were shaking.

"Why don't you come to visit? I've missed you so much," Aunt Vie said.

"I missed you, too, Aunt Vie." And even though I didn't

know her like I knew Grandma Sugar, who I've seen almost every day of my life, I heard stories about Aunt Vie, about Sweetings. And I remember talking to her on the phone a few times. I just thought when I saw her again, things would be how I imagined.

Was it okay to miss that? I felt my throat tighten. Maybe it was what Mama felt: a feeling that changing the past wasn't possible but you didn't want to feel helpless. The grown-ups were all doing what they could do. It wasn't Aunt Vie's choice. It was that disease that was stealing memories that belonged to her, to us.

There had to be something that I could do.

I closed my eyes and imagined a way I could help. Mama said straightening the house was enough. But it couldn't be. That wasn't helping beat up this disease. That wasn't stopping it from stealing from other people either. A few kids walked by and just like that, I had an idea.

Aunt Vie squeezed my hand. "Marlashonda Jean. You'll come by more?"

My face fell. "Marlashonda Jean?"

"Such a lovely name. But I know you like Markie better."

I figured that Markie worked with Aunt Vie at the diner. Or even if she'd started working there after Aunt Vie couldn't, I knew Markie had to know Aunt Vie. Grandma said Aunt Vie knew most people in the community. But the way Aunt Vie said Marlashonda and wished that she was there with her, they had to have spent time together. Markie knew Aunt Vie much better than I did. And Markie didn't mention it. Didn't ask about her. My chest heaved. She had those memories and didn't even seem to care.

"Markie Jean?" she called, as if answering my unspoken question.

"Yes, Auntie," I said. Now I felt stupid thinking that Markie was the "summer me" because she worked at Sweetings and had more freedom than I had. Those things didn't stack up to what I was realizing now. Markie had something I would never have: time with Aunt Vie before the bully took over. And that tingle of jealousy was prickling my skin again.

"You won't forget me, will you? You won't forget about me, Markie Jean? I did the best I could." She squeezed my hand tighter. Her eyes were watery with tears that must be falling on the inside.

I didn't want to press her, upset her. But she seemed alert. If she remembered Markie. Maybe I was in her mind, too.

"Do you remember me? Georgie, Aunt Vie? Georgie on my mind? Do you remember that?"

She patted my hand and looked beyond me like all the memories that were escaping her were in the leaves of that oak tree.

Before I had a chance to ask again, Mama stepped onto the porch. In a singsong voice she said, "Got your favorite, Auntie."

I cleared copies of the *Daily News* and *Essence* from the wicker table between us as Mama sat down a tray containing four glasses and a pitcher of lemonade, cloudy with pulp.

Aunt Vie kept rocking. I stood up and let Mama have my seat.

"Everything go okay?" she asked.

"Yes, ma'am," I said. "Is it okay if I go up to the diner now?"

I didn't want to hear about Markie's connection to Aunt Vie from Mama. I was going straight to Markie.

"That's fine," Mama said. "And you know the rules, right? Diner and back home."

"Yes, ma'am," I said.

Clearly neither Grandma Sugar nor Aunt Essie had told her that I'd left with Markie yesterday. And anyway, Mama was focused on Aunt Vie now. Her rocking was so forceful that Mama reached out and grabbed the arm of the rocker.

"The lemonade is here, Aunt Vie," Mama said.

Before I headed to the diner, I realized I'd left my notepad. I needed to start planning out my way to help Aunt Vie.

"Left something upstairs, Mama. I'll be right back."

Once I was upstairs, I could hear Aunt Vie's rocker clanking against the house. When I got to my room, I opened my door and picked up my notepad off the desk. I flopped on the bed. I flipped to a clean page and wrote the one word that had been circling in my head. FUND-RAISER. Before I'd mention it to Mama or any grown-up, I'd do my research. To get Peaches out of the hospital, I did all that I could. But Aunt Vie needs a different kind of help.

When I was back downstairs, I heard Aunt Vie's voice louder than I'd ever heard it.

I walked toward the door until I heard Mama's voice. The sadness in it made me stop, unsure if she'd want me to intrude and make matters worse.

"Where is Hannah? Where is Hannah?" Aunt Vie shouted. "Tell me what you've done with her, Essie."

Ms. Hannah. I'd never met her, but Grandma Sugar said that she was Aunt Vie's closest friend.

There was no use in me trying to help Mama convince Aunt Vie that Mama wasn't Aunt Essie. From the living room, I could see each of them, and I couldn't do anything but stand there. The tears were coming just because I knew how Mama must be feeling. She wanted her auntie back. She made lemonade and wanted to sit and drink it with her. Two other glasses for company that happened along. But that bully was there. It snatches everything away from everyone. My *whole* body was tense. *Calm down, Auntie. Please, calm down.*

"She'll come and visit soon, Vie," Mama said.

Her words were soft and soothing. My heart pounded. I stood there helpless. I hated that disease as much as I hated the meningitis that tried to take Peaches from us. I balled up my fist until my nails dug into my skin. "Please calm down, Auntie. *Please,*" I said aloud this time, though I knew that she wasn't in control.

"You've never liked Hannah. You and Lilly both. Let us be. Let us be."

Instead of rocking, Aunt Vie leaned forward and tried to stand. Mama's hand grabbed Aunt Vie's wrist. Then there was just my heart beating. The world in slow motion. Aunt Vie yanked her hand away and she slapped Mama across the face. Mama's cry of surprise and pain froze me where I stood. I'd never seen anyone hit Mama. And I wanted to shout out but I was scared to frighten Aunt Vie more. Then I saw Aunt Vie sit down. And slowly start rocking again. I ran outside. Mama stood holding her jaw.

"Are you okay, Mama?" I whispered with a voice I fought to find.

I wrapped my arms around her waist. She held me closer. Her chest trembling. "She didn't mean it, Georgie," Mama said. "She didn't mean it. It's the disease. My auntie would never hurt me. She loves me. She's done so much for me. I should have come home sooner. Why didn't I come home sooner?"

"It's okay, Mama," I said. Aunt Vie sat rocking. "You're here to help now. We're both here." Cars continued to ride by. The neighbor from across the street was standing at our gate. Mama held up her hand. He nodded and backed away. Mama kissed my forehead, then spoke into my hair. "I'm okay now. Are you?"

"Yes, ma'am." I knew I wasn't, but I knew she wasn't either. That's just what people say sometimes when they're trying to make the hurt go away quicker.

"Just go on down to the diner. The heat. This heat is too much. I'll get her back inside."

Aunt Vie stared at me. It wasn't that she didn't recognize me, but like I wasn't there.

I went to hug her, but Mama put her arm out to block me like she does in the car when she comes to an abrupt stop.

"Not now, Georgie. Let's not startle her," she said. "And let me be the one to tell your grandma and auntie about this, you hear?"

"Yes, ma'am," I said. She didn't have to tell me why. I'd heard them talk about Aunt Vie's mood changes and "how long" they'd be able to keep her home.

"Get going. We'll talk later."

"Okay," I said.

I wanted to forget the slap. But I was scared to forget anything. I heard about Alzheimer's before, but it was different seeing its effects up close. Aunt Vie had spent all her years meeting all those people on the wall in her diner. They'd all left something for her to remember them by.

And what about her family? Her sisters? Mama? Memories of them, of me and Peaches, were lost in her mind. At that second, I tried to remember every face I'd ever seen, everybody at Sweet Apple. All the good times we shared. It seemed only right that I tried my best never to forget anything. To never take memories for granted. My head ached as I fought. Maybe Aunt Vie couldn't make more memories herself, but I could find ways to make more memories with her. And I knew there was something else I could do.

We did it all the time at Sweet Apple. Once, we raised money for St. Jude Children's Hospital by walking around the track. When I was sitting with Aunt Vie and those kids walked by, it made me think of it. People pledged money based on how many laps we walked. Nikki and I completed twenty laps. Mama and Nikki's parents committed to five dollars a lap. Daddy "went big" with ten dollars a lap. I knew I wanted to do a fundraiser to help with research to find a cure. And I knew just the person who would help me.

6

MY BAD

As I walked to the diner, I had so many questions floating in my head. Aunt Vie knew Markie, so Mama probably knew Markie better than she let on. Why wouldn't Markie come see Aunt Vie? I needed to talk to Markie. When I arrived at the diner and opened the door, James Brown blared from the jukebox. A balding man stood with one hand pressed against it and the other hand fanning himself with a dollar bill.

"You gotta update this jukebox, Mrs. Essie," he said, "but I do love that lunch special."

I looked at the chalkboard behind the counter and read the special: *Red Beans and Rice. Pork Chop or Chicken (Baked or Fried). Cornbread. Unlimited Homemade Sweet Tea or Lemonade. Bread Pudding or Peach Cobbler.*

"Did you fly here, girl?" Grandma Sugar came over and smoothed hair that had loosened from my twists. She then kissed my cheek and held me at arm's length.

"You okay?" she asked.

"Oh, just hot," I said. "I'll cool off soon. Is Markie here?" I asked, looking around.

"Now, did you come here for Markie or to help out today?"

"To help," I said, which was a little bit of a fib.

"Well, could use help wiping down that counter over there and taking the dishes to the back." She handed me a towel.

"Yes, ma'am," I said, and she was off greeting a customer. I cleaned the counter while sneaking peeks out the window, looking for Markie. I piled all the dishes on the tray. Forks and spoons sprouted out of the glasses like antennas. I took them through the swinging doors to the kitchen.

Aunt Essie was standing over a skyscraper of gumbo pots. Steel pans hung from hooks on the ceiling. A griddle that had just recently been scraped clean was still sizzling and three fry baskets hung over pools of hot grease.

"Hey, Georgie," she said. "How you doing this morning?"

"I'm fine, Aunt Essie," I lied.

"Glad your mama let you come over to help today. We're putting gumbo on the dinner special. That normally brings in the crowd....Sit those over there. Somebody'll get 'em. Check with Markie Jean and see if she needs help."

"So she's here?" I said and kissed Aunt Essie's cheek.

" 'Fore day this morning," Aunt Essie said. "Behind that partition there." She nodded to the right, just after a baker's rack stacked with cast-iron skillets.

I sat the tray on the counter and peeked into the pot. "What's all in it?"

"Snow crab, andouille sausage, and, of course, the Holy Trinity."

"Green peppers, onions, celery."

"Bingo."

"Grandma Sugar taught me that. She puts chicken in her gumbo, though."

"There's about as many variations of gumbo as there are beads at Mardi Gras," she said and laughed.

I took another whiff and tossed my head back. "Smells delicious," I said. It did. I was hoping that Markie would hear my voice and come and see if it was me. *Nothing.* So I left Aunt Essie to her stirring and crept around the partition. There, with a gold pair of earphones on, was Markie bobbing to a beat. I hadn't figured out how I'd ask her about Aunt Vie and tell her about my ideas, but I'd know when the time was right.

I was pressed against the table for a few seconds before she looked up.

She uncovered her right ear.

"You into bounce?"

"It's okay," I said.

"That's a no. You're either into it, or you're not."

"Guess not, then."

"If you stay here for any real time, that'll change. Town is small but folks love good music."

"Let me check it out."

"No can do, lil buckaroo. I don't have the clean versions."

"Oh" was all I could manage. Although it was unlikely

that Mama would drop from the ceiling and demand to hear what I was listening to, if she did and I was listening to "explicit lyrics," I was a goner—as in Radio Disney until I was eighteen.

"Bet my best friend, Nikki, dances to it. She's fire," I said.

"What about you?"

"I'm okay," I said.

"One short arm and two left feet. Nobody is picking me for any dance team anytime soon. But I know kids around here who can outdance anybody you see on TV without even trying hard."

The bell in my head was dinging. I tried to calm myself. Markie didn't even know it but she may have been giving me exactly what I needed.

"What are you doing?" I changed the subject, so I could think things through.

"Making grab and gos for the people who don't have time or that much money to sit down for a full lunch. It's a day-old fried chicken sandwich, a slice of pound cake, and a cold drink to wash it all down. Costs less than the lunch special."

"Sweeting's *Extra* Value Meal," I said.

She pointed her index finger at me and clicked her tongue. "There you go." Markie whipped open another brown paper bag and it filled with air. When it stood on its own, she plopped everything in the center of it. To form a crease in the top to close, she pressed it against her hip and flattened it. It was about her twentieth impressive maneuver.

"It's cool, the way you do that," I said.

"Do what?"

"Open and fold that bag. Easy, like you buttered your biscuit when we first met."

She tilted her head as if that would turn me sideways. "What world do you live in that those things are cool? Just say what you *really* mean: It's cool that I can do it with one hand...Well?"

"It's cool that you can do those things with one hand."

"Was that so hard? I'm a regular kid with a jacked-up arm. That's it. I make the best of it. Someone told me once that everybody got lots of obstacles they face every day that make life a little harder. One of mine is visible. That's it."

"Someone like my aunt Vie," I said.

She nodded and said, "Yes, Aunt Vie."

"You're close to her, aren't you?" I blurted out.

"Yeah," she said. And secured a grab and go.

"Why haven't you asked about her? Come to see her?"

"My bad."

"What does that even mean?"

"Means 'my fault.'"

"I'm talking about what does it mean about Aunt Vie," I explained. "I thought she was remembering me today. But it was you."

"Really?" She sounded like a kid for the first time. Then I guess she thought about my feelings and said, "Oh, sorry. She'll remember you soon."

I stepped closer and lowered my voice. "Something bad happened."

That made her stop working and face me. "What?"

"She...she slapped my mom." I remembered my wish

earlier not to forget anything. I hadn't thought about bad memories.

"Dang. I'm sorry that happened, but don't say it was her. That was the opposite of her," Markie said.

When Markie said "opposite" I thought about my parents' divorce. It stole our family from us, but then returned it in a new way. A way we had to learn to love. Maybe Aunt Vie's sickness would do the same thing. I just didn't yet know how.

"While I'm in Bogalusa, I want to do something to help her and other people with Alzheimer's," I said.

"Like what?"

This was my chance. A fundraiser was too generic. What could we do to raise money and give the town a chance to join in? My idea had marinated long enough.

"A talent show," I said with confidence.

She nodded. "Sounds cool. I'll certainly be down to help. You've put on one before?"

"No, but I can't think of a better reason to learn. I'll have more to share tomorrow...Oh, one more thing." She raised her eyebrows and waited. "About when we first met. Guess I sorta acted like a doofus."

"You mean the staring." I nodded. "No sweat. I'm used to it."

"Doesn't make it right," I said. "Anyway, I'm here to help."

"Well, get an apron. They don't play about aprons and gloves when you're in the kitchen. Just get one glove. I pulled two out by mistake. So I got an extra. Ba-dum-bum ching," she said and hit an air cymbal.

"Ha. Good one."

In the far corner there was a coatrack where the aprons hung. I picked up a green one that had a picture of an alligator with a chef's hat on and shrimp, crab, sausage, and all kinds of seasoning dancing around a pot. *How to Make Gumbo, Louisiana Style.* I put on the apron and tied it behind me. I said a quick prayer that my day would only continue to get better.

7

DRIVING-DRIVING?

Markie put on a playlist that had the radio version of some of her favorite songs. She dropped the headphones to her neck, so I could listen in as well. Aunt Essie would call, need some grab and go's, and I'd rush out with neatly folded bags. When I came back after one delivery to the register, Markie had taken off her glove and was on the phone.

"Okay...okay...I'll bring something in a few minutes," Markie said.

Aunt Essie came through the kitchen to go to the pantry.

"Ms. Essie," Markie said, "are you gonna need me much longer? Rosella wants me to bring lunch."

Aunt Essie glanced at the joker-faced clock in the kitchen.

"If you and Georgie could make about five more that should hold us."

"Georgie, you can leave when Markie Jean does. Probably won't pick up again until around three or four."

"Can I stay? You can show me how to do something else."

"Like how to play a mean game of Scrabble," she said and laughed. "This is summer! Your grandma and I want you to enjoy some of it. Vie would, too." Aunt Essie sighed. "It's so hard trying to figure out how she'd want me to do some things, you know. But kids being kids, I know she'd want that. Markie Jean, Georgie can come with you, yeah?"

"Yes, ma'am," Markie said, not making eye contact. Scared either of them would change their minds, I rushed to get more bread for the chicken sandwiches. When I returned from the pantry, Markie was zipping up her backpack. I noticed that two of the grab and go's were gone. Since I didn't know whether Aunt Essie took them or Markie, I didn't say a word.

Markie hadn't said much since her call. Once we were outside, we headed back toward Aunt Vie's. Right before we got to that daycare, Boga-Littles, at the intersection of Fifth and Columbia, she hooked a left. And I mean hooked. Markie turned the corner like she wanted to punch a tree trunk.

"I can go back if you want," I said.

"It's not that," she said. "Not this time, anyway."

About five minutes later, we were at a corner store with *Need It. Got It* hand-painted on a slab of wood.

Three guys stood next to a green-and-gold car that twinkled in the sun. Another guy wearing a Southern University T-shirt straddled a bright red sports bike. They all had huge cups filled with what looked like slushies. Before Markie went in, she turned to me and said, "Hey, you need to wait here."

She stuck her hand in front of me like a stop sign. If she was that serious about it, I wouldn't try to go anyway. "Be out in a sec. And those guys are cool. One is the owner's son." I couldn't say I wasn't a little nervous. I stepped back some and held on tighter to my purse. But then that made me feel horrible, like I was doing it because I thought they'd steal it. But I just needed something to do with my hands. I folded my arms and rocked to a beat that wasn't familiar.

"You're new around here, Lil' bit," the one with the Southern T-shirt said.

"Yes, I'm from Atlanta, Georgia," I said.

Two of them laughed. I knew I sounded silly saying the city and state.

He nodded. "Moms graduated from Morris Brown. Welcome to Boga," he said.

"Thank you," I said, though I'd never heard anyone shorten it like that before. I guess whenever someone likes something, they give it a nickname. That's as far as the conversation with me went, and the guys were back to joking around while the sports bike's engine revved.

Before I could even decide on a stance that didn't make me look like such an oddball, Markie was out of the store. I unglued myself from the concrete and got in step with her as she nodded a goodbye to the guys. Two long subs stuck out of one bag, and she had a tiny black bag that was tied in a knot.

"Be easy, shorties," one said.

"All right, y'all, too," Markie said while I gave a tambourine wave. "Listen up. We're going to where I stay. Rosella doesn't welcome company, so just wait in the yard."

"No problem."

On East Fourth Street, we passed two places that had pool tables I could see through the open doors. The second one, Al's BBQ Pit, had two barrel-shaped barbeque grills side by side in the front of the restaurant. The smoke coming from it was as thick as the paper mill, but the smell made my stomach grumble.

When we turned onto Martin Luther King Jr. Drive, about two blocks from Al's, clotheslines appeared, looking like mini telephone poles. Some had no wires. Others had wires with shirts and pants hanging from them. The house Markie went toward sat on cinder blocks and leaned to the left. The screen was new but torn like it had been slashed. Its color was canary yellow and various shades of dirt. A Big Wheel was upside down against the house, and alongside it was a purple tricycle with plastic fringe dangling from the ends of the handlebars. There were curtains in the downstairs windows, but upstairs, sheets hung as Woody and Buzz Lightyear watched over us.

She huffed. "Be right out."

I stood at the edge of the patch of grass in front of the house. I wanted to give Markie all the privacy I could. I was sure that guardians weren't different from parents when it comes to embarrassing kids.

Markie knocked, then turned the knob. Soon as the door opened, a baby wailed.

"What took you—" was all I heard before the door slammed.

I didn't know how long Markie would be, so I called Nikki: voicemail. Before I tried Tangie, the door opened and closed and Markie said, "Let's go."

As we stomped down the street, she kicked a weed sprouting up through the concrete. In a vacant lot two blocks away, boys were zooming around on four-wheeled dirt bikes.

"Wish I could still drive. All this walking is for the birds," she said and tugged at her headphones.

"You mean you were *driving*-driving? Or just doing parking lot stuff?"

"Parking lot stuff? Like when your daddy lets you pretend to drive while he is in the next seat steering for you?"

"No," I snapped, though that was exactly what happened to me.

"Look around, it's not like I was on the autobahn, but I handled these roads pretty well."

I made a mental note to look that up. She said it with such ease, it seemed like something I should know. "And you could drive with one arm," I said.

Markie steered an imaginary wheel with her palm open like Daddy does. Mama was always at ten and two like on a clock.

"I whipped it like you wouldn't believe."

Even with the temperature feeling like it was ninety-five, I got a chill just thinking about her driving. "That must have been cool."

A puny German shepherd walked next to Markie, and she rubbed its head. After she stopped and opened her backpack, she dug around and pulled out a foiled-wrapped piece of chicken. She unwrapped it and tossed it to him.

Seconds later she'd zipped up her backpack, and we were on our way again. The dog trailed as Markie cut down a narrow street with box-shaped houses with no porch or gates. One house had about five bikes lined up out front, all leaning on their kickstands.

"You girls need a bike, now?" a man said. His accent was the first Jamaican one I'd heard in Bogalusa. He sat on a butterfly-shaped folding chair. "Gotta be tired of footin' it in this heat. This heat made for riding. Thirty-five dollars, nearly new. Two for sixty-five." The skin of the apple the man was peeling spiraled down. His red, green, black, and gold knit cap held what I imagined to be a mountain of hair.

"We good," Markie said.

"These beauties might not be here when your mind change, now."

We walked for a few seconds, then Markie backtracked and stood in front of the bikes. Only when she stopped did he stand and slink toward us. His beard was tangled but it glistened.

"This one best for you. Easy steering, new chain."

"Twenty," Markie said.

"Put too much work in for that. Let it go for, say, thirty. I see the lion in you. Thirty just for you."

Markie opened her backpack and took out a coin purse. It was crocheted around the top and the rest was shimmering emerald beads. She clicked the metal fasteners and pulled out her roll of money.

"Where did you get that coin purse?" I demanded.

"It was a gift," she said.

I bit my tongue. There was a feeling raging in my stomach that I fought back. It looked like the one Grandma Sugar had, but I wasn't sure.

"Twenty-five. That's all I got," Markie said to the man. "Had to return beaucoup bottles to earn half of that, rest is tips."

He thought for a second. "You're not pulling my leg, now."

"No, this is it."

He lightly tapped the kickstand with his sandal and rolled the bike toward Markie. I followed the coin purse as she eased it into her backpack.

She handed him the money. "Thank you," she said.

He nodded and went back to his apple and his butterfly chair.

Markie held the handlebar and I helped with my hand on the seat.

"Probably going to have to practice getting my balance before I can ride it. It's been a while since I've been on a bike. But this will come in handy soon."

"Maybe Mama will buy me one to keep here, then we can ride together."

"Yeah, okay," she said like riding with me or with anyone was the furthest thing from her mind.

I took my hand off the seat for a second and wiped it across my shorts. "Was that coin purse Aunt Vie's?"

"Was. She gave it to me."

I waited until a car whose muffler was scraping the ground passed us. "You sure?"

"What does that mean?" Markie didn't raise her voice or break stride.

"Grandma Sugar has a similar one. They both collected coin purses."

"Aunt Vie loved thrift stores, especially in New Orleans. I get a knot in my stomach when I think about her. So I try not to. Maybe that's not right. But it's sorta all I can do right now. I have other things I need to deal with."

"Like what? Every time I ask you about you, I get nothing."

"Sometimes I don't feel like talking about anything. You learn that when you realize that some people don't really listen. It was never that way around Aunt Vie, though. But then things started to change." She steered the bike straight ahead, her eyes fixed.

"When I'm going through a rough time, talking to my best friend helps or even my stepsister. Sometimes, you might not believe this, but talking to my baby sister even helps."

"Is that your way of saying you want me to talk to you?"

I chuckled. "Yeah, I guess that was my long way of saying that."

"I've been thinking about a lot of things lately," she said and glanced at me. "Nothing I really need to talk about but do. I could use your help."

Honestly, I didn't think I was getting through to her. I was pretty much up to help her any way I could. Selling peanuts, working closer with her at the diner, maybe even helping her run errands for Rosella.

"Sure. Shoot," I said.

"You don't even know what it is."

Soon as she said *that*, I bit my lip and hoped I hadn't done what Grandma Sugar says you should never do: "let your mouth write a check your actions can't cash."

Last time she said it, I told her that one of our teachers said that checks were just about obsolete, everybody was using plastic or a smartphone. She said that may be true, but getting in over your head wasn't going nowhere, no time soon.

I doubled down. "Don't get quiet now. What can I help you do?"

"Find my mama," she said.

I stopped walking and she whizzed on by me like she hadn't said a word.

8

POLYTETRAFLUOROETHYLENE

After Markie knocked me out with "find my mama," she disappeared for two days straight. I felt guilty for hammering her about not visiting Aunt Vie, then dropping my plans for the talent show on her like she didn't have enough to deal with.

"When is Markie coming back?" I asked Grandma Sugar.

"Since she just works for tips, she doesn't have a set schedule. I'm sure she'll show up soon."

I wished I had the easiness Markie had with the customers. I wasn't the quickest in cleaning tables. I didn't have her finesse while serving and I spilled more than I refilled. Aunt Essie relegated me to wrapping silverware in cloth napkins. The way Markie glided around and schmoozed with customers was just like racewalking—it wasn't as easy as it looked.

On the third day, I was just about to turn onto Columbia when Markie jogged up to me. She wore an *I Eat Unicorns* T-shirt and shorts with oddly shaped pockets and draw-strings along the sides. I was a little embarrassed that I had on the same drab short set I'd worn when we first met.

Though I kept walking with Markie without talking, I was practicing the conversation in my head as loud as cica-das. There had to be a way to do both: find her mama and get the fundraiser plans underway. With the diner in sight, she crossed the street and veered to the left.

"So you say something as serious as 'find my mama' and then vanish. What's up with you?"

"Are they expecting you this minute at the diner?" she asked.

"Not this minute," I said. Since Mama was okay that I was going to the diner every day, I made sure I was out the door as early as possible. I liked walking before the sun was on full blast.

"Wanna hang out with me for a while?"

I knew the answer right away, but I waited like it took some contemplation. Daddy said he never accepted a cus-tomer's offer without contemplation.

"You're going to spill it about your mama?"

"Maybe. If I'm up to it. But no promises. Why tell you all that when you might be gone in a few days?"

"I'll be here longer than that," I said.

"You think so, huh?"

"Why? You heard something different?"

She cuffed her hand around her ear. "I hear lots of things."

"Well, so do I and none of them sound like we're leaving anytime soon. I bet I'll be here long enough to do two important things." I held up two fingers for emphasis.

"I'll bite. What?"

"Help you find your mama and put on the biggest and best talent show Bogalusa has ever seen. You and me, we can help each other."

"Not bad," she said and shrugged.

Since that was better than a "no," I didn't push her and kept walking.

We turned off Columbia onto a street called Big Tree. But the thing about Big Tree is there weren't any trees at all. A few people were out taking down laundry. Rows of single-story apartments lined the street. Some doors had welcome mats in front with folding chairs out on each side.

"What's the name of these apartments?"

"Apartments? Is that what they call them in Atlanta? They're projects here." Then, like I'd never heard the term before, she said, "Government housing."

Three blocks down the street, we entered a park. Or what was supposed to be a park.

"What's this place?" I asked.

"McClurie Park."

Swings had been flipped around the top bar of the swing set that was connected to a dirt-covered slide; the missing bars on the monkey bars, the one-eyed caterpillar sitting atop a rusty coil spring, all must have been new back when the diner first opened, which, according to Grandma Sugar, was in the early 1960s.

Markie strutted over and situated her Chucks on the bleacher with green, peeling paint, then reached down and snatched a few buttercups out of the ground, flicked the heads off. I wished I'd thought of doing that first. It gave her a cool, unbothered look that I wanted. Then she threw the headless buttercups up in the air, except for one that she stuck in the corner of her mouth and chewed.

"Bet you got better places to hang out in Atlanta than this place?"

"Depends on where you go," I said. I conjured up images of Centennial Olympic Park with its musical fountains that danced underneath the sun.

Another buttercup took a nosedive. "I hang out here sometimes when I don't feel like going over to Cassidy Park or to the library."

I risked getting a splinter and sat on the bleacher. A huge oak canopied over it, so the shade was just as good as any porch.

"How far is the library? If you're looking for someone, that's a good place to start finding information, right?"

"Not like I haven't tried that already. The library is just a few blocks. If you want to go there, you're on your own. I bet you're a summer bookworm, anyway."

"What if I am?"

"Do you ever see worms come out in this heat?"

"No, but what does that have to do with books?"

"Worms come out when it rains. That's the best time to read. Sun is for fun. Aunt Vie used to tell me that just to get me out the house sometimes." She squinted, looked up, and then took deep breaths like the sun gave her super-powers. "You perked up at the thought of the library like you're ready to write a book report. Thought you wanted to get out of the house to have some fun and adventure."

"And I *thought* you were going to open up. I'm going back to the diner." I moved as if to leave.

"Okay, okay," she said. "For a while, Aunt Vie was my foster mom. But I messed up a lot. Big time."

When she didn't tell me how, I didn't push.

"Where are your folks?" I said, knowing if I didn't ask then, I probably never would.

"You know." She slid her hand across her throat.

"Oh no! They both died? Like a car crash or something?"

"No, my mother abandoned me. Not like in a dumpster or nothing, but she left me with a neighbor and never came back."

"Wow. How old were you?"

"Two or three, I guess. Didn't even bother with an adios. Au revoir. Cheerio. Arrivederci. All the same to me: 'See ya and I wouldn't wanna be ya.' I remember her in flashes, though I don't know if they are real or something I've imag-ined. I don't even have that for my dad. They're out there somewhere, living the good life. They're probably only dead to me...."

"I don't know what to say," I admitted.

"You're not supposed to. Your parents didn't kick you to the curb." To emphasize, she kicked her leg out and watched her imaginary ball as it ripped through the park. "Gooooal," she announced.

I sat on my hands. It stopped me from wrapping my hands around my stomach like I'd do if Nikki was here. She knew what that meant. Emotions were trapped in there. They made your stomach hurt more than too much Halloween candy.

"It felt like my dad had died after the divorce. It hurt so much not seeing him every day."

I folded my lips in. They tasted salty like I'd been crying. Markie was quiet for a minute. I almost didn't believe that I had said what I thought I said.

"That's too bad. Not quite the same, but I feel you," she said.

"You're right. Just thinking out loud. It wasn't even close."

She kicked the air ball again. "But what's it like, though?"

"What's what like?"

She shrugged, then filled her jaw with air, letting one cheek go flat, then the other, before releasing. "Having parents? I mean, of your own. What's that like?"

I dropped my head, so I didn't have to meet her eyes. "We saw this video in science class of a mama bird feeding baby birds. They're tiny and their mouths are huge. The mama feeds each of them. That's all they have to do is sit in the nest and open their mouths. In my mind, though, the daddy bird is there, too, helping."

I left out how I asked for a bathroom pass after that and went in the bathroom and cried.

It made me sad to think that the daddy bird wasn't there. I felt so childish I never even told Nikki about it.

"I'll keep that image in mind. Thanks." Then she said, "Lucky birds."

She sat down and took some peanuts out of her pocket and put the bag between her knees. She pointed to them and I shook my head. Seconds later, she was popping off the shells and tossing the casings in front of us. Didn't take long before birds appeared. Lots of them. It made me mindful of how much coconut oil I had in my hair.

"Do you know that some animals kill and even eat their young? Filial infanticide or filial cannibalism, take your pick. Or if there is a deformed cub or a weak one slowing the progress and taking food away from the healthy ones, the mama abandons it—free lunch for predators."

Then she giggled.

I frowned. Maybe it was that nervous laughter that you do when you're really about to cry. But no. Her eyes were sandpaper dry. Not a tear anywhere around.

"What's funny?" I said.

"Free lunch. Diner. Get it?" She arched her eyebrows.

"I guess."

"Anyway, I think my mama didn't want to be weighed down with a short-armed girl that in her mind was never gonna be good enough or strong enough, so she left me. Maybe my dad didn't even know about me. Or maybe he's the one who made her do it. Who knows? Can't say I blame her."

I wished Tangie was here. She's sixteen. She'd know what to say.

"It doesn't mean she doesn't love you. Maybe there was a reason. A reason you don't know about."

Two young boys walked by. One had a huge beach ball under his arm. The other played a handheld video game. The machine-gun fire crackled with every footstep. Birds flew away in globs.

"Okay. Does your baby sister play with dolls?"

"All the time," I said and shrugged.

"How many of them have an arm that looks like this?" She pumped her right shoulder like she could unhitch her arm from her body. When I glanced, then looked away, she grabbed hold of her little arm and waved it until I faced her again. "Nope, not this time," she said. "Take a good look. Go ahead. It's a part of me like your right arm is a part of you. I won't be mad or nothing."

For the first time, I looked at her arm straight on. It was puffy and twisted some, like a doll's arm pulled out of its socket and put back on backward. When you stared at it closer, there were two fleshy nubs that looked like the tip of a baby's finger.

"Is this one of the arms of her favorite doll?"

"No," I said.

Once Grandma Sugar told us that she could barely find Black dolls for Mama when she was growing up, so most of Mama's dolls back then were white. But neither of them had ever bought a doll that had a short arm or leg. Then I realized what Markie meant: I don't know if I would have played with it even if I had one. But I wanted to think so.

"It's okay," she said.

"What?"

"What you're thinking. You're an easy read, Georgie." She giggled. "You wouldn't last two days in the system." She put her hand to her face. "Every feeling you have is right there."

It wasn't like I hadn't heard something like that before. Mama called it "wearing your heart on your sleeve." Sort of a gross image when I visualized it.

"Didn't think I had to hide 'em."

"Another reason you're a lucky bird. Hiding your feelings is something you haven't had to learn for survival." She dug in her backpack and pulled out a couple of pieces of gum and offered me one.

"Thanks."

"Anyways, once the people who supposed to love you most in the world abandon you cause you're not good enough, your feelings are polytetrafluoroethylene."

"Poly...what?"

She cleared her throat and rolled her neck. "Paa-lee-teh-truh-flaw-row-eh-thuh-leen—Teflon. Just like that animal stuff. When no one wants you in their stupid lab group, you learn more. When no one wants to play with you at recess, you read more. But I bet you never, ever have had that problem. Anyway, nothing sticks to me. Shorty and I here can deal with anything."

"Shorty? That's a cool nickname," I said.

She gave her arm a playful pinch, then sorta hugged it, but let go quickly like she remembered I was there. "Not better than G-baby, but I like it."

"Yeah, right," I said.

"No, seriously. Not being facetious."

"That's like fake, right," I said, not sure what to think about that poly word.

"Something like that," she said.

I locked it in to look up later.

After tossing all the peanuts to the animal kingdom surrounding us, she dug a rock out of the dirt and threw it at the swing set. The rock pinged off the metal pole like a gong.

"Probably should get back to the diner now," Markie said. "Don't want anyone worried about you."

"C'mon, Markie. You haven't given me the go-ahead about helping you find your mama or helping with the talent show. We can do both of them together."

She nodded. "Been thinking about that since I mentioned it. Gotta feeling you have what it takes to pull off the talent show, but what if the help I need takes you out of your comfort zone?"

"Um. Well. Being uncomfortable is how you grow. I'm getting used to this town. Wherever the search takes us, no problem," I said, as cool as I could fib. It wasn't just a problem, but a huge one. Gargantuan. But that wasn't the only issue at the moment.

As we strolled out of the park and back through the apartments, more doors were opened and the number of kids milling about had grown. Once we were out on Columbia, I stopped like I'd come to the edge of the earth. "Whoa! I think..." I craned my neck. "I think that's my daddy's SUV." Excitement bubbled over before I could stop it.

"Those *are* Georgia tags."

"He didn't tell me he was coming today." Then I thought to add, "You're welcome to come to the house."

"Nah, looks like a family thing. He's probably trying to

surprise you. Don't want to be a hanger-on. Give me your number, I'll hit you later."

I rattled it off. "Call or text me and I'll lock yours in," I said. "We can do this!"

"Gotcha. I'll let you know."

"Cool," I said. "And I'll show you some plans, too."

She shot up a peace sign and that was as good as a green light. Seconds later I heard my phone bleep.

It almost felt like magic that I'd seen Daddy's SUV now. All of Markie's talk about family had me missing Daddy and Peaches. But as soon as I said that, I remembered what that meant—babysitting. There was no escaping it. If it would be a challenge for me to operate out of my comfort zone, it would be impossible with Peaches in the mix.

I decided to bookmark all those thoughts and focus on Peaches. I was glad that I'd put on an extra dab of Teen Spirit and had on my sneakers, because I zoomed past Boga-Littles and practically ran all the way.

9

CAN YOU TIE YOUR SHOE?

Daddy's SUV looked like a black rhinoceros in front of Aunt Vie's house. He sat on the porch talking to Mama as Peaches opened and closed the front gate, flicking the latch up and down like eyelids.

As soon as Peaches saw me, she opened the gate and ran along the sidewalk to meet me. I lifted her up like I'd pick a flower from a garden.

"How did you get here?" I said and twirled her. We'd never been away from each other for more than a week, excluding the time she was in the hospital, which I didn't like to think about.

"Daddy asked me how much I missed you, and I told him this much." Peaches spread her arms out until she was in imaginary airplane mode. "He said that's too much, and we came here."

I hugged her and inhaled the scent of her favorite snack, strawberry fruit chews. And I triple-kissed both of her cheeks. I shoved my curiosity aside and said, "Is that lip gloss?"

"Yep, Mama Milly bought it for me." I glanced at Daddy. He waved and walked over to meet us at the gate. Mama stayed seated in the rocker. That was the first time I'd heard "Mama Milly." I left it alone. "Mama said I can wear it during the summer for play but not in school."

"Sounds fair," I said. Then she lifted her T-shirt away from her body and put it to my nose.

"Perfume?"

"It's body wash for kids, just like you and Tangie have. Mama Milly bought me this plastic purse that had three mini-bottles of it."

"Smells scrumptious," I said.

"This place doesn't smell scrump...scrumptious," she said.

"I know. You'll get used to it."

Daddy wrapped us in his arms, which I had long since decided was the safest place on earth. He kissed my cheek and his beard tickled my face. His hair wasn't cut, and it poofed from his Braves cap.

"Georgie, take Peaches upstairs and freshen up. Aunt Vie is napping, so keep it quiet," Mama said.

"I'm going to take my favorite girls out for ice cream, then I have to get back on the road."

"Mama's not your favorite girl anymore, just G-baby and me, since Mama Milly isn't here."

"We're all his favorites," I said, skating out of the awkwardness.

"Mama is Daddy Frank's favorite girl now." Peaches had started calling Frank "Daddy Frank." I hadn't gotten there yet. I sorta wished I could, though.

"You two hurry along, now," Mama said.

As we marched in the house and upstairs, Peaches said, "Daddy don't pack like Mama. He left all my good pieces home."

I had to giggle at the word "pieces." That was what Mama and Grandma called clothes.

Once in the room, I flung her suitcase on her twin bed.

"Mama will get you some more clothes if you need 'em. Take your stuff out and put it in the drawer and make sure everything is folded and neat." I hoped she didn't notice that my suitcase was in the corner, still packed.

"Daddy said that I'd see my great-aunts. Where are they? I don't see anybody. Where is Grandma Sugar and... and Aunt Essie?"

"They're at the diner. We'll ask Daddy to stop by." I would have wanted to eat at Sweetings, but the thought of sitting there with Daddy and Peaches with Markie serving us felt odd. Like that saying Mama uses sometimes, "pouring salt in a wound." *Not after that conversation we had*.

Before we left with Daddy, we peeked in on Aunt Vie. She was still sleeping.

Peaches walked over to the bed. "She looks just like Grandma Sugar," she said. "I can't wait to talk to her when she wakes up."

"She'll probably be up when we get back," I said.

"If you tell somebody a lot of stuff, they can't forget it all, huh."

"No, I don't think so."

Seems like I had a plan and Peaches did, too.

Two days later, I wore Peaches out with a gazillion billion board games and listening to her read to me books I'd memorized. We both loved *I Love My Hair!*, but if I heard it one more time that day, I was going to pull mine out. Okay, I was exaggerating. I'd do what I needed to do to get her to nap time. The most I'd been able to communicate with Markie was a few texts.

"Why does Aunt Vie sleep so long? Why do we have to be quiet all the time around her?"

Peaches didn't understand why Aunt Vie couldn't remember her name. When I noticed that Mama didn't use the word Alzheimer's, I didn't, either. After the incident, Mama wasn't about to leave us alone with Aunt Vie.

Once it was time for Peaches's nap, I turned the fan on low and placed it next to the window. As I adjusted it, I glanced outside and there was Markie. I waved but she didn't look up. If I called out to her, Peaches would know that I had company and the nap would be indefinitely postponed. She had an extra battery pack, especially for these occasions.

Markie seemed be staring at something on the porch. Then she walked up to the gate. I hurried down the stairs, expecting to see her on the porch, but when I got there, she was walking away.

I lit out the front door.

"Hey, wait up!" I shouted. All of Peaches's toys scattered around the yard inside the chain-linked fence made me feel like I was inside a huge baby's crib. "Markie," I called. But then it was like I hit a force field that wouldn't allow me to step out without Mama knowing I'd left the house. I started walking backward, back inside the makeshift crib. To my surprise, Markie followed. Once we were on the porch, I checked to make sure Mama wasn't lurking at the door. I sat on the top step and Markie sat on the one below.

"Guess that was your dad, huh." I told her it was. "Heard he brought your sis."

I nodded. "She's upstairs napping. Been up since five a.m." I lowered my voice. "Did you ever talk to Aunt Vie about finding your mama?" I needed to get to it.

She rolled her neck like she'd slept wrong. "Why you ask that?"

"No reason. I just know she'd help if she could."

"Sometimes it was something I thought I never wanted to talk about. Sorta changes the older you get. I only wished I wanted her help before things started slipping."

"Don't beat yourself up about that. We need to do the best we can right now, though. And work together."

"Got it!"

"We do what we can to find your mama and get cracking on some details about the fundraiser." I extended my hand.

Like at the diner when Grandma Sugar introduced us, she left my hand hanging out there for a moment.

"Aren't you going to have your hands full with your sister now?"

"I'll work it out."

She swooshed her lips from one side to the other. Contemplation. "Okay, deal," she said, and we shook.

No sooner than I'd "sealed the deal," which is Daddy's favorite line when someone signed a contract, the screen door opened and there was Peaches. She'd put back on her play clothes but still had on her hair bonnet that she only wore because I wore one.

"Thought you were napping," I said.

"I was. It's not like sleeping. It doesn't take as long," she said.

I stood up. "Guess not."

"Mama said fix me a snack."

Before I shouted, "Pour yourself some cereal for now," I remembered that we weren't *home*, home.

"I'll be there in a second."

Peaches hung on to the screen for a minute and finally stepped out on the porch, barefoot. "What's your name?" She walked over to Markie and extended her hand.

"You two are serious about this handshaking," Markie said.

"That's the way my daddy meets new people all the time." Peaches studied Markie for a few seconds more. "Your arm was born like that?"

A giant fly could have entered my mouth. "Peaches!"

Markie darted her eyes toward me. "Kids say what's on their mind. Gotta respect that." Then she turned her attention back to Peaches. "Yeah. It was."

"That's okay. But maybe a doctor can fix it for you if you want."

Markie shrugged and mumbled, "Who knows."

"I was sick and I got better. They can fix anything. That's why I'm going to be one when I grow up."

"An airline pilot is out?" I said.

"No, it's not. I can do both. Mama said so." When she cleared that up, it was back to Markie. "Can you tie your shoes?"

"It took me a long time to learn but I can," Markie said.

Peaches darted her eyes between Markie's arms and her sneakers. "Really?...Let's see."

"No, we're not going to see. Let's get that snack." I held the door for Markie. "You coming in?"

"Nah. I'll wait here."

"Okay. Be right out."

I asked Peaches was she really hungry, or did she just want some cereal. I beamed when she said, "Just cereal." Then she added, "And toast."

I slid a bowl, spoon, milk, and Cheerios in front of Peaches with more ease than I had served anyone even a bowl of grits and some biscuits at Sweetings. Then I dropped two pieces of bread in the toaster and put the fresh strawberry preserves on the table. I popped the toast up before it was barely brown.

"Are you going somewhere with your friend? That's why you're rushing. You're not going to eat with me?"

"I have company," I said. She dropped the spoon in the bowl and folded her arms.

"Mama catch you folding your arms and dropping that

silverware like that at this dining table, you won't get away with it like at Daddy and Millicent's."

Millicent didn't have any kids and had never been married before Daddy. Since she wasn't our *real* mama, whenever Daddy wasn't around, Peaches could pout all she wanted. I encouraged it, actually. That's when I called her "Millipede"—my mean, secret nickname for her—because I thought she was the reason Mama and Daddy's marriage was *terminada*.

I hated to admit that I was happy when Peaches threw tantrums with Millicent. I wanted to throw one, too, but I was too old. So I just wouldn't talk to Millicent. The silent treatment. (Unless Daddy was around.) But now I felt guilty for the way I'd treated Millicent, especially after she helped Peaches so much when she was sick.

The ceiling creaked. "Mama's probably on her way down now."

Peaches unfolded her arms and slowly started to pour the Cheerios.

"Why can't you eat with me?"

"C'mon. You know why. Plus, this is your snack. We've already had breakfast." Then I glanced toward the stairs. "When Mama comes down, tell her that I went out with Markie, okay?"

She nodded, not looking me in the eyes, which meant she was fighting back tears. I knew she wanted me to tell her to go get ready and come with us, but I'd been keeping her entertained all day yesterday and this morning. We weren't going to be in Bogalusa forever. And I had lots to do.

"Are you going to the store?"

"Maybe."

"Bring me something back," she said.

"If I go, I will," I said and hurried out. But I was too late. Markie had already left without me. I couldn't risk going after her and coming up empty. So I moseyed in the house and listened to Peaches plan out our entire day while I envisioned my next steps in my head.

A few minutes later, "Who was that out front, Georgie?" Mama asked as she entered the kitchen holding a basket of towels.

"Markie," I said.

"What did she want?"

"To know if I was coming to the diner. Have you ever seen her in action, Mama? She's really good. She remembers orders without writing them down and can even run the register."

Mama switched the basket from one arm to another.

"Well, she's older than you," Mama said.

"She's only twelve and a half," I said.

"That's not the only measurement," Mama said.

"Georgie wouldn't let me see her tie her shoe," Peaches said. "I tried to tie mine with one hand, and I can't do it."

"I haven't been around her much, but your grandma and Aunt Essie have told me about her. She might be a little mature for you. You understand?"

"No, I don't," I said. "Why don't you want me to be friends with anyone unless you know everything about them?" I pushed my chair back and folded my arms. "That's just another way you're babying me."

"Protecting you is more like it," Mama said.

My voice was low. Almost like the deeper I said the words the more Mama would listen.

"So she is the reason why you wouldn't let me go down to the diner before?"

Mama switched the basket again like a huge basketball. She shook her head. "Georgie. That's not true. Sorry if it seems that way. Your grandma and Aunt Essie work to help her. I just don't want you getting in the way of that."

"How? By being her friend?"

Mama went into closed-eyes mode, which is what she does when she tired of my questions. I usually back down when she does that. But I planned to keep cranking them out this time. "Peaches is here now. I'd rather you just watch her."

"So I have to stay in the yard all day again and play with Peaches."

Peaches held her spoon full of Cheerios in midair. "I thought you missed me, G-baby," Peaches said and nearly ripped my heart out.

I took a deep breath. "I do but that doesn't mean I don't want to hang out with other kids, too," I said. "You know, kids closer to my age."

Mama cleared her throat. "How about this. After you two fold these towels and straighten up the kitchen, why don't you two walk down to the library?" Mama plopped the basket on the floor. All I knew was that, with or without Peaches, the library wasn't the porch. I know Markie said that she'd already used the library resources to search for her mama, but it wouldn't hurt for me to explore a few ideas.

It wasn't a pass to go hang out with Markie, but it was something.

"Okay," I said.

This was my ticket out of the house, and I snatched it. As soon as Mama was headed upstairs. I texted Markie: Meet me in the library. 30 minutes.

Mama wanting me to take Peaches to the library and me needing to go to the library was one of those moments that our homeroom teacher likes to talk about. Serendipitous. I always liked that word. It just sounds like it's full of sunshine.

The library was about a ten-minute walk. *Avenue F.* Right on *F like Frank*. I followed the directions just as Mama gave them, holding Peaches's hand as instructed, but only until we were out of her eyesight. Nobody wanted sweaty palms in all this heat, and Peaches wasn't in darting-off mode like she was when she was younger. She stayed close to me, like Mama put magnets in our pockets.

"Think they'll have computers?" Peaches asked.

"If it's like the library at home, you know you can't get on the computer by yourself," I said. I couldn't even have my own computer in my bedroom at home. We had the "family computer" that probably had every single parental control on it ever invented. "Let's stick to books for now."

A few blocks down, two pickup trucks parked along the curb. A young boy sat on the back of one truck bed and behind him was a garden of watermelons stacked. In the other truck bed were two rows of window air-conditioner units. The man selling those had an unlit cigar in the corner of his mouth. He took it out right before talking to a lady inspecting a unit.

"Take it home. If it don't work, just bring it right back here or over to my shop. Still over there on Fourth."

An older woman swept the sidewalk in front of Gina's Dress Shop and Dry Cleaners, then went inside as a car pulled in front of it. Peaches had been quiet as we walked. I thought she was busy taking in our small-town scene.

"You mighty quiet, Peaches. Everything okay?" Her romper dress had daisies peeking out of the pockets. It's one of her favorites. If they'd forgotten that, Daddy probably would have had to send it.

"How old do you have to be to start forgetting stuff?" she asked.

I pursed my lips hoping the right words would come. "You don't always have to be old. We all forget stuff sometimes."

"The stuff that's in our heads. We'll lose it? Like the names of all my friends and TV shows and stuff?"

"Maybe for a little while, but it will come back to you."

"Then why can't Aunt Vie remember my name even after I said it over and over?"

Now I looked up like Mama does, even when she's in the house and sees nothing but ceiling. I searched the sky for words.

"Aunt Vie can't help it."

When she skipped-stepped to catch up with me, I slowed, remembering that she was still taking medication from the meningitis. I was so busy trying to get the right answers that I was walking faster than I realized. Her questions were on rapid fire.

"That's what happens when minds get old?"

"No. It's a disease." Didn't matter if it was hot, I reached out for her hand.

"Like the one that made me sick but it's in the brain."

"That's close," I said.

"You think the doctors will be able to help her?"

"I hope so, Peaches."

"Me too," she said. I squeezed her hand tighter. "We're going to help her."

"How?" she said.

"You'll see soon. Okay."

She nodded. Then I slowed down even more. Whatever activated in the brain that made a moment turn memorable, I hoped it worked its magic now.

10
COURAGE TO SOAR

Walking into the library, I shook a little bit to help my body adjust to the sudden blast of cold air. The library was small and neat. Unlike the massive three-story Auburn Avenue Library in downtown Atlanta, where posters of authors like Virginia Hamilton, Ernest Gaines, James Baldwin, and Toni Morrison graced the walls, I didn't see any authors at all. Instead of writers, there were rows of black-and-white pictures of Bogalusa when it was the "Magic City" and a lot of posters of people at the Washington Parish Free Fair that hung on the brick walls. On the side of a few bookcases were posters of *The Cat in the Hat* and *The Classic Tales of Brer Rabbit*, which Grandma Sugar said shouldn't be stories for children at all. The ceiling lights were domino-shaped tiles, some flickered and a few were dim. Before we got situated, I checked for a text from Markie. Nothing. That was disappointing but I could still make the most out of my time here.

"Let me know if I can help you find anything," the librarian said and tucked a flowing strand of reddish hair behind her ear.

"Thank you," I said.

There was a Kiddie Corner that Peaches beelined to, forgetting about the computers. I followed. Hanging above the circular tables were gigantic, tissue-paper bees, butterflies, and ladybugs. Peaches sat at a table loaded with books and dove in.

"What's our rule?"

"Don't even think about leaving this table until you come back, Jack."

On "Jack" we gave each other a high five.

"I'm going to look around." Before I could leave, a little girl with jawbreaker-sized pink hair knockers sat down across from Peaches. They started chatting as I eased away to the circulation desk.

"Can I help you?" The librarian tucked her hair again, revealing dangling, red-eyed frog-shaped earrings. Then there were three frog tattoos that formed a bracelet around her slim wrists.

"Is this the sign-in sheet for the computer?" I asked.

"Yes. There is a thirty-minute time limit. We can extend it if no one is waiting. And please use headphones for any audio."

There were two computers available, so I signed my name. Peaches was still directly in my line of sight.

"Anything else?"

"Yes, what's the best way to...to help someone find someone?"

"Is that person missing?" Her voice rose in alarm.

"No...well, not really. What if someone was adopted and wanted to find their birth mom?"

"Okay, that's a bit different." She placed her frogged wrist on her chest. "Whew. You scared me. There is a section on adoption. That's a good place to start. It's not an easy process, though." The way her voice singsonged, I knew she thought it was me. "How long are you visiting for?"

I told her the summer as she tapped away on her computer. She nodded and then wrote down a few section numbers on a piece of scrap paper. "Most of these are back in that right-hand corner. I'm here to help if you need me."

"Thanks," I said and headed for the open computer. Knowing that a line could form at any moment, I got straight to it: how to find your birth mother.

Social Media
Adoption Registries
DNA Registries
Go through the Court System
Hire a Private Investigator or an Adoption Detective

Markie's situation wasn't really an "adoption" but I didn't know what else to call it. I didn't even want to know what would come up if I typed in "how to find a mother who abandoned you." So I didn't. Of all the steps, the one that I thought was the most helpful was "hire a private investigator." Then I scanned to the cost, "$50–$150 an hour on average." What if I helped Markie buy and sell more peanuts? Even if we could get one to work for an hour, that could help. Before I got excited, I decided to verify something that I thought I remembered from one of those TV court shows.

I opened another tab and typed, "How old do you have to be to hire a private investigator?" I hoped against hope that I wouldn't see what was in front of me: eighteen unless you're an emancipated minor. Emancipated meant "free." I knew I wasn't in that group, and even though it may have seemed like it, neither was Markie.

I spent the next twenty minutes reading and printing articles that could help Markie. Even though I hadn't heard my phone ding or vibrate, I checked it for a text from Markie. Nada. But I had to keep moving, so since I didn't know when I'd be back in the library, it was a good time to look up my other idea. I typed in "talent show, fundraiser," and the screen populated. A link that read "Talent Show Fundraiser" had a girl my age underneath it. I clicked. I scanned the article to ensure it included a list of steps. I printed out one or two others, too.

Maybe a full talent show was ambitious, but I had to try. It would beat a car wash or a bake sale. How much could I really raise with those? For a few seconds, I closed my eyes and did what Daddy says he does when he needs a big sale. "Positive envisioning." He said that "envision" means "cause to be." I tried it when I wanted my parents back together. It didn't work. But now that I see them being friends and not arguing as much, maybe it did, just not exactly the way

I wanted. It was worth a try: Kids were doing whatever talent they could do and the best they could do it. Parents, friends, teachers, everybody in the community came out to watch them, take pictures, make memories. Aunt Vie was there—even if she couldn't remember us, we'd spend that night remembering her. And throughout the evening, we asked for donations. We'd raise millions of dollars—I opened my eyes. I was getting carried away. I stood and checked on Peaches. I had my eyes closed just for a few seconds, but it felt much longer. She was fine and still talking to her new friend.

After I'd done as much research as I could on the computer before others stood waiting, I paid for what I'd printed and went to check out the section on adoption that the librarian had recommended. Then I ambled around in the library, running my hand along the edges of books like piano keys. At the edge of one shelf, I turned the corner and there at the end of a long stack, sitting at a table with about five or six books scattered around, looking like she was up to something, was Markie. I marched over to her.

"So you couldn't have responded to my text?"

She glanced up. "Oh, sorry. That was you. Thought it was Rosella. I was going to check in a bit."

"Got it. Why did you leave?"

"Didn't want to get you in trouble. Saw your mom in the upstairs window. Didn't look too pleased."

"She's stressed. That's all," which was right in that sweet spot between truth and a fib.

Courage to Soar," I said aloud, anything to change the subject. "Simone Biles. That's a good book."

She pulled her backpack closer to her. "Have you read it?"

"No. Just heard good things 'bout it. You're not even a little surprised to see me." I grabbed a seat.

"Hmm, Atlanta's population is close to five hundred thousand. Bogalusa's is a little under twelve thousand. So not really."

"Oh, you've been looking up Atlanta, huh?"

"Gotta keep my options open."

"You were in the library before me. Who's the summer bookworm now?"

"I'm on a mission. It's different."

"What's up with Simone Biles?" I said.

Markie started stacking her books. "She was adopted, and I wanted to learn more about her story. But it was by her grandparents. And I, obviously, have none of those around here."

"I'm researching ways to find your mama." I put my notebook on the table.

"And what's that gonna do?"

"It's to record information."

"That's what this is for," she said and held up her phone.

"I like writing stuff down. Anyway, how is where you live now? Doesn't seem like it's the greatest."

"Decent. Temporary, like the others. Nobody wants me forever," she said.

"That's not true. Aunt—"

"Don't mention her. I meant nobody since her. I didn't know then what I know now."

"What's that?"

"Not everyone finds a forever home. I bet anyone would take you in a heartbeat."

"Who knows?" I didn't want to go there with her again.

"I'm just hyping myself up with these books. Can't wow them with cuteness, like you. But you'd never be in foster care. If both your parents and your stepparents dropped dead, I bet you got a handful of people who'd fight to take custody."

"Maybe," I whispered 'cause just the thought of it nearly frightened me speechless.

"Well, thank you for not saying 'no.' That's, at least, a little bit of honesty. Keep it up, you might be on your way to knowing just how good you got it."

"It's not that I don't know that. But you make everything in my world seem like a dream and it's not."

"I'll trade with you any day."

I didn't know if I was supposed to say how I would change with her. Nikki and I say it to each other all the time. But I couldn't with Markie. And I think she knew that. When she grabbed *How to Win Friends and Influence People*, I said, "My daddy's read that one."

"Not for the same reasons I gave it a shot, I bet. Waste of time anyway. I'm ancient in the adoption world. Finding my birth mom is some hope."

I tapped my pen on my notepad. "Well, let's get to it. We need to start with the basics." I stood up, zeroed in on Peaches, who was helping the other girl flip through a picture book, then I sat back down. "Mother's full name?"

Markie stared at me. I pressed my pen on my notepad, ready for more of her resistance. Then she said the words so slowly, they almost floated away before I could write them. "Irene Whitlock."

"Middle name?"

"Marie."

Then I asked for her "last known place of residence?"

"Duh, if I knew that, would we be having this discussion?"

Unlike before, her smart remarks bounced off me. "Bogalusa, Louisiana," I wrote. "Description?" I said.

"An older version of me, I guess. But with arms the same length. Taller."

"If you're not going to take this seriously, how is it going to work?"

"Okay, sorry. But don't you think I've tried the basics? The Google searches, all that? I have my own lead."

I tapped my pencil on the page. "Why didn't you say something?"

"Didn't know if you were really serious until now." Tap. Tap. Tap. "Okay, Aunt Vie's best friend lives on the outskirts of Bogalusa. Sounds far, but it's only about three to four miles from here when you know the right way. If there was anyone Aunt Vie would talk to about my mama, it was Ms. Hannah."

That's who Aunt Vie said her sisters were keeping away from her. "They were really close," I said.

"Yeah, I've been out there with Aunt Vie."

"Aunt Essie doesn't like her much?" I knew the answer to that but just wanted to hear what Markie had to say.

"Neither does your grandma," Markie said.

"Why?" Aunt Vie's words about them never liking Ms. Hannah pierced me.

"Could be because she's mixed. The white side of her family is known to have been pretty mean to Black people and some even belong to organizations that hurt them."

I shivered but caught myself before Markie noticed. I remembered what Tangie and I'd read.

"Like the KKK," I said.

"Maybe, back then. Aunt Vie told me that Ms. Hannah had no say so in choosing her family. And she didn't love them, she loved her."

"We have to get to her."

Markie leaned closer to me. "You're down with going today?"

I tried to calculate how long three miles would be. I pictured the track at Sweet Apple. When we walked around it four times, that was a mile.

"Yep," I said, not wanting her to know I was concerned about the distance.

Markie glanced toward the circulation desk and eased books toward her book bag. It was like we were back at Peanut Man's. As much as I tried to fight it, something told me that I was only beginning to figure out why Mama wanted me to stay away from her. "Hey, did you check those out already? I'm not about to look away while you steal books from the library. These aren't peanuts. You'd be taking books away from other kids who need them."

"Put a sock in it, Phillis Wheatley. These are already checked out."

"I hope so," I said, trying not to imagine a scene when the security buzzer went off.

I let that go for now and thought about the distance to

Ms. Hannah's. If four times around the track was a mile, then twelve times would be three miles. And it may be more than that. I imagined stretching out the track twelve times there and then back. One thing I knew for sure: I'd never get permission to go without an adult.

"How long would it take to walk that far?"

"Forever. But I have a plan for that," Markie said.

I soaked in her confidence. That reminded me of how I'd bathed in Nikki's confidence and did a few seconds of envisioning before the last cheerleading tryouts—I still got cut. Not a good sign. I pushed all of that to the back of my mind.

"Let's get Peaches and go."

"She can't come with us. We need to take her home. She'd be like dead weight."

"Don't ever say that about her," I said and clapped a book shut. My voice was deeper than it had been. Nothing that she'd said up until that moment shook me like those words. It didn't even matter that I knew what she meant. Just the word "dead" mentioned in connection to Peaches took me back to the hospital. To moments where I never thought she'd come home again.

"Oh, sorry. The meningitis. Didn't mean it like that."

"Yeah, okay. It is too far to take her, though. I'll figure something out."

She twisted her mouth to one side. "We can forget it if you want."

I used my lead attorney voice. "Not an option. We're going to talk to Ms. Hannah."

Markie went up to the desk and checked out another

book while I gathered up Peaches. Before I could even get a word out, she shouted, "I'm not ready to go!"

"Ssssh," I said. She buried her face in the book, her bush of hair round above it like a cottontail.

I slowly lifted her head until her face mooned over the book.

Peaches closed it but didn't move.

"Why can't I stay here with my new friend while you go with your new friend?"

"You know why. A little girl can get snatched anywhere. Even in safe places like the library. We always have to be extra careful."

Markie walked over and hiked her book bag up on her shoulder. "Ready?"

I guided Peaches and her folded arms to the door.

"Come back and soon," the librarian said and waved as we headed out.

Markie walked a few steps behind us.

"Watermelon slices, fifty cents," the boy who was on the back of the truck bed called.

"You want a slice, Peaches?" I asked.

She shook her head. "I want to go back to the library."

I grabbed for her hand, and she yanked it away. I put my hand on her shoulder, and she didn't resist.

After a few minutes, we were on Fifth Street and Aunt Vie's house was in sight, and Peaches stopped walking. I thought it was because she was tired. Even with her medications, she wasn't back to one hundred percent.

I kneeled on the cracked sidewalk. From the house across from us, what sounded like *The Price Is Right* show blared. I reached into my purse and pulled out all the change I had and held sixty-five cents in front of her. I expected Peaches to snatch it.

"Not moving. You're trying to bribe me."

I reached back in my purse and grabbed a dollar. She eyed it. "Just go in the house and tell Mama you're tired. Rest a little bit and when I come back, it'll just be you and me for the rest of the day. We'll play whatever you like, Beauty Shop"—Peaches was the beautician and I was a last-minute customer who needed an elaborate style—"Sorry!, Go Fish, whatever."

"Why can't we play now?" Peaches sulked. "It's because of her." She turned back and squinted her eyes in Markie's direction like she was a sliver of sun. And pointed like she didn't even know it was rude.

"You know better than to point like that," I said and gently pushed her hand down. "Listen, I don't have time to explain. Are you going to do this favor for me?"

"If she wasn't here, you wouldn't leave me. I don't like her. When we have a new baby brother or sister one day, I'm not gonna dump it to be with somebody older, especially a meanie. I'm gonna be a better big sister than you."

That stung. "C'mon, Peaches. Just take the dollar and let's go. I said I'd be back soon and it'll just be you and me."

She crumbled up the dollar in her fist and did a drum major march right past me.

When we got to Aunt Vie's gate, I said, "Go in and remember to tell Mama it was your idea. That you were tired."

"Yeah, okay," she said and had shifted gears to a flower-girl pace, stuffing the dollar in her pocket. I was just lucky no one was on the porch or looking down from the window. As soon as Peaches disappeared inside the house, I second-guessed my decision. If Mama didn't allow me to see Markie anymore, everything would be kaput. Even if Mama didn't feel it, something told me that Aunt Vie would love that Markie and I were connecting. I know that the things Aunt Vie told Markie are the things she would have said to me. The Alzheimer's can't steal those things. Maybe I felt this way about Markie and Aunt Vie, but Mama could squash it all.

I swallowed hard and caught up with Markie. Since Mama wasn't a fan of hers, I'd better make this time count.

11

TROUBLE

We were passing McClurie Park when the smell of pop-corn wafted around. A few kids sat in the yard of a house, watching a projection-screen TV that had been set up on the porch. Even though I couldn't see the screen clearly, I'd recognized Princess Tiana's voice. Close to a window was an electrical cord running to the red popcorn maker next to her. Sorta like the one Daddy had in his customers' waiting room. I tucked that idea away for when we got back home. Peaches would love it.

"You're gonna need some wheels. Wanna make it back before it gets dark, right?" Markie said, paying no attention to the outdoor theater.

"Definitely. I need wheels. But I don't have enough to buy one from the Jamaican guy," I said. I remember her saying to bring money when I was with her, that's why I had ten singles. Eight after I paid for the copies and bribed Peaches.

"No worries."

After we cut down that side street off Columbia, a few minutes later, we arrived at the baby-stroller house. The boy was sitting on the steps transfixed with a video game.

"What's up, Scooter. We need a bike."

"How long you talking?" He tapped his thumbs like drumsticks on the game. There was an explosion. Then he looked up.

"Two, three hours, max?"

"Need it back by six. Got a reservation on it. Let you use it till then for five." He spread his hand wide like a web.

"Bet," she said and went for her pocket.

"I got it," I said and opened my purse.

"That'll work," Markie said.

Scooter went behind the house and returned with a light blue bike with rust speckled along its handlebars like leopard spots. The seat was wrapped in silver duct tape. He wheeled it in front of me and seemed to watch my facial expression for approval. I nodded and handed him the money.

"That's the best one you got?" Markie said.

"Yep. Should have come earlier."

"It's fine," I said. Now I was thinking about the time. We had to retrieve Markie's bike, as well as ride to the outskirts of town and back before nightfall.

"Gonna charge a fee if you late," he shouted as we turned the corner.

A few boarded-up houses sat disconnected from the sun, shaded like black eyes. Bugs and dust lined our way as the livable houses disappeared, and abandoned homes and vacant businesses surrounded us. One home had a mangled dollhouse and a shredded lawn chair inside the gate.

"So is your bike at your place?" I asked as we rolled the second bike along the bumpy road, even though her house was nowhere in sight.

Markie slowed next to an auto shop at the corner. The sign was so faded that I could only make out *UTO SOP*. Cars had weeds sprouting around them as high as the passenger windows. A gutted school bus with its stop sign extended was scrawled with graffiti. And tire hills were home to birds nesting on top. The chain-link fence was high and rusted. *Private Property* and *Do Not Enter* signs hung on the gate with twisted wire.

She asked me if I had my cell and I just nodded, not wanting to show it.

"Well?" she said. I took my flip phone out of my purse.

"Don't laugh. It's prehistoric." I'd managed to avoid her seeing it all this time.

Markie side-eyed me again. "You embarrassed by it?"

"Wouldn't you be?"

She laughed. "Not much embarrasses me. Rosella gave me this phone to make sure she can get in touch with me. But only when she needs something. I'd take one like yours if I didn't have to deal with the drama," she said.

"Got it," I said, though we both heard the ding. I hadn't come up with a response to what she said, so I didn't say a thing.

"Stay here. I'll just be in there for five minutes or less."

"Your bike's in there?"

She nodded. "Are you going to be my lookout or what?"

"Five minutes. I'm setting my timer."

She was able to pull the gate back enough to slip through. "Cool with me," she said.

I glanced at my phone to make sure that the timer was working. Two kids sped by on bikes. A dog playfully ran alongside them, his patched fur slick with water.

When my phone rang, I mistook it for the alarm. Then I saw my stepsister Tangie's number flash. I didn't answer. I'd be too nervous to talk, and she'd know something was up. Five minutes passed.

I peered inside the gate, hoping to see Markie hustling out with the bike. Nothing. I called her number. It rang a few times and went to voicemail. Okay, I'll give her another minute. The same kids raced back by, this time with no dog trailing.

I walked around the gate to see if I could see any sign of her. The windows were caked with dirt. I called again—voicemail.

Back at the front of the gate, I stared at the private property sign like a red light. She was more than five minutes over her time. I pulled the gate open as far as I could and wormed my way in. Some small squirrel skittered underneath a car that had two flat tires. At least I hoped it was a squirrel.

I couldn't fit the bike through the gate, so I leaned it against the fence, hoping that no one would touch it. I sprinted into the back of the building and into the office.

"Markie!" I called. The floor creaked and a thin cat dashed across the floor, which was grimy with dirt and oil. I couldn't imagine how the bottom of my shoes must look. The back of the door had a poster of a white woman in a bikini, standing next to a race car and holding a jug of Valvoline. The dirty windows blocked the sunshine and the inside smelled of mildew and burnt rubber.

"Markie!" I shouted again. Instead of her voice, clanging rang out. I followed the sound and there Markie stood banging a large stone against a lockbox.

"Thought you were grabbing the bike and coming right out. What are you doing?"

"I'll give you one guess," she said and struck the lock again. "Wait. I bet you have a bobby pin, don't you?"

I wanted to say no. But to keep my hair from tickling my neck, sometimes I pinned the ends up.

"We could go to jail for breaking and entering, and now you want to add vandalism."

"Look around. Not sure there's something here that anyone would toss us in jail for. Plus, we're juvies. The most we'll get is a good talking to. Some sort of scare tactic. Trust me, they have their hands full with real crimes. We're like gnats. I need two pins. One for the lock pin, the other for a tension wrench."

I dug in my purse for another one.

"Straighten one out for me and bite off the plastic tip."

"Maybe we should just look around for a key."

"Tried that. Nothing." As I held the lock, she inserted the straight end. "Now hold it steady. When I insert this end, you must put the straight edge in that groove and turn. I need you to be my other hand," she said.

"Not funny. And I don't buy you're not worried about police."

"Lighten up, please." After about two minutes of fiddling around with it, it popped. And there were some old receipts and about ten dollars.

"Boom," she said and stuffed the money in her pockets. 'Alone we can do so little. Together we can do so much.' "

"Wherever that's from, I'm sure it wasn't meant for stealing."

"It's Helen Keller. I had a teacher who thought instead of me playing with the other kids, it would be better if I sat out recess and learned platitudes. She was really into Keller. Maybe having a short arm was the same as being blind in her world. Who knows?"

I surveyed the office. There was a pallet in the corner. A stack of books. And a few cans. On the desk was her backpack. And there was the bike leaning against the wall.

"Wait! Are you living here?"

"Let's just say it's my bunker, an aboveground fallout shelter. People like me need a place to hide out, take cover. When I hang out here, I have time to figure things out."

"If you don't like where you live, maybe Aunt Essie... she'll take you in. You don't have to stay here."

"Ms. Essie has enough to deal with. And you just don't

get it. I'm not a piece of luggage. Everybody doesn't have to take me with them, and not everybody wants to. Don't even know why I said 'luggage.' Most of the time, I'm moving in garbage bags. Aunt Vie even bought me a suitcase once, but someone stole it."

"That must have been rough," I said.

She hunched her shoulders. "You get used to not having something of your own."

"Bet that's a horrible feeling," I said. It made me feel silly about my biggest complaint being Peaches sharing my room. I wished that every girl could have her own room. But I didn't have time to think about that for long. As we were talking, the gate rattled. The grumbling of a truck was like the roar of a bear.

"Get down!" Markie hissed. We crawled under the desk.

"They'll see us. They'll see all of your stuff," I whispered.

"No, he hasn't come inside before. Whoever it is probably just needs something out of the yard. Just keep quiet."

Minutes passed. My knees were shaking. But I'd stay like that a straight hour if it meant we didn't get caught.

I couldn't squeeze my eyes any tighter than they were. Tiny red dots danced behind my lids.

The truck didn't rev up again and rumble out of the gate like Markie said. A man's voice was in the hall. Heavy footsteps weighed on the creaky floors.

"I got to recommend they secure this place up. Get a new alarm," a husky voice said. But as I listened to it, it became familiar, though I wasn't sure. "Hey, let me call you back, something's up in here."

I tried my best not to breathe. Not to make a sound. But there was so much dust. I bit my tongue harder than I'd ever bitten it before in hopes of not sneezing. Markie had her finger to her lips.

He walked around a second, though I know he had to see everything in there from the door.

It had to be about as close to fainting from fright that I'd ever been, including that time Daddy took Nikki and me to the haunted cornfield maze. I waited for hands to even lift the desk from above us or just yank us from underneath it. I balled myself up as tightly as I could.

Then his phone rang. But he didn't answer. It wasn't until his boots were right in front of us, until the phone was on the third ring that I realized that it wasn't his phone at all, but Markie's.

"Markie Jean! Come out from under there," he shouted. "I know it's you. What are you doing in here?"

Those flashes of light behind my lids were an eternity compared to the speed that everything else happened. Markie and I eased from under the desk. I came out with my hands up.

"He's not the police, put your hands down," Markie said.

"Ain't you two lucky that I'm *not* the police?" At that the voice and face were clear. It was Peanut Man. "Markie, you haven't answered my question: what are you doing in here?"

"She was getting her bike, sir," I said, which was better than Markie's silence, so I thought.

He nodded. "Let's let Markie Jean speak for herself." Then he took a handkerchief out of his painter overalls that had splotches everywhere. After dabbing his forehead, he faced her directly. I expected his voice to be gruff, but it was soft as if we were in the library.

When I glanced at Markie, her eyes were searching the floor. And her arm was folded behind her back.

Peanut Man lifted her chin. "I thought we'd come to an understanding. Was I wrong?" he said. Why wouldn't she say that before instead of acting like she didn't even know the people who owned the shop.

"We did. But I just needed to keep this stuff here for a while," she said.

"I'm just checking on the property. Told you I sold it, right? The new owner is one of those Guidry brothers and not likely to be as easy on you as I am. What's gotten into you? Saw you help yourself to the peanuts the other day. Didn't I tell you that you're welcome to take 'em and sell 'em anytime you liked?"

"Yes, sir," Markie said.

"So if I keep my word, don't you think you should keep yours?"

She nodded.

When he said that, I replayed that entire moment in my head: He went inside. She ran on the porch. She asked me did I want some. Did I say she was stealing them? Did she run just to mess with me?

"Let's get your stuff together. I'm going to take you home and talk to your guardian myself this time. Nothing personal but I can't let you think this is okay."

"No, Peanut Man, please. I'll take it all home myself. No need to worry her."

"That's what you said last time and the time before that. I didn't have a problem with you hanging out in here when I owned the place. But it's changing hands. And this is 'bout your third warning. I'm not a betting man, but I'd say that's three more than any Guidry's gonna give you. Let's get this stuff gathered up."

In a flash, Markie knocked down a rusted lamp. When it crashed to the floor, she took off.

Before my feet came unglued from the tile, Peanut Man's hand was firm on my shoulder, pinning me in place. I thought Markie would stop when she realized I wasn't behind her, but she kept running until I heard the gate rattle.

My adrenaline transformed into slush. I stood there melting on the spot.

"Didn't I see you just the other day?" Peanut Man asked. For the first time, I looked up at him straight. "You Mrs. Essie's grandniece."

"Yes, sir," I said. "I promise I won't come back if you let me go. I'll keep Markie from coming here, too."

"Nah. I've already been too lenient to let her hang out in here. But that was when I owned it. She'd tidy up and do some busy work. It'll be on my head if anything happened."

He took out his phone again.

"You said you didn't like cell phones," I reminded him. If he heard me, he didn't acknowledge it.

He pulled the phone away from his ear and put it on speaker. I didn't have to ask who he was calling. I knew. With every ring, my summer plans washed down the drain. Then "Sweetings Family Diner" pinged off the walls.

"Essie, this Peanut Man," he said. "I got something that belongs to you. Someone, I should say." A washing machine's spin cycle couldn't go much faster than the way the room spun. Then my head pounded like somebody was playing Whack-A-Mole right on my skull. "Tell her what's going on, young lady."

I squeezed my eyes so tight that I bet my whole face was the size of a fist.

"It's me, Auntie. It's Georgie."

"Lilly Mae," she called out to Grandma Sugar. I imagined them with the phone split down the middle of them.

"Georgie, what you gotten yourself into?" Grandma Sugar cried.

A few sniffles before I could even speak. "I was just looking around," I said, digging myself in deeper.

Peanut Man spoke. "Markie Jean ran off and left Ms. Georgie behind. I could deliver her right to the police station, but I know she got people. Plus I don't trust a few of them to teach her a lesson I'd want her to learn."

"Thank you for that. Do me a favor and drop her off at Elvie's. We'll take it from there."

"See you in a bit."

We packed up Markie's stuff and put it in his truck. It was a few garbage bags. One was filled with books, paperbacks mostly. I stuck my hand in and pulled out a worn copy of *Roll of Thunder, Hear My Cry*. I'd checked that book out of the library two years ago. And another I'd never heard of, *M.C. Higgins, the Great*. The others were science books. There was that lockbox on the desk. Peanut Man picked it up and put it in a bag.

"That's hers?" I said.

"Used to be mine. Gave it to her."

I felt stupid.

"What you gonna do with all her stuff?" I asked.

"Guess I'll put it in my basement. She'll be back around."

"Can you leave it at my aunt Vie's house?"

"Fine by me."

I knew nobody would object to that, even Mama. Keeping her stuff safe was the least of my worries.

When we took off, I stared out the window. And, right before the building was out of sight, Markie appeared. I'd totally forgotten about Scooter's bike. She straddled it and was holding something in her hand.

It was safe to say that we'd run into a major roadblock in the Find Markie's Mama plan.

And as far as talent shows, whatever Peaches and I could do in our porch crib would be about it once Mama was finished with me. I needed every ounce of brainpower to get myself out of the biggest trouble in all my eleven years. Daddy always told me, "You may get yourself into trouble with other people, but you end up figuring a way out of it alone." Had a feeling I was about to learn how right he was about that.

12

TRIPLE TROUBLE

Peanut Man wasn't as talkative as he was when we first met. If I hadn't heard him talking the other day, I'd have thought he was what Daddy would call "a man of few words." I honestly wished he hadn't had enough words to call Sweetings and tattle on me, but I guessed I brought that on myself. I was just thankful that his truck was about as old as one of Mama's old-timey shows, *Sanford and Son*. It puttered along, giving me time to think of what to say when we got to Aunt Vie's.

I wanted to disappear as soon as we got close enough that I could see the house. There on the porch were Grandma Sugar, Aunt Essie, and Mama. Triple trouble.

"I hope you know I did this for your own good," Peanut Man told me.

I didn't, but I said, "Yes, sir."

"Things have changed here some, but don't you ever forget there are people around these parts that will do you harm as easy as they take pie with coffee. And it's not just racist white folks like it used to be. This younger generation, well, some got too much time on their hands. Been trying to get them something like a Boys & Girls Club here for ages. Closest one is forty miles away."

"That's far," I managed to say.

He slid up against the curb of Aunt Vie's house and I figured that this was what it must be like to have Mama come up to the principal's office if I'd ever given a teacher at Sweet Apple Elementary any reason to. Mama was out of the gate and sidled up at Peanut Man's window before he could even cut off the engine.

"Sorry to visit under these circumstances," he said, taking his cap off and stepping out. Mama hadn't even looked at me yet. "I've been meaning to get by here and see Vie for a while now."

"Come on out here, Georgie," Mama said, her voice tight with anger.

"I have to help with Markie's stuff," I said.

"You don't have to do nothing but get yourself in the house, right now."

"I'll handle it all for you," Peanut Man said.

Mama eyed the bags. "And what's all this?"

"Markie was sorta living there," I said.

In one swoop, Peanut Man had the bike, as well as the two Hefty bags full of Markie's belongings in his hands.

"You can just put it on the porch. We'll get it to her soon enough," Grandma Sugar said.

I looked at my shoes instead of at Mama.

"You come on down to the diner, Peanut Man, whenever you're ready and take a breakfast or dinner home for your trouble. Take one home for you and Mattie Mae."

"I'll be sure to take you up on that. I'm glad it was my property and not someone else's. Changes hands soon, though."

"Ain't that the truth," Aunt Essie said. "Heard you sold it to one of them Guidrys."

He nodded.

"I know you would have found somebody better to take it off your hands if you coulda."

He didn't even bother with words, just nodded, and yanked out his handkerchief again.

Whatever punishment Mama had, I didn't want to be a spectacle for the neighborhood. I dashed into the house, winded at the thought of what was coming my way.

As soon as the screen door shut, Peaches was on the stairs, peeking down.

"Mama told me to stay up here. I messed up a little bit."

"It's okay," I said.

The door opened behind me and I was tempted to bolt upstairs.

"Can you even count the lies you've told today? And you have your sister lying for you, too." Mama peered up the stairs, though Peaches wasn't visible. "Read for a while like I told you, Peaches. Your sister and I have some talking to do."

Mama hung her head for a minute, which made me feel worse. When anyone made Mama the level of upset that she had to take a moment to speak, she hung her head. She'd do it often with Daddy, sometimes with Grandma. More and more, she was doing it with me. When she'd glanced up, she was seeking help. When she closed her eyes, she was summoning patience. When she hung her head, it seemed like she felt helpless.

"I don't know where to begin with you, Georgie. Before I can even talk about you being on Peanut Man's property, what in the world made you think it was okay to leave Peaches, your sister, here without saying a word?"

"I told her to tell you I'd be back." If I knew that my excuse didn't make sense, I knew Mama knew. It was all I had, though.

"You know doggone well that you're supposed to watch her. Not drop her off like soiled laundry and keep stepping."

"You brought me here for the summer and made it seem like I'd have stuff to do. But you don't want me out of your sight unless I'm with Peaches. You still won't even let me help with Aunt Vie, nothing."

"That's not true. I let you go down to the diner and look what happened."

"Daddy talked to you. That's the only reason. You didn't do it on your own."

"None of that has anything to do with you trespassing on someone's property. So you go right upstairs and think about it."

"She didn't want to go home. That's why she ran. All she wants to do is find her mama."

"And what does that have to do with you?"

"Nothing, she just talks to me about it. She was on her way to see someone who may know something about her mama," I said.

"Who was that?"

"I don't know."

It wasn't the time for me to mention Ms. Hannah, especially after I heard Aunt Vie talking about her before raising her hand to Mama.

Tears rolled off my chin.

"Maybe it's best that we go back to the way it was." Without asking I knew what she meant. She didn't even look at me. "I knew she was too old for you to hang around with."

"Stop saying that. She didn't get me into nothing. I know how to make my own decisions."

"That's it. You find another way to occupy your time while you're here. No more spending time at the diner. This friendship you're building with Markie Jean is making you act out. No more."

I trembled and bit my lip so hard it hurt.

"Katrina, don't you think you're being a little harsh?" Grandma Sugar said. She had eased in the door a minute ago but hadn't spoken.

"Let me handle this, Mama."

"We have enough going on in this house," Grandma Sugar said, standing next to me.

When she tried to hug me, I pulled away. She wiped my tears with her thumbs and rubbed my wiry hair.

"Stop treating me like a baby, Grandma, please," I said.

"Trina, you know how it is when kids are in a new town, nothing is off-limits. I'll talk to Markie Jean. I'm sure she didn't mean for all this to happen. You know all she's been through. But don't try to ground this child in the middle of summer."

You know all she's been through? What did Mama know? If she knew, why was she treating Markie like she was the worst influence on me ever? But Grandma Sugar's words hit Mama's cement wall and didn't make a dent.

"Go on upstairs, G-baby. You might not leave until it's time to drive back home."

"It's Georgie. And that's fine. I want to go back. Now. Let me go stay with Daddy or Frank and Tangie. Anywhere but here. I didn't want to be here in the first place."

"You're pushing it. You'll be here until I say so."

"Only because you need a babysitter. You're doing it again. You and Daddy. It's not fair."

"Doing what again?" Mama said.

I swallowed. "You don't care about what I want. I'm nothing but a baby until you need me to help with Peaches."

I turned and headed upstairs.

"This isn't over," Mama warned.

Once in my room, I plugged in my phone. Soon as I got a little juice, I checked it for a message from Markie. Nothing. It would only be a matter of time before Mama launched her full-throttle punishment. What if she called my bluff and Daddy came to take me home? I'd lied. I wasn't ready to leave Bogalusa. And those were words I'd never thought I'd say a few days ago.

I kicked off my shoes and flung myself on the bed. As soon as my head hit the pillow, everything I'd been through that day crashed down. Even though I tried to stay awake and wait for Markie to reach out, I'd been up since five this morning with Peaches. I drifted off to sleep. A couple hours later, I knew Mama was still cooling off when I woke up and there was a shrimp po'boy, sweet potato fries, a slice of chocolate cake, and a bottle of water on a TV table.

Even if Grandma Sugar or Aunt Essie would have wanted to bring it to me in my room under normal circumstances, Mama would have vetoed it and made me come downstairs. She wasn't ready to "see my face right now," that's what she used to tell Daddy when she was mad at him. "Go ahead and leave. I don't want to see your face right now."

The shrimp spilled out of the po'boy and I ate a few but it didn't taste as good up here in my room alone.

Right after I finished my lunch, Markie called. "Wow. I'm surprised you can answer. Thought your mama would take away your phone asap. Isn't that punishment 101?"

"She will when she remembers."

Markie told me that she was at McClurie Park and asked me to come back out.

"Ah, doubt it. Remember, Peanut Man brought me home."

"Thought you were helping me, being a private investigator and all. Is that only when your mama says it's okay?" I was quiet. For whatever reason, Mama hadn't unloaded her full wrath on me. Maybe Grandma Sugar got to her. Maybe even something I said. Did I want to ruin that? "You're no better than the grown-ups. They don't keep their words either. All that stuff about you willing to go out of your comfort zone was just a bunch of baloney."

"That's not fair," I said. "It's not like you haven't been messing with my head, too."

"Well, you shouldn't say you're going to help someone and not do it. If you're grounded anyway, what's the difference? They can't double ground you," she said. "Stuff your pillows under your blanket. That'll work. Meet me here at seven."

"I'll be there," I promised.

All the air seemed like it left the room. I was dizzy. Instead of figuring a way out of trouble, I was about to dig myself in deeper.

13

BAT SIGNAL

Six thirty. I hadn't conjured up a plan to get out and meet Markie. I sat there and nibbled on my cold po'boy feeling like a squirrel trapped in the attic. I flipped up my phone and pressed BFF, which was something like sending up the Bat Signal.

"'Bout time you called," Nikki said. "Must not be that boring there, you don't have time to talk or text."

"The time I tried, it went to voicemail."

"That was only one day. Got caught with eyeshadow. Not even the real stuff. Nothing but glitter, like Lu Lu wears."

I rolled my eyes like Nikki could see me. Lu Lu was the nickname of Lucinda Hightower, a Sweet Apple bully but not the kind who takes your lunch money. Those are easier to spot. We've reported a few to teachers with decent results. Lu Lu was the kind who'd pretend to be your friend if they want something you have. They were slimier than fake friends. A fake friend will talk behind your back. But those bully friends would even stick up for you as long as you had something they wanted.

"Hey, can we talk about Lu Lu later? I need your help."

"Why didn't you just say so? What's up?"

Nikki was excited at first, but when I told her that it wasn't about a boy, that faded. Of course she couldn't let that go without teasing me about Kevin Jenkins, who was the closest I had to a boyfriend ever. I considered him my "almost boyfriend." Once we were over that, her voice filled with genuine concern.

"The thing is that I'm sort of on punishment. If I don't go, I'll let a friend down. If I go and get caught, I can't imagine Mama ever allowing me out of her sight again. What do you think I should do?"

"Yikes. You've only been there a hot minute. How did you get involved in all that?"

"Long story. Let's bookmark it."

"Okay, but uh, she's not your friend."

"How do you know that? You've never met her."

"A friend wouldn't ask you to do anything that would get you in trouble."

"Nikki, are you serious? We've both been guilty of that and that's not even including you and Lucinda."

"Okay, okay, but not when you're already on punishment.

They'd care more about you getting off punishment, not adding to your time."

"Good point."

"I'm supposed to try and sneak out the house and meet her in just a few minutes."

"Don't do it, Georgie, please. There's still a lot of summer left. Don't let this insta-friend mess it up for you!"

Nikki was making sense whether I wanted to hear it or not.

"You're right," I said.

"Remember that summer I was grounded for more than a month. It was almost time to go back to school before I could even ride my bike."

"Yeah, I remember."

Nikki's mama called her in the background. "I'll let you go," I said.

"Don't do it!" she warned right before we both said "bye" and hung up.

I sat there and watched the clock on my phone hit 7:00 p.m. I couldn't bring myself to call Markie. A quarter after, Markie's number flashed on the screen.

I was tempted to answer but got ready for bed. If I was ever going to help her find her mama, getting in more trouble with mine wasn't the way. That, I was sure of.

The next morning, Mama knocked on the door. "You up, Georgie?" Before I could answer, the door flung open.

I yanked my sheet to my chest, covering my thin nightgown. Not that I had anything that Mama hadn't seen, but who doesn't want some privacy? Even though I had my own room at home, Mama never bothered to knock. To me, privacy was just as important as her calling me "Georgie." But one of Grandma Sugar's favorite sayings was "Pick your battles."

I slid my feet into my slippers, securing the sheet around me with clasped arms, then I glanced at the empty twin bed across from me.

"Peaches slept in your room last night?"

"She's trying to give you some space." Mama didn't sit on the empty bed, but she fluffed the pillow.

"Did you call Daddy?"

"Co-parenting doesn't mean I call him every time you get out of line, Georgie. We'll talk soon enough."

"Sorry about trespassing."

"You could have landed in much more trouble than you did. Both of you."

"Am I grounded?"

"I'm still processing this. Your great-aunt and grandma weighed in. If I try to confine you to this room, they said they'll free you." She gave me a half smile, sat down, and then glanced out the window. "Whether I like it or not, I have your Grandma Sugar and Aunt Essie to contend with in this house."

As Mom sat there, my courage built up to ask her one of a dozen questions that had been buzzing in my head. I swallowed hard and went for it.

"Why didn't you tell me that Markie used to be Aunt Vie's foster kid?"

Mom pinched the space in between her eyes like she'd taken off her reading glasses. We both listened to a car's bass so loud the windows vibrated.

"Turn it down," someone shouted. Mom waited for the commotion to pass before she spoke.

"Markie hasn't officially been Aunt Vie's foster kid for a while. Even though the state thought she'd be better off placed with another family, she and Aunt Vie remained close. Then once Aunt Vie's condition worsened, Aunt Essie moved back to Bogalusa and she used to let Markie sit with Aunt Vie."

I crisscrossed my ankles. Crossed them back. Anything I could do to ease my nerves as Mama continued talking. But she stopped and now was facing me. Still silent.

"Why she stop letting her? She loves Aunt Vie, I know it. It's not fair I get to see her and Markie doesn't. She knows Markie more than she knows me."

It hurt to say it aloud but it was true. Mama knew it, too.

"Things started missing, Georgie. Valuable pieces of jewelry that belonged to Aunt Vie. Aunt Essie suspected that Markie might be taking them but didn't know for sure. She found Aunt Vie's coin purse in that bag that Peanut Man brought here."

My stomach was caving in but I tried not to show it. I'd looked through her bags, too. Wasn't I just talking about my privacy? I was that word I missed on a spelling test last year. A hypocrite.

"She said she gave it to her, Mama. It's possible."

"She's a smart girl and knew that Aunt Vie wasn't in a position to give away anything. At the least she should have told Aunt Essie."

A part of me wanted to tell Mama how I thought Markie was stealing peanuts. How I was wrong about that. But it didn't seem to compare to finding that coin purse. Right now, it was all about trying to figure out how not to let what all I wanted to do in Bogalusa go down the drain.

I crisscrossed my ankles a few times waiting for the punishment that still hadn't landed.

"Do you think you can stick it out with us here?"

After a few seconds of contemplation, which was more like shock, I said, "Yes, ma'am."

Mama pulled me close. Instead of one of her favorite perfumes, she smelled of Dove soap and mouthwash.

"After yesterday, I think I need to spend some quality time with you two. This is your summer vacation. We're going on a little trip. Peaches is having breakfast now, then I'll do her hair. Just come down when you're ready. I have a few other things I need to finish up for Aunt Vie. We'll be on our way before long."

"Okay," I said. Mama kissed my forehead and left.

I tried to put Markie out of my mind as I got ready, but it wasn't working. I mustered up the nerve to call. It went to voicemail. Maybe it was for the best. Since I wasn't going anywhere and had miraculously avoided major punishment, that bought us a little more time. Mama wanting to spend "quality time" with Peaches and me was a good thing. She had been more stressed than I'd seen her since Peaches was in the hospital. I knew that Aunt Vie's condition was just part of it. Maybe this time away could help all of us. I'd rethink my plans with Markie when I got back. Starting from square one with her not trusting me wasn't an option. We just didn't have enough summer left for all that.

14
THE CAUSEWAY

As soon as we had Peaches in her booster seat, I buckled myself in.

Grandma Sugar, Aunt Essie, and Aunt Vie were on the porch to see us off. Aunt Vie looked like she was sleeping with her eyes open. Grandma Sugar leaned and whispered in her ear, and she shivered like Grandma's breath was a cold breeze. But when Mama blew her horn, something in Aunt Vie switched on. She started waving, not just with one hand but with both. That car horn meant something to her. My heart leaped.

"Aunt Vie's waving," Peaches shouted.

Mama tooted that horn again and the waving became even more frantic.

"Bye-bye! Bye-bye!" Aunt Vie shouted. I waved until we couldn't see them anymore and so did Peaches. I knew she probably didn't know it was us leaving, but whoever she saw in her mind meant something to her.

The navigational system started in and Mama said, "Don't need you today, Gladys," and reached to turn it off. She started calling it that last year when she learned a Black woman helped design it. She took it off the dash and stored it in the glove compartment.

"Peaches, don't have me stopping at the gas station before we get on the road good," Mama said.

"I already used it," Peaches said, not looking up from her game. "Two times," she added. I held my breath, waiting for Mama to ask me, too. It's hard to explain but it felt like she'd trusted me to be in charge of when I had to go without her reminder. Yeah, it was a little thing, but I'd take it. I made sure that my seat belt was fastened.

"You're not telling us where we're going, Mama," I said.

"You'll know soon enough." I loved the anticipation in her voice. It was rarely the three of us anymore since she married Frank. It felt good with it being "Mama and her girls" again. As Mama drove, I stared out the window happy that I recognized places that I'd walked with Markie. Along one side street, a fire hydrant was on and kids skipped and danced in the white water like a street-long Slip 'N Slide.

Mama seldom listened to the radio when we were in the car. But this time she tuned in a jazz station and let it play for a few minutes while she tapped the steering wheel. When she was ready to speak, she turned it down.

"Girls, you know how Aunt Vie lives in her home but stays in her room most of the time?"

"Yeah, she doesn't like to come out," Peaches added.

"Well, her sisters are starting to think it would be better if she lived somewhere else for a while. Somewhere they could help her and where she could socialize with people with similar conditions."

"But where could be better than home?" I asked. Mama didn't answer right away. "You're talking about a nursing home," I finally had the courage to say. "That's where Grandma Sugar says she never wants to go."

"Georgie, your grandma and Aunt Essie are the ones who have to make the decision about their sister. They'll do the best they can until they can't. That's what loved ones are supposed to do. But this isn't a regular nursing home, it's a—"

"Memory care facility," I said.

I glanced out the window, wondering what I was seeing that Aunt Vie had seen for years. I tried to lock it in my memory so I could tell her about it. Things that you never thought you'd care if you remembered or not, like what the specials were at Travis's Grocery. Or how telephone poles and wires played double Dutch against the Bogalusa sky. When I thought about Aunt Vie not remembering things in her own kitchen, I realized that it wasn't just about not forgetting the big stuff in life, like the names and faces of people you love, but the ordinary stuff, too.

"That's right," Mama said. "Memory care. How do you know that?"

"The ads come on all the time when we're watching *Judge Judy.*"

"Nothing is decided yet." Then Mama's voice cracked. She let the music play for a while and we enjoyed the ride. When I saw the sign for *Mandeville, LA*, which was about thirty miles away from Bogalusa, I guessed we were heading to New Orleans. For almost twenty minutes, Mama sang along to the radio and I joined in if I recognized a song. Then she glanced in the rearview to see if Peaches had nodded off to sleep.

"Good. She's napping," Mama said. "Georgie, I told them about the slap." She whispered the word "slap."

I squeezed my eyes shut for a moment. "What did they say?" I asked.

"Both of them told stories about Aunt Vie's aggressive behavior. This was the first slap. I mean, she's pushed my hand away but never something like that. But it's not only about protecting those around her, but protecting her, too. Right now, we still think she is manageable. Keep in mind that Aunt Essie's husband, your uncle Dean, drives long haul. And your grandma hasn't retired yet, though she's thinking about making this year her last. Aunt Essie can't handle things on her own. The truth is that we're leaving soon."

"How soon?" I said.

"I mean we won't be here forever. You know that."

Mama turned up the music again, but her words were in each beat. Then something crossed my mind. Something that Mama and all the grown-ups already knew: It didn't matter how much we wanted it, Aunt Vie would probably never again know any of us like she used to.

Toll signs for the Causeway appeared. Twenty-three miles of nothing but bridge and water. After Mama paid the toll, Lake Pontchartrain spread out around us. Unlike when we crossed it the first time, the more I stared at the water, the more my stomach twisted with fear. The water was calm, beautiful, but in the pictures…Hurricane Katrina had turned into a monster. Is that what it was like for Aunt Vie? Was forgetting things not a big deal at first and then it came on like a hurricane that washed away the memories of so many things she loved? I quick wiped tears away.

We didn't say anything for a while. My stomach felt like it does when I'm swinging too high and afraid the chain will break.

Then as if Mama knew I needed to hear her say something, or maybe it was her needing to say something, she turned down the music and sighed. "Aunt Vie was the first person to drive me across the Causeway. You'd never know it now, but your grandma was scared to drive. Aunt Vie took me to her favorite restaurant in New Orleans, Dooky Chase, once or twice a month. She modeled Sweetings after it. Sometimes her best friend, Ms. Hannah, would go with us."

I straightened up in my seat. And turned directly to face Mama. She glanced at me quickly and returned her eyes to the road.

"You knew Ms. Hannah back then?"

Mama chuckled. "It wasn't like dinosaurs were roaming around, you know." Mama shook her head and smiled but it only lasted a second. "We'd eat, shop, and just enjoy the day. Those two have been friends since I can remember."

"But Aunt Essie and Grandma Sugar don't like her," I said.

Mama knew I must have heard what Aunt Vie said right before she slapped Mama, who she thought was Aunt Essie. "You've never liked her. You never understood our relationship." But I didn't want to make Mama sadder than she was already feeling inside.

"It wasn't so much Hannah than it was the times."

"Her being mixed, biracial," I corrected.

"Yes," Mama said, without asking me how I knew that. "Maybe if she'd had a Black mama and white daddy, folks would have lived with it. Keep quiet about it like they do. But Ms. Hannah's mama was white and her daddy was Black. That didn't sit right with the white folks in Bogalusa, especially the menfolk, one bit."

I forced myself to swallow. "Did anything bad happen to her daddy?"

"Before I was born, he went missing."

"Like Emmett Till, Mama? Think something bad like that happened to him?"

In my mind Lake Pontchartrain was raging again. Mama's hand left the steering wheel and found my knee. Even though she didn't approve sometimes, Daddy talked to me about Black people who were victims of hatred. He had their names on a board in his office: Emmett Till, Sandra Bland, Trayvon Martin, Tamir Rice, Michael Brown. Those are the ones I could remember because I saw them on the news. Daddy said he never wanted me to see that picture of Emmett Till without him or Mama there so he showed me himself. He didn't keep that picture on the board, though.

But the one when Emmett Till is alive and smiling. I waited for Mama to sugarcoat things, like Daddy accused her of sometimes.

We both checked to see if Peaches was still sleeping. "Yes, baby. Ms. Hannah's daddy was never found, though. But that's what most Black people in Bogalusa believe, that someone...killed him."

Neither one of us wanted to say more about that. I didn't want to start crying, so I envisioned Emmett Till and every-one else, including Ms. Hannah's daddy, living their life in heaven. That helps, sometimes.

Mama hummed along with the music and I glanced out at the water. I took a deep breath and refocused on my plans. "Mama...if Aunt Vie and Ms. Hannah were close, you think that Ms. Hannah was close to Markie, too?" A cloud of seagulls floated above the water.

"I wouldn't see why not. If she wasn't, it was probably due to Ms. Hannah's people. The ones we know anyway. Why do you ask that?"

The squawking of the seagulls mixed with the radio as I tried to think of what reason to give. My stomach flip-flopped, scared to say anything that would give Mama more reason to keep Markie and me apart.

"Think she'd know how to find Markie's mama?"

"No. I doubt that very much. If Aunt Essie doesn't know, why would Ms. Hannah? Is that what Markie's been saying?"

"Not really," I said, trying to back out of it. "I just thought it just now. Why doesn't Ms. Hannah come around?"

"Aunt Essie said she came by when we were in Covington. She has this notion of taking care of Aunt Vie out at her farm. Of course, Vie's sisters aren't open to it."

"Why?" I said and cringed at how much like Peaches I sounded.

"Maybe they are scared of being cut off from her. As you heard, the relationship between all of them is tense. And what I say wouldn't carry weight against her sisters. We all just want what's best for Auntie," Mama said.

There were so many other things I wanted to ask that my feet were tapping on the floorboard like a woodpecker. But I saw how Mama's hands were back to gripping the steering wheel. I didn't want to upset her more than she already was.

Mama reached to change the station but decided against it. "I'd just about give anything if I could be sure that Aunt Vie knew that I was here."

I thought of Mama styling Aunt Vie's hair in the Bantu Knots. The way she leans on Mama when they're walking a little more than she leans on her sisters. Maybe they don't notice it, but I do.

"I think she knows, Mama," I said.

"I hope so," she said.

"When I sat out on the porch with her the other day, I thought she remembered me. You know, really remembered, like when you told me she used to sing "Georgie on My Mind" but she was remembering Markie. She loves her. And I think Markie loves her, too."

"That may be so, baby. Let's let Aunt Essie and Mama figure out how they want to handle things. Best we stay out of it. Neither of us really know Markie." I felt a kick to the back of my seat. And I told Mama that Peaches was up. Mama nodded.

Peaches caught the tail end of the conversation. "I don't like Markie."

"You don't know her," I said.

"She's bossy," Peaches said.

"You have a good nap?" Mama said, adjusting the rearview. "And hush up about who you don't like."

"Okay," Peaches said, leaning toward the window. "But she's a meanie....Daddy loves this bridge, Mama," Peaches said.

"So do I," Mama added.

We exited the Causeway and rode for a couple of miles.

As I looked out the window, some of the land around us was vacant. And then vibrant buildings appeared, some painted purple, others bright orange. The colors so vivid it was like the paint was still wet. A few of the buildings were old and others were new with fancy shutters and iron railings. A memory of Katrina flashed. That news footage of everything underwater. There were people holding signs saying *Help Us* as they stood atop roofs with water up to their knees. I looked up like I expected to see the ghosts of them there. Daddy said that reporters even called residents refugees when New Orleans was the only home they'd ever known.

"Is this the French Quarter, Mama?" I asked as we searched for a place to park.

"Not quite. It's the historic area called Tremé. This restaurant hasn't been opened long. A friend of mine suggested it. She's going to meet us here in a bit. Haven't seen her much since college."

I thought about the way I was feeling and said, "It's probably hard for anyone who lived here not to still be sad about Katrina."

"That's that bad hurricane with your name, Mama?" Peaches said.

After a quick rearview glance, Mama said, "Yes, baby. Most of the people here had to rebuild their entire lives."

Mama veered into a parking lot that had a low fence around it. There wasn't anyone taking money or anything like in lots in Atlanta. Mama eased into a numbered space. Once the three of us were out, we walked up to what looked like a huge, gray mailbox and Mama got a ticket. We both took Peaches's hand and made our way across the street to Ray's on the Avenue. There was a flurry of fried chicken and fish aromas mixed with some vegetable that I couldn't distinguish. I almost expected Aunt Essie or Grandma Sugar to come stepping out.

Inside, Ray's wasn't as big as the diner. There were several square black tables with a tiny candle in the middle of each, and chairs were along the wall underneath a counter like the ones at our diner for people to sit, drink coffee, or read the newspaper.

"Good, they're not here yet," Mama said.

"She's bringing someone with her?" I asked.

"Oh, no...no. I meant she's not here," Mama said and looked behind us. "Just excited to see her, that's all."

A waitress rushed over to us. "Good afternoon. Welcome to Ray's. Will you be dining in or is this to go?"

The waitress's gap-tooth smile was welcoming. At the end of her left eyebrow was a tiny hoop earring. Six earrings of varying sizes lined each ear. If it wasn't impolite to stare, I wouldn't have taken my eyes off her. She was like one of those drawings where you see something new every time you look.

"We're dining in," Mama said.

The waitress told us we could seat ourselves.

Mama headed for a table in the middle that sat five anyway. When we were seated, the waitress hustled over and brought us huge menus as big as coloring books.

"May I get you ladies some cold drinks?"

"Do I have to have *water*, Mama? Can I get a soda?" Peaches said.

"Let me bring watah for everyone and I'll come back and take the orders."

"That'll be fine," Mama said.

"Be back in a second, beh-bey."

The way she said "baby" was like a song I wanted to sing out loud. I heard a few people say it before, but it wasn't the long and slow way she said it, like that last note you don't want to end.

As we looked at the menu, Mama checked her phone again. Then she turned up the volume and sat it on the table instead of inside her purse. Something was up. She never did that. Phones were a no-no on the table. She and our stepdaddy, Frank, agreed with the phone rules. Daddy, not so much. Now that I think about it, it was odd that this friend of Mama's didn't invite her over to her house.

Not long after the waitress had returned with our waters, she was back to take our orders. After going around the table, we'd decided on Ray's Soul Platter: fried fish, shrimp, and chicken wings, hushpuppies, and bread. We ordered a bowl of Ray's Famous Gumbo so we could compare it to Aunt Vie's. The waitress hurried away and reappeared with a basket of cornbread muffins, and we started munching.

"Peaches, I asked Georgie this already. Do you think you can make it in Bogalusa for a couple more weeks?"

"But what if I miss Daddy too much?" she said.

"We'll work something out," Mama finally said. "Your daddy suggested we video call. You know what that is, right, Georgie?"

"It's how one of my friends communicates with her dad overseas. And how we have author visits. I tried to get you to download one of the apps on our home computer when Daddy..."

"When Daddy what, Georgie?" Mama said.

"When he moved to North Carolina. You know...before he came back to Atlanta."

"It's okay to say it, baby. Things are much better now. We weren't in—"

"A good place," I said aloud, though I hadn't meant to.

"Guess we say that a lot," Mama said but didn't smile. She glanced at her phone again.

We all stopped talking for a while and chomped on muffins. Mama's phone rang. "You girls stay right here. I need to step outside for a moment."

When Mama left, Peaches said, "G-baby, you think that if Daddy and Mama Milly have a new baby they'll let the baby come live with us for a little while? I mean just for a weekend, like we do at Daddy's?"

"I don't know about that. She'll be a new mama and want the baby around her all the time. We can probably go over there and stay." That seemed to be okay with her, for now.

Mama was still away when the waitress returned with our food.

Once the waitress laid out our spread, Peaches immediately stuffed two shrimp in her mouth. "That's it. Let's wait for Mama to say grace together," Georgie said.

Mama was acting strange. She had a surprise for us all right, but I was starting to believe that it wasn't a friend of hers, but somebody we knew, too—Daddy. That could be what this was all about. She'd called Daddy to meet us to give me another talking to about getting in trouble. Why wouldn't she just say it? Guess the surprise would be for Peaches. It just meant another lecture for me.

When Mama sat down, we blessed the food and officially started eating. She motioned for the waitress, who scurried over with a pitcher of lemonade in one hand and water in another. Her three-finger New Orleans Saints ring sparkled against the pitcher. That was Grandma Sugar's favorite football team.

"Refills?" she said.

Peaches nodded immediately, taking advantage of Mama's relaxed mood. And after the Causeway conversation, I was happy she didn't seem as sad.

"More for you, young lady?" the waitress said to me.

"Yes, please," I said, while expecting to hear Daddy's voice any minute. Even though there was a lecture coming, I was still excited to see him.

"Oh, can you bring back a menu, please?" Mama said.

Okay, that meant just Daddy, no Millicent.

"Coming right up," the waitress said.

"My friend is just having dessert. I'm sure she'll want to show us around a bit. And I want us back on that Causeway well before dark," Mama said to no one in particular.

"I don't wanna drive in all that water in the nighttime, Mama," Peaches said, chugging more lemonade.

After the waitress cleared some of our plates, Peaches and I made our way to the restroom.

When we got back to the table, Mama wasn't there. The waitress came over and said that she'd be right back, then she handed us dessert menus. We barely finished the Soul Platter and deemed Aunt Vie's gumbo the winner of the gumbo battle, although Ray's was, as Mama said, "nothing to sneeze at."

I couldn't resist banana pudding topped with home-made vanilla ice cream.

"You think you want to share one with me, Peaches? I bet it's huge."

"I want my own," Peaches said.

Seconds later, Mama's back. "Ahem. Ahem. We have company coming." Mama raked a flyaway piece of hair into her messy bun and smiled.

"We don't see nobody, Mama," Peaches said.

I didn't take my eyes off the doorway. And—believe it or not—in walked Nikki. I hit my knees against the table, almost knocking over my lemonade. Mama was still standing as I ran over to meet Nikki before she could even get halfway to us. I wrapped my arms around my best friend.

"How did you get here?" I said.

"Our mamas worked it out for me to ride with my cousin who goes to Xavier." Then she leaned in and whispered to me, "You almost messed it up if you would have snuck out again and got caught."

"So glad you're here. Need more help," I whispered. "Tell you more later."

"I'm ready to jump in," Nikki said.

Mama didn't know it yet, but she'd just helped me shift my plans into high gear. Not too sure if Nikki would vibe with me trying to help Markie find her mama, but if there was anyone in the world with the skills to pull off a talent show, it was Nikki Denise Shepard, aka Know-It-All Nikki, the best dancer in all of Sweet Apple and maybe even one of the best in the entire city of Atlanta.

The three of us working together might be filled with a little drama or, okay, a lot of drama, knowing Nikki and Markie. But my confidence that we could get this done was one hundred and ten percent. And like what I thought was a sign when I read the word "vacuum" at the car wash, there was another sign. On the wall of Ray's, right above a poster of a band, was that phrase Markie said the first day I met her: *laissez les bons temps rouler.* That was my clue, maybe for today anyway, to forget about the challenges waiting for us across that Causeway, enjoy my best friend, and let the good times roll.

15
ME TOO, SUN

The next morning, sun freckled in through the lace curtains, dotting along the floor and walls. Newspapers hitting porches and walkways sounded like footsteps. And grumbling engines headed to work mixed with the whistling of birds. I'd woken up to those sounds for more than two weeks now. For a moment, I almost didn't recognize Nikki across from me in the twin bed. I flung the cover back and rubbed my eyes.

"'Bout time," she said, unwrapping her silk scarf from around her micro braids.

"How long you been up?"

"Just for a few minutes. Trying to figure out why it smells like rotten eggs in here."

"The window is open. I told you about the paper mill already. It's always worse in the morning," I said.

"No shirt, Sherlock," Nikki said and I giggled.

"Are they tight?" I said, remembering the time I helped put beads on Tangie's braids.

"They're loosening some." She scooted down and faced me, resting her hand on her chin.

"You said you had something to tell me, but you fell asleep," I said.

She stretched toward the ceiling. "It's about your boyfriend...Kevin?"

"Stop calling him that....Okay, how about 'almost boyfriend,'" I granted.

"Almost" really isn't a thing, but whatever. "Sure you want to know?"

I bit my lip. Whenever Nikki started anything with "Sure you want to know," it was something that I didn't want to know.

"Let's hear it," I said.

"I saw him two days ago walking with Lu Lu. Your archenemy."

"Mine? Don't you remember...?"

"Okay...okay, we're over that. Anyway, I still saw them together."

"You didn't say anything?"

"Nope, 'cause I was in the car with my mama."

"So what? Doesn't mean he likes her."

"Well, you'll see what is going on with them when you get back home. I've told you, so my best-friend work here is done."

No time to add that to my list of things to worry about. Bookmarked. "Actually, your best-friend work is only beginning."

"Whatever it is, you know I'm in." She cuffed her ear. "Listening ears on high?"

"Okay. Remember, I told you Markie's mama abandoned her. We need to help find her mama."

"Correction. You need to help," she said and sat up. "My mama gave me one thing to do while I'm here and that was to stay out of trouble...."

"What if I told you that was just half of what I need your help with."

"Still listening."

"I've told Markie. But this is your *lane*. Know how Sweet Apple and the Boys and Girls Club are always holding fundraisers for trips and stuff," I said.

"Ah, yeah. That's how we were able to go to regionals and stay two nights at the Best Western."

"We can put on a fundraiser here. But instead of selling candy bars or hosting a bake sale, we'll have a talent show. Bigger than this town has ever seen."

"Talent show? That's my middle name."

I stood up.

"I told you this was all you. We'll call it Bogalusa's Got Talent?"

"OMG. You do need me. That's absolutely the most boring name in the universe. But I get it."

"And the funds we raise can go to..."

Nikki sniffed. "To getting the funk out the air?"

I didn't want to tear up thinking about it like on my Causeway ride. I wanted to be stronger.

"I can one-up that. Help kick Alzheimer's behind."

"Like our St. Jude's walk," she said.

"Yep. Helping Markie isn't the only way to help Aunt Vie." I took a knuckle to the corner of my eye before a tear fell.

"Wow. This really means a lot."

"It does."

I didn't want to tell her about the hurt when Aunt Vie thought I was Markie, or how I saw Aunt Vie raise her hand to Mama and break her heart.

A minute later, she flipped through my notebook reading what I'd planned so far. And I pulled out the pages that I had printed from the library about talent show ideas.

She glanced at them. "Looks like I got here just in time. I've got better ideas than these right here," she said and tapped her forehead.

"I don't doubt that at all," I said.

It took us about thirty minutes to shower, do some upsweep style with Nikki's hair, and get downstairs. We wolfed down pancakes and sausage in record time. Grandma Sugar said that she had a million things that would keep Peaches busy so that Nikki and I didn't have to have her tagging along.

"Oh wait," I said before we jetted out the door. I sprinted upstairs and grabbed one pencil and put that behind my ear and stuck another one in one of my twists in case Nikki needed one.

No sooner than we were outside, the paper-mill smell

was so thick, we could skate on it. Before we left the gate, I went to the backyard and wheeled out the bike.

"We need that now?" Nikki said.

I looked up to make sure Mama wasn't somewhere in earshot. "It'll be too risky to come back and get it."

"Gotcha," Nikki said.

I wheeled it next to me. A neighbor shaking a throw rug over her porch railing waved.

"Tell your mama I'm coming for tea before she leaves," the lady said, draped in a broccoli-green housedress.

"Yes, ma'am," I said.

While we walked, the smell of the paper mill gave way to the scent of boiling peanuts, but Peanut Man was nowhere in sight. I didn't know what I'd say to him when I saw him again. Even though he delivered me to Mama, he could have made more of a big deal about it.

"Where are we going?" Nikki said and adjusted her spaghetti straps. A tubetop-like T-shirt was underneath as her bra stand-in.

"To the park where I was supposed to meet Markie yesterday. It's a good place for us to talk even if she's not there. I really need you to do me a favor and be nice to her. I mean...don't be *mean*."

She stopped in front of me. "Are you really serious? Not only were you about ready to get grounded for her, now you're telling me how to behave. What's up with you and this girl?"

"She's just had a harder time. Harder than—"

"Don't go there. Don't compare our lives to hers— that's not fair. I wasn't going to mention this, but I gave up attending a cheerleading camp in Athens to come here." She pointed to the ground like she meant that very spot. "You could at least act like you appreciate it. Before you have me playing backup dancer to the girl."

"Didn't mean it like that. I do appreciate you coming. Wow. I know how much you love those." I took my hand off the bike for a second and stretched out my cramped fingers.

"Really. I'd never know it. Before we can even have any fun together, everything is about *Markie, Markie, Markie*. And from the looks of things, she's gonna get both of us locked in your room, no phone, no TV. And, news flash, her mama didn't abandon her yesterday. So why the urgency now? I say we strictly focus on the talent show." She pulled out her lip gloss and we started walking again.

Every word Nikki said was like a mosquito bite. "You're right. I'm doing a little too much. But there's lots of reasons why she's more concerned about her mama now. Aunt Vie is one. She's really close to her. And you know that's changing."

"Okay, you left out that information," Nikki said and smacked her lips. "Want me to push the bike?"

As we walked, her eyes rolled over everything like she was videotaping.

"This place is quaint. Q-u-a-i-n-t. Quaint. Did I spell it right?"

"Think so. But why are you spelling it in the first place is the question."

She pulled out her cell and we listened to Siri spell "quaint."

"After the fake eye shadow, there's another reason why I almost found myself grounded for the entire summer. C in English. C minus really. That back-to-school laptop is off the table until I get my vocabulary words up." Nikki stopped again to straighten her jean shorts that cuffed at the knee. I took that time to tell her about how much Aunt Vie loved spelling. And that it was a given we'd play Scrabble with Aunt Essie before too long. For the rest of the time, we talked about this and that and walked.

We were almost at McClurie Park when someone called, "Georgie! Georgie!"

Of course, I knew the voice immediately. As soon as they stood next to each other, Markie's black T-shirt with the Batman bat on it clashed with the burst of glittery stars on Nikki's top. I was there in my pastel "fashion fail" short set—Georgie in the middle.

"When you guys were putting my stuff in the truck, this fell out. I wanted you to see it."

"You went back in there," I said and reached for the picture.

Nikki took hold of the bike.

"I won't do it again, but I had to see if everything was out....And glad you brought the bike with you. Good thinking."

"I guess you're Markie," Nikki said.

"Yeah, sorry to start right in. You're Nik." Markie's eyes landed on Nikki's fresh-out-the-box Ugg sneakers. I could tell Nikki noticed because she changed her pose to give her a good look.

"Nikki. Only my big brother calls me Nik and it reminds

me how much he gets on my nerves. Pleased to make your acquaintance."

"Same here," Markie said.

While I glanced at the picture, I could hear Nikki spelling out the word "acquaintance" under the chatter of kids in the background. I'm sure it was going to annoy Markie in a few seconds.

As I held the picture in my hand, Aunt Vie's eyes met mine. Her hair was tucked under a red chef hat that matched her coat. Sweetings was embroidered on the left pocket. She was standing in the diner's kitchen over a pot of gumbo, just like Aunt Essie. And next to her, a few years younger, was Markie.

"Would you hold on to it for me? If one of the kids where I live gets ahold of it, that's that. I snapped a shot of it, but some pictures you always want the original."

"Sure. I'll keep it until you're ready for it," I said and put it in my purse.

"So why the no-show the other day?" Markie said.

"If she did show, I probably wouldn't be here now. Glad I advised her against it," Nikki shot off.

Markie laughed. "Wait, Georgie. I thought you wanted to be a lawyer. She sounds like your attorney."

"I'm her best friend, so sorta kinda," Nikki said. She'd decided to get on the bike and pedal-walk it.

Markie skipped ahead a bit and started walking backward in front of Nikki and the bike.

"Like your straightforwardness, loyalty. I can respect that. I know she's told you about the talent show. Your bestie has been talking you up. Says your dancing skills are 'fire.'"

"Yeah, I'm all that," Nikki said and tossed a few loose braids in a playful way that made Markie and me laugh. "Doesn't look like your coordination skills are half bad."

Markie was still walking backward and not even tripping on the uneven sidewalks.

"I'm better at handling this uneven pavement than most. Don't have much choice. If I fall, Shorty here can't do much to help me," she said. "So I try to prevent it, you know. Coordination doesn't carry over to dancing, though. I can't even square dance on beat. I bet you're on beat in your sleep," Markie said.

"Come up with some of my best routines when I'm sleeping." Nikki's eyes toured our surroundings. "How long you've lived in this town?" Nikki asked.

"Not in the same house, or with the same family, but pretty much since I've been alive. I lived in New Orleans once, but I don't remember that."

"Could your mama be in New Orleans?" Nikki said and fanned herself.

I side-eyed. If she noticed, she ignored me big-time. I didn't think I had to tell her to let me be the one to tell Markie that I'd brought her in on it.

"You told her?" Markie said.

"Cool out," Nikki said. "That's what best friends do."

I didn't think that my mediation between them would have to start so soon. Markie never told me not to tell anyone, but maybe she didn't think she had to either.

"I mean she's really only interested in the talent show, but there's no way I can totally leave her out of things. Even if I wanted to," I said.

Markie stared me down. Her jaws puffed out some before she spoke. "You don't think you should have asked me about that?"

I didn't even have to think about it. She was right. I nodded. "My bad for telling her before I had your permission."

With us clustered together on the bleachers, I got down to business. I told Nikki how far Markie and I had gotten before the plan fell apart. "So we need to get to Ms. Hannah's. ASAP."

As long as the grown-ups had their issues with Ms. Hannah, I doubted that she'd come around anytime soon. Not only was I going out to her place to help Markie get answers, I needed to tell her how much Aunt Vie missed her.

"Okay, here's what we'll do," I said to Markie and Nikki. As I spouted the plan, they both leaned in. We just needed to get going. The sun wasn't going to hang around and wait for us.

"Markie, think Scooter has two bikes to rent?"

Nikki held up one finger. "You two only need one more bike. I'll hide out at the library. There's gotta be one somewhere around here, huh?" I nodded. "Good. If we're going to do this talent show right, I need to know"—she tapped her temple—"I need to know the 'lay of the land.' Or, in other words, what's poppin' in Bogalusa. I could *easily* spend a couple hours researching."

Once that was settled, we headed out of the park. As we walked, we discussed different scenarios and hatched out our Plan B, which we all hoped we didn't have to use. Minutes later, we were in front of Scooter's.

"Hey, Scoot. Needa bike," Markie said.

"All out," Scooter said.

"Really? We'll even take that wreck you had the other day," Markie said.

"That's on the road," he said.

Scooter stepped away and picked up a clipboard that sat atop a metal plant stand. He flipped through two or three pages. I marveled at his organization. "Hold up. Think I got something for you."

"Now that's more like it. You know I'm one of your best customers."

I thought Nikki would have more questions, but she was scrolling through her phone, not fazed at all by all the "goings-on." Seconds later, Scooter reappeared with Roller-blades swung over his shoulder.

"Okay. Okay," Markie said. "These will work. Look about my size. Whoa! Velcro, too. Good looking out, Scoot." Markie grabbed the skates.

Nikki walked over to us. "Things really just got real. Three miles in Rollerblades on these roads. Good luck."

"Don't need luck when you got skills," Markie said.

"How much, Scooter?" I asked.

"Two fifty. Half the price of the bike."

As I paid Scooter, Markie sat on the curb and put on the skates.

"And why are you paying?" Nikki wanted to know.

"She paid for the other things, Nikki. Trust me. It's fair."

"Don't know about all that, but okay," Nikki said.

"Back by seven," Scooter shouted as Markie, Nikki, and I headed off to the library. Markie turned, spun, and jumped. "This is what you call skills on wheels." Then she shouted as she skated past us, "This is how you roll with the punches....Picture me rolling." And even Nikki, who hadn't cracked a smile since meeting Markie, had to laugh.

The three of us stood in front of the library. I had to admit that I was glad that Nikki was staying behind to concentrate on the talent show.

"Nikki, you're sure you're okay with not coming?" I asked.

"Whose idea was it, Georgie? Plus, you know my allergies and stuff. With all that dust, I'd have to stop every second. That's not what we need."

"Okay," I agreed. "But Nikki, please don't leave this library."

My mind flashed to the time Nikki, Kevin, and I rode our bikes to the hospital so that I could see Peaches. We left Nikki waiting outside for longer than we meant to. She got angry and went riding on her own. But she got lost. When Kevin and I couldn't find her on our own, we had to get Nikki's big brother involved. I thought she could be gone forever. Remembering it made my eyes blur with tears. The last thing I needed at the moment.

"Trust me, I've learned my lesson." That's all I needed to hear and Markie and I were on our way. "Good luck!" Nikki yelled.

I glanced back and waved.

"Thank you," Markie shouted to Nikki as I sped up.

I could almost hear the sun saying, "I'll stay up here as long as I can. I hope you're home by then."

Me too, sun. Me too.

16

SUMMER SABOTAGE

"How did you get so good?" I said. Keeping my sentences short and pacing my breathing.

"There is a rink about one hour from here. Aunt Vie and I used to go. She skated sometimes but mostly she just cheered me on and played hooky on the diner."

For the next few minutes, it was just us and our breathing.

Then I thought that this was my last chance to find out what I needed to know from Markie before Ms. Hannah came into the picture.

"Why haven't you gone to her before?"

She took a breath. "I wanted to. Maybe I just didn't want

to go by myself. And going with you is the closest I can get to going with Aunt Vie. You're patient like her."

"Wow! Thanks," I said. "My mama told me a little more about Ms. Hannah the other day. Lots of *deep* stuff there. But they need to work something out so Aunt Vie can see Ms. Hannah." I rehearsed in my head just how I would tell Ms. Hannah how much Aunt Vie missed her.

We'd been going full speed for about a mile. The path was rocky but not as many cars as I thought there would be.

"You know, I never wanted to find my mama. I wanted her to come looking for me like you see on TV. Doubt that's happening."

I'd taken a deep breath but didn't speak. Her words floated around us.

"But why do you think Ms. Hannah knows something?"

We stayed on the sidewalks when we could, but that wasn't always an option.

"I don't know for sure. But I know that Aunt Vie loved her sisters, but when she needed someone to talk to, she went to Ms. Hannah. What if...what if...what if something happens to Ms. Hannah, too?"

"Like what?"

"I don't want to say. You got mad at me the last time."

"Oh. What if something bad happens to her like she passes away or something."

"Yeah. And I'd never tried to talk to her on my own."

"I understand," I said.

"If we're going to make it there, we got to pick up the speed and the mood. Sappy isn't my bag," she said and laughed.

"Not my bag, either," I said, loving how cool "bag" sounded. We picked up more speed. When I pursed my lips, I could tell how dry they were. I stopped. I needed to put on my ChapStick. I'd hate to meet someone Aunt Vie loved so much with my lips dry as tree bark.

The constant movement gave me that prickling heat feeling all over my body, which acted as a spark to make me move even faster.

Then as I was just getting used to the noises of birds and the air flapping, Markie said, "Want to know what Aunt Vie would do when we'd go walking?"

"What?" I almost wanted to stop so I wouldn't miss a word.

Markie started whistling. I mean not the sort of whistling people do to call someone but in tune. I listened.

"Aunt Vie whistled?"

"Not out in public. But when she was in the house she would. She and Ms. Hannah whistled together. Aunt Vie said that her daddy used to tell her, 'A whistling woman and a crowing hen surely don't come to no good end.'"

The rhyme made me laugh but I knew that it wasn't really funny.

I wasn't sure if I ever met a girl who whistled. Daddy did sometimes. But if I whistled, especially in the house, Mama or Grandma Sugar would tell me that it "wasn't ladylike."

"Want to know one of her favorite songs to whistle?"

As soon as I heard the first two seconds of it, my feet could have stopped pedaling and I could have cruised on this melody the rest of the way.

"'Georgia on My Mind'? Really?" I said. I didn't even

want to tell Markie how Mama said that Aunt Vie used to sing "Georgie on My Mind" when I was a baby. Maybe she knew. Maybe that's why she told me.

About ten minutes into our whistling, my mouth was dry. Just off to the left a sign read *Nettie's Local Grocery* in bright blue letters. "Can we stop there?" I asked.

"Yeah, I could use a thirst quencher," Markie said, then she swirled to an impressive stop and bowed before tumbling forward.

"Markie!" I shouted, letting the bike fall to its side. I was sure she was going to go facedown.

"I'm good," she said, barely recovering.

"You could have just come to a regular stop, you know. Didn't have to be super fancy."

"Where is the fun in that?" she said.

As soon as we opened the door, a squawking that sounded like it was coming from speakers swirled around us. There, with its talons gripped to the register, was the largest parrot I'd ever seen. It spread its wings and it squawked even louder. The blue looked like the color of where ocean and sky touched on Mama and Frank's honeymoon postcard from Negril.

"Calm it down, Nettie," a lady said. "Don't mind her, she's testy today." The lady held out her arm, which was wrapped in a rubber sleeve, and Nettie landed on it, then quieted. "That's a good bestie," the clerk said. Two sets of eyes followed us to the refrigerated section. The store smelled of Vienna sausages and crackers.

Markie opened the door and grabbed a purple sports

drink. I chose a flavored water. Once at the checkout, I stared at the gigantic jars that sat on the counter. One contained chunks of pinkish meat floating in light red liquid, the other contained humongous pickles. Markie stared directly at them and turned the pickle jar around.

I tapped the unlabeled jar. "What are those?"

"You must be new around here," the cashier said.

I nodded, not taking my eyes off the jar. "Those are pig lips. Out of feet and tails. I'll have some tomorrow."

"Oh, my grandma eats pig tails, sometimes," I said.

"Yeah, but she probably cooks them with rice. Mine are pickled for easy eating," the cashier said and laughed. "What can I interest you in?"

I put my water on the counter.

"This is all for now," I said.

"You should try one of these," Markie said about the pickles swimming in red water. "You in?"

"Why not," I said.

"Two please," Markie said, shooting up rabbit ears.

"These are fresh and sweet," the lady said. She smiled, showing gleaming white teeth. The bird hopped from her arm to directly on top of her head. Her turban-like wrapping provided the cushion. When she turned to ring us up, there was a tattoo of what I thought at first were praying hands on the side of her neck. But I realized they were wings.

"These are Koolickles," Markie said as the lady put them into two wax pouches. She handed both to me, but Markie reached for her own.

"I'll leave all the naming to you young folks. They're

just sweet, sour, and good pickles to me. That's all Nettie knows."

"Your bird eats them, too," I said.

She laughed. "Not hardly. Too picky. She's my namesake. Only namesake I got. You two stay out of trouble, ya hear?"

"Yes, ma'am," we said as Markie paid. I tried to hand Markie my half, but she wouldn't take it. The lady gave us napkins. Markie tossed her napkin on the counter, placed her Koolickle on it, then stuffed the drink in her pocket.

We went back to face the heat with drinks, Koolickles in tow.

"Aunt Vie used to eat dill pickles with a peppermint stick down the middle of them. But she wouldn't try these," Markie said.

As soon as I bit into it, it was a mouthful of sugary deliciousness that I know Nikki and I would have never tried in Atlanta. It was simply a dill pickle soaked in what tasted like cherry Kool-Aid. I pushed the bike with one hand and tackled my Koolickle with the other. Markie walk-skated by my side. In an open lot not far from Nettie's there were a couple milk crates. We sat there while I finished my Koolickle. Markie nearly inhaled hers.

We'd gone about another mile and a half it felt like before we reached a fenced-in plot of land with only one house in the distance and a barn.

"Please tell me that's Ms. Hannah's," I said.

"That's it."

It still took us about ten minutes to get up to the gate. Markie opened it and we were officially on Ms. Hannah's property.

"Should we look around for her, or just go up and knock?" I said.

Even before we could get to the door, music pierced the air. It seemed to be coming from the trees.

Markie and I stared at each other.

"Where is it coming from?"

We walked closer to the house.

All the curtains were closed. The house was mostly brick with well-manicured hedges and not a weed in sight. The columns at the front of the house had all type of carvings and nicks in them. I leaned the bike against the porch step.

"Ready," I said. "You want me to knock?"

"Nah. I got it. Doubt she's in there, though. Probably somewhere on the grounds."

Before she knocked a second time, there was galloping. I turned to see a sight that I'd never seen before in real life, ever.

17

SLOW DOWN

The horse in front of us was so black that it shone a deep shade of purple. Its mane was thick and braided with green and red twine. Ms. Hannah looked majestic atop it. Her silver hair was parted down the middle and two braids, one on each side, hung past her shoulders.

Seems like somebody would have mentioned that Ms. Hannah was a real-life cowgirl.

"Well, you two are a beautiful sight." Then she focused in on Markie. "So, you must be ready now?" Ms. Hannah said, tugging on the horse's reins. Two buttons were undone on her denim shirt, revealing a thin gold necklace.

"Yes, ma'am," Markie said.

"And you're sure? That's not how you felt a few weeks ago."

Markie never said anything about talking to Ms. Hannah a few weeks ago, which only surprised me a little. I was learning that Markie didn't lie straight out, she just omitted things. *Important things.*

"And let me guess who we have here....You must be G-baby, Katrina's daughter." Ms. Hannah got down from her horse.

"She likes the name Georgie better," Markie said in a respectful correction.

"Well, that makes sense for a young lady," Ms. Hannah said. The horse high-stepped and neighed. "Hush up, now. Nobody leaving you out. This here is Bessie." Ms. Hannah stood next to Bessie and smoothed her mane. "Markie, why you acting like Bessie's a stranger?" Markie walked over to Bessie and stroked her side. "She likes to meet new people," Ms. Hannah said to me, "especially Vie's family." I stepped over and rubbed Bessie, too. It was like the warmth of my hand in an oven mitt.

"Well, it's good to see you again, baby." Her "baby" didn't make you feel childish, but like she was welcoming you into a special club. "I'd know you anywhere, you and your mama have Vie's same deep-set eyes. Everything fine with Vie?" she asked. "I mean, as well as can be expected?"

"Yes, ma'am," Markie said.

A few chickens appeared from around the corner, along with a pig that was shaking off flies.

"Shoo! Shoo!" Ms. Hannah said as she tied Bessie's

harness to a metal rod jetting from the column. "Now, I take it that you two have to get home sooner than later, so we best take care of business. Have yourselves a seat on the stairs if you like. I've got some fresh lemon tea brewing. I'll be right out."

Ms. Hannah must have known just where to walk because the steps didn't creak as much. I was nervous that if for whatever reason Bessie decided to take off, she'd pull that wobbly column right along with her and we'd be lost under the front porch rubble. As soon as Ms. Hannah opened and closed the door behind her, I turned to Markie.

"Think we'll make it back before dark?"

"I do," she said. She barely mumbled the answer. I knew she was thinking about what she wanted to ask Ms. Hannah.

Bessie watched us as the chickens and pig circled around her and then went off about their business.

When Ms. Hannah returned with the tea tray, we stood. She sat it on a table and then filled our glasses, then one for herself.

"You were her best friend," Markie said.

"I am. I am her best friend. Closer than sisters... kindred." Ms. Hannah sipped her tea. "One day you two might find what binds you as friends. It's seldom random when two spirits connect. I love Vie with my whole entire heart, but that doesn't mean we agreed on everything. I wanted her to put pen to paper when things were getting foggy for her. She didn't. That's why her sisters don't understand how much she'd want to be out here, roaming this land with me."

I sipped my tea and let the ice cube rest on my lip before

I spoke. "She'd love that." The land was flat but green. There was a white wooden fence that separated the land like the lines you see in the middle of the highways in Atlanta. Unlike the porch, the fence looked freshly painted. Beyond that was a two-story red barn with stacks of hay along its sides. The barn was trimmed with white, too, as if outlined with chalk. Where it looked like windows could have been were giants Xs like in the squares of ticktacktoe.

"Markie Jean, how are you doing in your foster home?"

She shrugged. "My foster mom...she's okay. But she might be getting married soon. I heard 'em talking. Even though she gets a little money for me, might be easier on them if I wasn't around."

"Did she say that to you?" Ms. Hannah said.

Markie's words drenched me with cold water. She'd never said any of that to me before. A part of me felt selfish for getting upset that she shut me out.

The ice cubes in Markie's glass clinked. But she didn't sip, just watched the tea swirl in the glass. "I'm almost thirteen now. It finally hit me that maybe it's time to know what I can."

Ms. Hannah darted her eyes between the both of us, and they landed on Markie. "Hold your hand in front of your mouth." Markie did that. "Now say anything you want." Markie looked at Ms. Hannah, then at me.

I shrugged. "Go ahead."

"My name is Markie. I'm twelve and a half."

I wanted to fidget, cross my ankles, something. But I sat freeze-tag still as if Ms. Hannah's connection to Markie would break with any sound.

"Good. Did you feel your breath against your hand as you spoke?" Ms. Hannah said.

"Yes, ma'am," Markie said.

"Now, try to take them back."

Markie pursed her lips. "What back?"

"Those words. You felt them, right? Now try to take them back."

"I can't," she admitted.

When I understood what she meant, my whole body tingled. The kind of jitters you get when you know you're seeing and hearing something that will stay in your mind forever.

"You have to know that's how it feels to know the true power of words. If Vie made decisions not to reveal certain things, those of us who may know a thing or two also know that once told, they can't be untold." Ms. Hannah looked out at her field, then left her tea on the table and stepped back out into the yard and rubbed Bessie. I'd took a huge gulp while waiting for Ms. Hannah to speak.

"You're twelve and a half?"

"Yes, ma'am," Markie said. Ms. Hannah returned and picked up the mason jar and held it to her forehead.

"Remember I said that Vie and I didn't agree on everything?" Markie nodded. "Well, what I'm about to tell you is one of those things." Markie and I exchanged glances. "How she came about the decision to want you in her care when she did is a gray area. I don't think she'd ever been completely straight with me about it. One day we were sitting right here and she told me that she was starting the process to be a foster parent."

"Because of me," Markie said.

Ms. Hannah nodded. "I didn't know it at the time, though. Even the person closest to you can keep thoughts to themselves. I just know that Vie was determined to care for you. There was a distant cousin who showed interest but that didn't pan out. She's long since left Bogalusa."

"It's just not clear to me how I got into the system."

"I'm not one hundred percent sure of that myself. What I know is that you were with your mama in New Orleans for a while. Then she came back to Bogalusa. Maybe tried to settle here again. She left you with a neighbor, I believe. From my understanding, the neighbor called Child & Family Services after there had been no contact with your mom."

Ms. Hannah's silver hair crept over her right eye. She raked her hands through it, turquoise earrings gleaming. It was only her eyes, which were greenish brown, and the sharpness of her nose that reminded me of a white person.

"No one knew where the cousin went?" Markie said.

"Keep in mind that some people came here to work for the mill. 'Paper people' we call them. They weren't born and bred here. And even if they were, it was probably their parents that had the opportunity in Bogalusa. Things dried up for the younger folks. A slow economy and drugs took a toll. All the connections were gone, and they have no reason to stay. Sometimes they leave things behind, though."

It was like an electric surge shot through Markie. Her back straightened and her knees bounced.

"Did my mama leave anything behind? I mean, besides me."

Now, Markie looked down like she'd realized how excited she had gotten and prepared for disappointment.

"Yes, actually. Give me a few minutes. I'll be right back."

When the screen door closed, this time I moved closer to Markie. I thought she'd lean in for a hug. But she didn't. Nikki would have. But Markie drained her tea, then clasped the jar between her knees and dug into it and retrieved a thin ice cube. She rubbed it on her face and neck.

"What do you think it is?" I said.

She sighed. "Who knows. Probably some letter, trying to explain why she left."

"That wouldn't be so lame, would it?"

"Only a person with a mama—two, matter of fact— would ask that."

I cut my losses and didn't answer. We both watched a black ant march across the ground with a speck of food.

Then I was thinking what if Markie's mama had found her way back to town and was staying with Ms. Hannah until she "got on her feet." That's what happens to grown- ups sometimes, like with my daddy's cousin Arthur. He stayed in our guest bedroom and worked for Daddy at the dealership until he could afford his own place.

What if Ms. Hannah opened the screen door and out strolled Markie's mama? I'd never say that to Markie because it even sounded unbelievable to me. Still, I crossed my fingers but hid them under my leg. That couldn't hurt.

When we could hear Ms. Hannah heading back out, Markie said, "I guess a letter wouldn't be that lame."

There was only the sound of one set of footsteps. I uncrossed my fingers. Seconds later, the front door opened, and Ms. Hannah took two long strides toward us. In her hands she held a medium-sized canister, like it was a birthday cake.

Markie didn't reach for it.

"That's for you, Markie," I said.

When Markie still didn't move, Ms. Hannah set it lightly on Markie's lap.

"What's in it?" Markie asked.

"Personal belongings of your mama. How Aunt Vie got them and when, I'm not clear about. But she knew enough to put them away for safekeeping. I'm sure Vie probably had planned to sit and talk with you about the items one by one. Even if she didn't know the history behind it, she wanted to be there to share the moment with you. Life doesn't always present the perfect moment, so we have to make it."

Markie shook her head. "I don't want to do it now. I don't."

Her voice had that sound right before tears gushed. I was so used to my voice sounding that way, even Nikki's, but not Markie's.

"That's okay, baby. Do it in your time. You take all the time you need," Ms. Hannah said.

"Georgie, can you please put this in my backpack for me?" It was the first time she'd asked me to help her maneuver something. "If it doesn't fit, we can toss something out."

I jumped up to grab the canister. It was heavier than I expected.

"It's fitting," I said. "But you sure you don't want to open it now? There could be clues. I thought this is what you wanted."

Markie stood up and stared at Ms. Hannah.

"Does anything in there tell me where she is or why she...why she left me?"

Ms. Hannah closed her eyes for a moment like she was seeing everything inside the box. She put her hand to her chest, and it was the first time I noticed the gold necklace had a half a heart charm on it.

"No. It's mostly just memories of her. Trinkets that will help you know her."

Markie sniffled and dabbed her eyes with her knuckles. Then she puffed her chest out like that somehow was a way to stop tears. "The fact that she never came back is all I need to know," Markie said. "Why couldn't she keep me with her? Why just leave me like that? That's not what parents are supposed to do, especially the mama, right, Georgie? Remember what you said about the birds. Remember? I hate her. I hate her."

The sadness in Markie's voice made my knees tremble. Once I put the canister in the backpack, I was going to wrap my arms around her. But Ms. Hannah was there. She had her arms around Markie and eased her to the door. I followed.

"Georgie, please, let me talk to her alone for a bit. We'll be out as soon as we can."

"Okay," I said. I couldn't imagine feeling Markie's pain without bowling over with tears. When I shared that bird image with Markie I didn't know that I was hurting her. I didn't even think that Markie wanted to be one of those baby birds, too.

Though I couldn't see her face, I didn't hear anything

but an occasional sniffling. I didn't ever want to know what it felt like to have to be so strong that you couldn't cry when you needed to. I used the edge of my T-shirt to wipe the tears from my eyes and sat down on the steps and waited. Bessie stood there attentive like she was waiting for Ms. Hannah to return, too. I stood to go rub her mane again but thought to look at my cell phone. *Good. No messages.*

Stroking Bessie made me think what it would be like to ride her across the land like Ms. Hannah. I wondered if Aunt Vie rode horses, too. A few minutes later, Markie and Ms. Hannah came out. From what I could tell, Markie had something in her hand and put it in the pocket of her shorts. But unlike when I'd seen her put other things in her pockets, she buttoned the flap.

"Wish I could stay out here with you," Markie said.

"We tried that and what happened?"

"I kept running away," Markie said.

"That didn't help, but the DCFS people didn't think an 'old, crazy horse lady' was your best guardian. Time heals some wounds, only prolongs others. You have to give yourself a chance to learn which one it will do for you." Like me, Markie widened her eyes trying to decipher the meaning. "Some hurts will heal. Some may not. But we have to be open and continue doing the best we can, not limit ourselves."

"I understand," Markie said. "When I'm ready, I don't have to look through the box alone."

Poking my thumb to my chest, I said, "I'll be there if you want."

"See," Ms. Hannah said. "And you're always welcome here."

"Thank you," Markie said to both of us. "I guess we need to get back to town."

"I'll be happy to drive you two."

"Think that'll be cool, Markie?" I said.

She shrugged. "I rather just go back the way we came."

"As long as we make it back before late, that's fine."

"We will," Markie said.

Ms. Hannah watched us prepare to leave. "You two sharing a bike?"

"Georgie is riding the bike, and I have these." Markie pointed to the Rollerblades that she'd dropped near the porch.

"We can do better than that. I got about three bikes in the shed. Keep one for the rest of the summer. Leave it at your aunt Vie's for when you come back again."

"Thank you, Ms. Hannah," we said.

Markie and I followed her to the shed. We waited at the door and she rolled out an older bike but with a near perfect yellow finish. It had a brown wicker basket attached to the front.

"This is the one Vie loved to ride when she was out here. This should get you home quicker."

The thought of Aunt Vie and Ms. Hannah riding around like Markie and me made me smile.

"Thank you," we said.

I took a second to call Nikki. No answer. That may have been usual for some people to let a call go unanswered in the library, but Nikki once got grounded for texting during Sunday service. So I waited for a text back. *Nothing.*

Ms. Hannah trotted Bessie alongside her as we headed

out to the front of Spirit Farms. "You two go straight back now. And give Vie my love."

"Wait one second, Markie," I said. I turned back and rode until I was in front of Ms. Hannah. "She misses you. I know things aren't good with my aunt Essie and my grandma, but I hope that doesn't keep you away for long." The way Ms. Hannah gently touched my face and rubbed my cheek I just couldn't bring myself to tell her about the slap.

"Thank you for that, Georgie. That means more than you know. You get on back now."

Markie and I waved and set off on the main road.

Once we were on our way, I thought the ride back would give us time to let it all roll around in our heads, sink in.

I just couldn't imagine how Markie could ride with that mystery box in her backpack. Just the thought of it was weighing on my mind like the thousands of rocks on the road. But I started to really panic when my thoughts flashed forward to Nikki waiting for us at the library. Patience wasn't high on her list of attributes.

"Slow up," Markie called out, but beating the sun going down was one issue. Nikki was the other. Maybe I should have convinced Markie that Ms. Hannah's offer to give us a ride was best.

"We gotta get back soon. You don't know Nikki. This whole thing will backfire. I don't even want to think about what would happen if my mama found out." So I kept pedaling as fast as I could.

"It's not dark yet."

"Yeah but the library is closing. And we need to get back *before* dark. Way before."

I was standing up and pedaling like time itself was chasing me and I was determined to beat it.

"C'mon, you need to slow down. . .please," Markie said again. "This bike doesn't handle so well on this road."

Then there was a sound like Markie's bike was doing doughnuts. I turned in time to see the bike splayed out and Markie sailing across the sky like a low-flying kite.

18

OMW

We made it back to Nettie's shop before I realized how banged up Markie was.

When Nettie saw us, she scurried from behind the register. "My word, what happen to you?"

"My word. My word," the parrot mimicked Nettie.

"Oh, now you want to talk today," Nettie said to parrot Nettie.

"She fell off..."

"Fell off...fell off," parrot Nettie said.

"I didn't fall....I hit a rock. There was a huge rock on the road," Markie said.

"However it happened, let's get you patched up." Nettie pulled out a chair from behind the register and helped me ease Markie down into it. Blood started streaming faster from one gash. Nettie pulled what looked like a metal toolbox from behind the register. She opened the register and removed a tiny key to open the box. When she flipped it open, there was a roll of gauze, a gleaming knife, a ruby bracelet that sparkled, and at the back of the box was a handle of a gun, as black and smooth as Bessie. The barrel of it was buried under rolls of quarters and a stack of money. My eyes bulged.

Nettie noticed and said, "A woman can't be too careful running a store alone," and pulled out a roll of gauze, two Band-Aids, and a travel-size bottle of alcohol.

"Is that gonna sting?" Markie said and seized up like a potato bug.

"Yeah, it is. And it's gonna hurt you more than it hurts me, so let's get it over with as soon as we can. You don't want an infection."

Markie's right leg had the deepest gash. She didn't bend her leg and walked on it like it was wooden. Nettie sent me to get us some waters. When I came back, I asked Markie was she going to be able to ride the rest of the way.

"I know you're not talking about a bike. Plenty of pain if you do," Nettie said.

"Plenty of pain. Plenty of pain," the parrot emphasized.

Markie stood up and shook her leg like it had fallen asleep. "I'll be okay. I've been through worse."

"How far you have to go?"

"Sweetings," I volunteered.

My phone rang. I yanked it from my purse. It was Nikki but she was whispering.

"Where are you?" she said.

I pressed the phone closer to my ear. "On our way. We had a spill on the bike."

"She's here. At the library."

"Who are you talking about?"

"Your *mom* is in the library. She's sitting at the Kiddie Corner with Peaches and another little girl. I can't go to the restroom or leave. There's no way she can see me without you."

Panic swirled in my voice. "I'll text you when we're closer to see what's happening."

"What if she spots me?"

"Plan B."

"Got it. Bye," she said.

"No good news," Markie said.

"Nada," I said.

I had to think about Markie and the fact that she'd learned a little more about her background. Maybe not the outcome we wanted, but it was better than nothing. But I'd dragged Nikki into all of this. If Mama spotted her, she'd have to lie to cover for me. I felt guilty about that. I'd already used my "get-out-of-being-grounded card" with the Peanut Man incident. I could kiss our talent show goodbye. Mama wouldn't believe that I came up with the idea before Nikki got here. She'd think it was a scheme to avoid staying in the house. It was more than that. Much more.

The way I envisioned it would be good for all of us. The entire town. But I could hear Mama's voice: "You should have thought about that before you went traipsing through Boga-lusa without telling a soul." I'd never want her to think that I'd stoop as low as to come up with the show to raise money for Alzheimer's as a way to avoid trouble. One thing for sure, she'd send Nikki packing back to Atlanta for her part in the cover-up. The other thing is that Nikki would be doubly mad at me because she'd missed the cheerleading camp.

A car pulled up in front of the store and a lady and two teenaged boys walked in. Nettie sent us on our way with two pineapple sodas and chips.

"Come back and visit again, now," she said to us as we left. "And slow down."

Markie tried not to hobble, but she grimaced each time she bent her knee. Maybe it was to prove me wrong, but she got on her bike and rode without complaint. She set the pace and we didn't talk. The good news was that just like with most trips, the travel home seemed shorter than the travel to the original destination. The bad news was that less than a few blocks from the library, I got another text.

We pulled over for a minute.

"It's closing. She's still here," Nikki texted. "Hurry... I think Peaches spotted me. I shushed her but you never know."

"OMW."

"There's a path to come up on the back of the library," Markie said. "Then we can just connect with her out front and act like we were together all the time."

Riding as fast as we could, it still took us about fifteen minutes to see the library. My phone didn't beep. No new text from Nikki. After coming up to the rear of the library, I realized it was too late to hide from anyone. Not a bike was on the rack, not a car in the tiny lot. It was closed.

"We're too late," I said.

Nikki texted. "At Aunt Vie's. Hurry."

Markie and I could have both rode to Aunt Vie's, but if I was already in trouble, the last thing I needed was for Mama to see me with Markie.

"I best ride back to Aunt Vie's alone."

"Good call. I'll ride up to the diner and leave the bike there."

As we were parting, I said, "I hope...I hope there's something in that box that you love."

Markie nodded. "Thanks for coming with me. Sorry we haven't used your detective skills yet. I appreciate the support, though."

"That's what friends do," I said and shrugged.

Markie nodded and adjusted her backpack. "You better get home," she said with a softness that made me want to cry. "Hug her for me, please."

"I will," I said.

With gullies to the left and right of me, I rode so fast that I paid them no mind, not even the barking dogs. As I got the house in view, I didn't know exactly what to expect. Peaches was playing with the same little girl she'd met the first day. And sitting in the chair, wiping her eyes, was Nikki. We were officially in Plan B: the fake cry. Whenever we'd gotten ourselves in a bind, or needed time to think, we had to pull the cord on the "fake cry." Nikki was giving it her all. It felt like I was riding straight into a wind tunnel. But I kept going.

"Where have you been?" Mama's voiced echoed throughout the entire street.

Now, it wasn't an issue of whether I was in trouble but how much. Judging by Nikki's crocodile tears—a ton.

19

HEEBIE-JEEBIES

My feet hitting the sidewalk sounded hard enough to cave in the cement. Nikki glanced up and wiped her eyes. Mama rubbed her arms the soothing way she does when someone is hurt or upset.

"Georgiana Elizabeth Matthews," Mama said.

"Uh-oh," Peaches said.

"First, you're lucky you got yourself here before dark. Roll that bike right to the backyard. We'll get it to Markie, but you, young lady, won't be on that bike or any other."

"Yes, ma'am," I said, trying to get some clue from Nikki what story she'd used. I leaned the bike against the back of the house and slinked around to the porch.

"Explain yourself. Why didn't you stay with Nikki? You two have been friends for too long to abandon her."

Nikki folded her arms and cut in. "I didn't want to stay with her, Auntie Trina. All they wanted to do was ride that bike and stuff. It was too hot. I was scared that my...my asthma would flare up, so I found the library."

Okay, good. That's close to the Plan B story.

"I would have gone with you," I said, trying to do my part.

"I just think I want to go back to Atlanta," Nikki said.

Nikki, you're overdoing it. We have a whole talent show to put on. Take it down a notch.

"Is that how you want your best friend to feel, Georgie? She traveled all this way to spend time with you and you pretty much ditched her for someone who's already gotten you in trouble."

"You can stay and play with us, Nikki. Nobody wants to be around G-baby's meanie friend," Peaches said.

"Georgie, you and Nikki go on inside and see if you can come to some type of agreement." Then she zeroed in on me. "If you were home, you'd be begging for Nikki to come over, and now that she's here, you toss her aside. I'm not sure what's getting into you. You need an attitude adjustment and quick. That Markie is gonna get you in something you can't get out of." Then she spoke directly to Nikki. "I'd planned for us to all eat together at the diner this evening to celebrate you being here. Even if you want to go home, we can do that anyway."

"Yes, ma'am," she said. "Thank you. I'd like that."

"Go talk it out. I'll be up in a little while," Mama added.

Nikki walked in without me and didn't hold the door. She was the best at all the finishing touches.

"She can't always have everything her way," I said to Mama to add to the tension.

"Just go on inside and talk to her," Mama said.

Nikki had already gone up the stairs when I came in. I followed up after her and closed the bedroom door.

"Whew." She wiped her forehead.

I shushed her and pointed to the window. Nikki turned on one of her music apps and Chance the Rapper rang out.

"I'm not sure what favor I'm calling in for all that, Georgie. But you better believe I'm going to think of something."

And she'd earned it. In Mama's world, there is absolutely no excuse for us losing track of each other when we're supposed to be together.

"Name the favor. You got it. So what happened?" I said, unable to sit.

"More like what didn't happen—you and I aren't grounded for all eternity. Thanks to me." She held her index finger above her head and pointed. Then did a quick shimmy move. And adjusted an imaginary crown.

"C'mon, tell me." I peeked out the window to see Mama still on the porch. "Obviously, my mama spotted you in the library."

"Maybe that's what you and your little friend Markie would have let happen. But I took control of the situation. Got in front of it—I 'found' her. Then went on to tell her how you and Markie were all about that tomboy life and I wasn't having it."

"So you told her we left you at the library?"

"Have I not taught you a thing? Ugh. That would have still gotten you in more trouble than you are now. I put it all on me. Me going to the library without you was never going to get me in as much trouble as you riding to the unknown 'outskirts of town' was going to get you."

I rolled my eyes upward. "That is so true."

"So right now, I'm upset with you because you were showing Markie more attention than me. I was so angry that I left and found the library. Instead of petrified when I saw your mom, she thinks I was relieved. . . . And the Oscar goes to. . ."

"Nicole Denise Shepard for Best Supporting Actress. . ."

Nikki put her hand to her forehead and fell back on the bed. A dramatic fainting spell. Then she popped up. "Supporting? Really?"

"Okay, Best Actress," I said.

"Forget the jokes, Georgie. That could have really been a mess. I hope it was all worth it."

"I think so. Ms. Hannah gave Markie a box with some belongings from her mama. She hasn't opened it yet. Things got a little emotional," I said. "But I'm glad you were on the case with the talent show. It was a good decision for us to split up. How did you do at the library?"

"It was busy. I could only stay on the computer for thirty minutes. But that was more than I needed, really." Then she held up her phone. "Took mega notes and even borrowed some paper from the Frog Lady librarian. I'll email them to you."

"No biggie. You'll be here helping me put the show

together. Thanks to you, I'm not grounded, so it is still a go. Time to ramp things up. Think it can be bigger than I thought at first."

She didn't say anything. I thought for sure she'd start practicing our routine before I'd finished my sentence.

Now she pushed down on the bed, leaned forward. "Georgie…what if I told you that I was sorta telling the truth about wanting to go home?"

"You mean, leave?"

"Yeah, I don't see this ending well for us. I'm really try-ing to stay out of trouble for the rest of the summer. And this is all for a girl who I still think is playing you."

I did a Mama move and searched the ceiling, my head as far back as it could go. "Stop saying that. You weren't there today."

"Okay, I'll give you that. But you're taking too many risks for her. Everything is about Markie. I'm supposed to be here to spend time with you. That's not what's happening."

After all that riding, it was Nikki's words that made my knees weak. I sat next to her on the bed. I didn't have any Plan A or B for this. Now that Nikki was here, I just couldn't imagine her leaving so soon.

"But I thought we'd worked this out. I wanted you to come with us, Nikki."

"Okay, so I'd have to go on a six-mile, round-trip bike-athon to spend time with you. Is that fair? I don't think this is the end of it. There will be something else tomorrow. I feel it. And you said that she didn't even bother to open the box you risked getting grounded to help her get."

There wasn't a way I could describe that moment to

Nikki, so I let it be. As she sat, she started rocking. That's her calming mechanism when something is bothering her. The last time I remember her rocking like this was when we were both waiting on news about Peaches.

"What's going on with you? I mean I know Markie isn't your favorite, but I didn't think you'd go as far as leaving. I know you haven't spent a lot of time with Aunt Vie yet, but I told you how much putting together this show means to me. And I do need your help."

"You don't know everything, though. There's something else."

I scooted closer to her. "Spill it. Like what?"

She glanced down at the sneakers, then pursed her lips and swished them from side to side. "Know how you're going to a new school next year?"

The thought of that made my stomach twist. I'd never attended a school without Nikki.

"Yeah? But we'll still see each other....Wait...is your mama making you go to Woodward?"

"Something like that. They just hit me with the news not too long after you left."

"And you're just now mentioning it."

"D-e-n-i-a-l. Denial. Wasn't ready to talk about it."

"Got ya. This just means that we can get through the new school heebie-jeebies together." Nothing I said connected with her. No smile. Not even a playful side-eye. Nothing. "And I know you're probably going to hate wearing a school uniform, but you have your own style. You can make anything look fly. You'll rock it."

She nodded and gave me a half smile. "That's true." Then

her expression drooped again. "It's more like that the school is in…"

"Can't be any farther than Snellville."

"I wish….It's in California."

It was like someone piped all the paper-mill fumes into the room and I couldn't catch my breath. "Wait… *California*?"

She didn't say a word but her tears said it all. If I were in my own room, I could grab one of my pillows or one of my stuffed animals to stop the tennis balls that seem to be smashing against my chest.

"My brother says he's not going, but he's almost eighteen. I don't have a choice. I knew my dad was looking for work, but neither of my parents ever even hinted that it wouldn't be in Atlanta."

"We never get a say in anything. That's how I felt about the divorce."

"I just wanted this summer to be us. You and me. And I get here and there's all this drama going on. I don't want to go home, but I don't want to be on punishment on my way to California either. I have to leave everything, everyone I love. It's just not fair. So I came here to be with my best friend. You keep saying how much you need me for the talent show, but I just need you. This is harder than I thought."

I leaned over and hugged her. She hugged me back and I felt that I'd let her down. I was so fixated on Markie, I didn't even see she needed me.

"I was getting used to the fact we wouldn't be at the same school next year and now this," she said. "What about our Period Party? I'm not having one with my mom. Nope, not doing it," she said and folded her arms.

I tried to laugh. We'd planned to do sleepovers and dish on all the details of when our periods came.

"We can still do that over the phone or video, Nikki. We'll be there for each other. You'll see. I want you to stay. I'll do better. Promise."

She pointed her sneakers upward and nodded.

Before I could even think to hug her again, there was a knock on the door. I figured it would fling open any second.

"Come in," I said. The door opened and there stood Mama.

Under her breath Nikki said, "A wait-to-come-in. Nice."

Nikki and I hugged again. "I'm staying. We talked it out," Nikki said.

"Good. No more of this separating. Stick together or both of you stay in the house."

"No problem, Mama," I said.

Nikki nodded.

"You two get freshened up for dinner. I'm glad it's going to be a celebration of you staying with us, Nikki."

"Seafood gumbo on the menu?" she asked.

"You know it," Mama said and laughed. Then she reached behind and tucked in the tag of my T-shirt. As she was doing that she said, "I had your aunt Essie get in touch with Markie Jean. I'd like her there this evening as well. 'Bout time we chat if you two are going to be hanging out together more often."

"Okay," I said and felt a chill. What was Mama going to say to her?

Soon as Mama left, Nikki gave me that sly smile of hers and said, "Question?"

"What?"

"This is not an all-girl talent show, is it?"

"Whoever has talent," I said but still distracted.

She played around with ways to restyle her braids. "That includes this cute boy I saw at the library?"

I sighed. "Yeah, I guess. If he has talent."

"We'll have to find him and ask," she said, her eyes wide and fearless.

"Is that what you're thinking about? Didn't you hear my mama say she wanted to chat with Markie? What if she didn't buy anything we said today?"

"Impossible. First, I was good. Two, my mama hasn't called."

"Good point." They had a mama-to-mama hotline.

"So whoever has talent is in?"

"Yeah. I just want it to be an exciting show that raises *beaucoup* dollars."

"It will be, Georgie. You're good at rallying people. Even when you get cut from the cheerleading squad, you're the first one to encourage the other girls who didn't make it to try again. I mean, as much as I can say about this Markie, I could see why she wants you as a friend. Who wouldn't?"

"Is that a compliment from you?"

"Sort of, I guess."

She put her arms around me, and I held her close. "You're about to give them the best talent show that Bogalusa has ever seen."

"*We're* about to," I said, holding up her printouts from the library.

The thought of all we had to do to get it off the ground was enough to make me collapse.

Then the door opened. And there stood Peaches. I could see the end of a dollar bill crumbled in her hand.

She stepped in and walked over to me, looking behind her most of the way.

"What's up?" I said. "You should be getting ready."

"That meanie is in the backyard. She gave me a dollar to come get you."

"What should I do?" I said to Nikki.

"Let's see what she wants," Nikki said. "Might be good news."

"She said only Georgie. If you come I gotta give her back a whole fifty cents."

I chuckled at the thought of Markie saying that to Peaches.

"Humph, she's something else," Nikki said. But after all the conversation we'd just had, I wasn't moving unless Nikki was okay with it. If not, I'd pass. "Go see what she wants. I need to call home anyway."

"Are you sure?" She nodded. "Okay. I'll be right back," I said and followed Peaches outside.

Peaches stayed in the front yard, and I went around back. Markie was dressed like Sunday school.

"Thought I should wear this. What do you think?"

"A dress? It's just to the diner. And you...you still have on your sneakers."

"Gotta keep it a little real. Can't go all girly-girl. That's just not *moi*."

"I get it."

"Think your mama wants to see me to blast me out about Peanut Man? Maybe I can't work at the diner anymore?"

"We'll know in a little bit. Are you going to come in and wait for us to get ready?"

"No, I'm going to go now. Hey…do you think they are bringing Aunt Vie?"

"My mama is getting her ready now. And guess what?"

She just bugged her eyes and waited. "What?"

"Nikki made lots of progress on the talent show while we were gone. Located places that might be interested in donating. Figured out what type of talent would get the town most excited."

"Isn't that all the stuff I'm supposed to do?"

"Doesn't matter who does what. What's important is making it a reality. You said you knew some kids with talent, right?"

"Yup," she said.

"Round them up and bring them to the park tomorrow. We need to get moving."

"Your bestie okay with me being involved?"

"She's with it…." I said, fibbing for what I've heard Grandma Sugar call "the greater good."

"Don't believe that but nice try." She paused and looked down at her Chuck Taylor's. "I haven't opened the box yet." She shoved her hand in her pocket. "I'll let you know what's next. If anything," she said. "And no clue what your mom wants to talk to me about? Could be like a Meet and Greet like at school."

"Yeah, could be," I said, and she seemed to really like that idea. "Hey, I've gotta go. I'll see you at the diner."

"I'm Meet and Greet ready," she said and I wondered if she'd ever even been to one of those snooze fests. But with Mama, Nikki, and Markie there, along with our special guest, Aunt Vie, snoozing wasn't on the menu.

20

I'M OUTTA HERE

Before Nikki and I stepped foot in the diner, we could see everyone, including Markie, from the diner's window.

"Wait. She's wearing a dress? And you have on a dress. Doubt that's a coincidence."

"Yeah, when I realized how much she wanted to impress my mama, I didn't want her to feel so off. I tried to get you to wear one, remember?"

"Yeah, no thanks. And how hard is she really trying, wearing those crazy-looking sneakers?" Nikki said. "Sheesh."

"That may have been all she had," I said, but Nikki was opening the door, purposely moving on without me.

Mama marched up to us. "Georgie, I was just talking

to Markie." My insides did about ten jumping jacks on the spot. "She's told me what has had you two so occupied lately. What a thoughtful thing to do! I can't believe you didn't tell me about this. Whatever I can do to help, let me know."

She pinched my cheek. *Ugh.*

"So you're not mad that I didn't tell you what we were doing?" I said.

"Georgie." She said my name the way you do when you pat a puppy's head. "Why would I be mad at you for helping Markie Jean organize a fundraiser to combat Alzheimer's? I've been hoping that you'd find something meaningful here and you have. More than I could have imagined."

The wind knocked out of me. I didn't know how much I wanted to be the one to tell Mama about my idea until that second. Markie stood there holding one of Aunt Essie's famous root beer floats. I wanted to dunk Markie's face in it.

"We've just started the planning, Ms. Katrina. Georgie is handling more of the fundraiser portion," Markie said, throwing me a bone. "She's a whiz on the computer, researching places likely to donate on short notice. I couldn't plan it without her."

"Umph," Nikki said and folded her arms. "Isn't that good of you, Georgie?"

"I'm going to spend most of my time with talent acquisitions, you know."

Mama chuckled. "Can't have a talent show without someone acquiring the talent."

"I didn't know we were ready to share the plans yet," I said. "Do you think it's doable, Mama?"

"If you three put your heads together and stay out of trouble, it's certainly doable," Mama said.

Markie took a sip of her float, then said, "I was scared that we'd squandered our chance when we were at Peanut Man's. I shouldn't have been keeping my personal belongings there, but they are better there than where I live. My foster mom's kids have no respect for other people's property."

"Well, we have your belongings at Aunt Vie's. Whenever you want to pick them up, let us know. No hurry."

Markie stood directly in front of Mama and complimented Mama's blue sundress with white daisies. She seldom wore it without telling someone that it was a Michelle Obama knock-off.

"And you look quite nice yourself," Mama said. Then she wagged her index finger between the two of us. "You even got Georgie in a dress."

"Thank you kindly," Markie said, and tugged at her dress like she was prepping to bow. "I knew Aunt Vie would be here, so I wanted to look presentable." (That could have been direct shade at Nikki, who had on jeans and a T-shirt.) "I mean I know she won't *know me*, know me. But she'd try to get me to wear a dress sometimes," Markie said and rubbed the fabric so hard it was like she smeared something on it.

"She'll be here shortly. My mother took her and Peaches riding for a while. They should arrive in just a bit," Mama said. "Aunt Vie loved riding." Then Mama shook her head. "I mean loves. She loves riding."

Needing to put the talent show business out of my mind for a moment, I said, "Do you think she liked riding horses?"

"I've never known her to. But who knows with Aunt Vie?"

Something about the thought of Aunt Vie being able to get away from the diner now and then to ride bikes, ride horses, or just sit on the porch with Ms. Hannah without a care made me happy.

Then Mama placed her hand on Markie's shoulder. "I do apologize that it's taken me a minute to chat with you. Do you remember me visiting Bogalusa at all?"

"Not much," Markie said. "Aunt Vie always talked about you, though."

My ears sprouted up. Markie had never even mentioned that she'd seen Mama before. Maybe she thought that I knew she had. I remember coming down for the family reunion one year, but no Markie. Not that I could remember. *Did she see me?*

Mama looked at Markie.

"How did you get that scrape?" Mama turned Markie's face to the right.

The dress covered the gash on her knee.

"Doesn't take much. You know. . .when I trip on the sidewalk. Can't support myself as well as some." She hunched her shorty shoulder.

Nikki scoffed and I poked her.

"Oh, I understand. Glad you're okay," Mama said, as I'm sure Markie expected.

When Mama went to talk to Aunt Essie, the three of us huddled in a corner.

After holding them in, I could finally let my words fly. "Why did you tell my mama the talent show was your idea?"

"That was a low move," Nikki said. "What kind of friend are you?"

"The kind that's trying to get her mama to not think I'm the bad news blues. Should I have opened with the trouble I've caused? She could have suggested that I not work here anymore. I had to have something positive, you know."

Nikki tapped her temple. "Nah. I'm not buying it. I can tell that you use your brain. I bet you could have thought of another way. You just wanted to steal Georgie's thunder."

Markie took a gulp of her float, unlike the tiny sips she took in front of Mama. Then she shrugged. "Well, what's done is done. And Ms. Katrina is all for us spending time together making the show happen. Who's to say that we won't need that time for other things as well?"

Nikki poked my shoulder. "See, told you. She's got something up her sleeves."

"Really? *Sleeves*? Are you trying to be funny?"

Nikki froze for a second with her mouth slightly open. "Don't try that with me, you know what I meant."

Markie laughed. Nikki tried to keep a straight face, but she knew Markie had got her for a moment.

Before we got deeper into our back-and-forth, the diner door opened and in walked Grandma Sugar with Aunt Vie on her arm. Peaches was at Aunt Vie's other side as they walked in. Peaches had been glued to Grandma Sugar and Aunt Essie, helping them any way she could. That kept me from watching her, but it also made me happy to know that she'd have lots of memories with all of them.

Then my eyes returned to Aunt Vie. She was dressed like Sunday morning with full pearls, a rose-colored dress, and a hat that dipped and swirled with flowers and starbursts orbiting around it.

"Oooh," Markie said with such gentleness that Nikki unfolded her arms.

Grandma Sugar guided Aunt Vie over to us. I made sure not to rush to her or do anything that might frighten her. She inspected all of us, then said to Nikki, "Why aren't you dressed for tea?"

Nikki rocked on her heels. "I...I apologize."

"Hello, Aunt Vie?" I said. At any moment I expected her eyes to widen like they did the time she thought I was Markie, but nothing. Aunt Vie squeezed Grandma Sugar's arm tighter, like I said something threatening to her. Then she took Markie in and walked closer to her before she spoke.

"Why don't you have on the proper shoes with that dress? Why have it on at all? Is that the way your mama raised you?"

Markie shrugged, then said, "You used to let me wear sneakers with my dress. I hate dresses. But you liked them so much that I'd wear them just for you. And you let me keep my sneakers on so I'd be comfortable. Then you told me one day that I never had to wear a dress again. Even when I was a grown-up if I didn't want to. All girls don't have to wear dresses."

Mama had told me that it's unhealthy to compare your body to other girls'. That's not what makes a girl, *a girl*. Markie didn't like nail polish, glitter, or frilly things like Nikki and I liked. Was Aunt Vie the one to tell her that was okay? There was more silence in the diner than there was in the entire world. Even the hum of every appliance had quieted. Seemed like we all waited for Aunt Vie's response.

"Who are you? What are you talking about?"

I sucked in my breath and held it.

Aunt Vie tried to yank her arm away from Grandma Sugar, but she held it firm and led her away from us. "What is she talking about? Who is she? Tell me who she is!"

Grandma Sugar led Aunt Vie to the kitchen. Mama rushed over to Markie. "Are you okay?"

"Yes," Markie said.

Mama patted Markie's shoulder like a baby's back. "Sometimes faces and memories come back to her when we least expect them. Other times, it breaks our hearts when she doesn't know who we are. It doesn't mean she doesn't love us."

"I said I was okay," Markie snapped. "I don't need you explaining anything to me. I've been here. I've seen it all happening."

Mama hadn't taken her eyes off Markie.

I cleared my throat. "Maybe we can all go to the movies. Wouldn't that be fun, Mama?"

"Now, that's a good idea," Nikki said. "Do they have the kind of chairs that recline? I love a good recliner."

I leaned back and kicked out my leg. "Right, nothing beats a comfy recliner."

Mama wasn't fazed. She was still deciding how to respond to Markie's attitude. Her words were a gut punch and Mama wasn't the only one who felt it.

"I'm outta here," Markie said.

"Wait! I'll drive you. It's getting late," Mama said.

"I don't want you to drive me. I'm not one of your little babies. I'm fine."

Nikki stepped in front of her. "Hey, Aunt Trina said that this was my celebration. So stick around."

I nodded my head toward the back table. "Yeah, Aunt Essie closed the diner just for us. It's too soon to leave now. Let's just go have another float."

Mama's face was sunken. And she barely opened her lips wide enough to speak. "Maybe one more before dinner. I'll let you girls talk now." Mama slunk away and went to Grandma Sugar and Aunt Vie.

Peaches wasted no time running up to Markie. "You made my mama sad," Peaches said. "I'm not talking to you anymore. Don't care if you give me one of your wrinkly ole dollars."

Aunt Essie grabbed Peaches's hand. "Okay, calm down, sweetie. Markie didn't mean to raise her voice like that, did you, Markie, yeah?"

I grabbed on to Nikki's arm. If Markie sassed Aunt Essie, I just don't know if I'd be able to hold it together.

Markie turned her right sneaker to its side. "No, ma'am."

"Why don't you three go out and get some air? Give Aunt Vie a moment to get settled. She hasn't been in the diner in a bit. Okay? And we'll save the floats for after dinner. Got peach cobbler, too, if you like."

We all muttered, "Yes, ma'am," and headed toward the door.

The air outside smelled like wet dirt. But there were no other signs of rain. The three of us stayed under the awning, pretty much where Markie and I stood the first day we met.

Markie was staring at her phone. She put it down to her side when I planted myself in front of her.

I pursed my lips, which tasted of mouthwash. "What was all that about, Markie? You have to know this is hard for my mama, too. She didn't deserve that."

"She was going out of her way to be nice to you," Nikki said.

Markie shrugged. "If that's what you want to call it."

I sighed and stared her straight in her eyes. "What would you call it?"

"Nothing. You're right. She didn't deserve that. This is harder than I thought. It's crazy that I miss being with Aunt Vie so much. I'd give her nothing but trouble with my attitude sometimes. Running away. Acting out in school. That's how I ended up going back and forth in foster care. Maybe that's why she kept what was happening from me until she couldn't anymore."

"We have to focus on what we can do now, Markie. That's what I'm learning," I said.

While she retucked one of her dangling braids, Nikki said, "The good news is that Auntie Trina is all about the talent show. I know we want to do it ourselves, but we'll need grown-up help with some things." Nikki was working double time to make us see the positive side of all of this.

"Why don't we all go back in and enjoy the rest of the evening, visit with Aunt Vie. Sometimes I don't like to say it aloud, but I hate that I didn't get to know Aunt Vie better. I wish Grandma Sugar and Aunt Essie would have told my mama earlier about her condition."

Markie stepped off the curb and faced us. "Doubt it

would have changed anything. Your mama wasn't ready to come."

"Why would you say that?"

"It was a while ago, but I overheard Aunt Vie talking to your mama and asking her to visit. There was always an excuse. Even before the divorce. Aunt Vie would call and talk to your mama, but only your grandmother visited. Maybe your mama feels...guilty."

I thought back to Mama's conversation on the Causeway. "Maybe she feels a little guilty for not coming back before now. Grown-ups aren't perfect." As soon as I said that, I wanted to shove it back in my mouth. I thought about what Ms. Hannah said about words. *Those words were out now. I couldn't take them back.*

And, like I feared, the words burned like fire under Markie's feet. "I know better than both of you that grown-ups aren't perfect. That has nothing to do with the fact that I think your mom knows more about a lot of things."

Nikki sighed. "Ugh. You are ruining this whole night. Are you saying that Aunt Trina knows something about your mama? Maybe you do need to just go home and let us enjoy ourselves."

For a moment, instead of dealing with the conversation, I wanted to put my hands to my ears like a child. My head was spinning. "If she knew anything about your mama, she'd have said something by now."

"You two just don't get it."

Nikki was in the one-hand-on-the hip mood now. "Get what?"

"Who's stayed away from me for about the entire time

since she's been here? Who was sending Aunt Vie money to help with 'diner upkeep' but rarely has been back here? You said it, not me. Your mama feels guilty, but it's about more than what you think."

"You're crazy. You think my mama knows something about yours and wouldn't tell you?"

"Explain why she doesn't like you around me."

Nikki's voice was even higher than before. "Ah. Cause she probably figured you would get Georgie in trouble."

Then Markie shot Nikki a side-eye. "And you want me to believe that you two never get into trouble. It's just me. Really?"

When Grandma Sugar got my attention, she waved for us to come inside.

I took a deep breath. "C'mon, let's get back. We can talk about this at the park tomorrow."

"Nah, I'm good," Markie said. "It'll be less drama if I went on home. I'll be at the park with those kids like I promised."

Whatever energy I needed to ask her to stay, I didn't have. "See ya, tomorrow," I said and turned to go back inside with Nikki.

21
FAKE-YONCÉ

Didn't matter if Markie took credit for the talent show or not, it was still on me to make it happen. Nikki labeled Markie a "button pusher," and I had to agree. I wasn't about to let any of that mess with the talent show.

Nikki and I wolfed down breakfast and left the house before Peaches was up.

"We haven't talked about our part in this show," Nikki said.

"What do you want to do?" I said.

"Do you really have to ask?"

"Which routine?"

"The one that would show these Bogalusa kids what's what."

When we entered McClurie Park, Nikki set her purse on the bleachers, went in the center of the park, and did a backflip, testing out the ground the way Mama would a mattress.

"Ground's level," she said. "Least there is space to practice. Actually, it has a certain *je ne sais quoi* that appeals to me."

"Yeah, me too," I said. "If we hold the talent show here, there'll be space for whoever wanted to come out."

"And no rental fee," Nikki said.

I pulled out my notepad to write down the details. "Actually, since it's a fundraiser, I'd better check if there is any fee to the town to use the park. Plus, we might need an emergency permit." My stepsister, Tangie, was the queen of impromptu "emergency" permits whenever she helped her boyfriend organize rallies. *Mental note to ask Tangie about permits.*

Nikki looked around the park again and sighed. "You know, this might be our last chance to turn it up together for a while."

I twisted my lips to one side and back again. "*California.* It doesn't seem real."

"When you see that *For Sale* sign my daddy plunked in our yard, it will." At that Nikki took out her glitter lip gloss and dabbed her lips. They sparkled like a planetarium.

About ten minutes later, Markie arrived—alone.

I stood and greeted her. Then got down to business. "Thought you were bringing some talent?" I said.

Nikki waved, her hand limp as a wet towel. "Aren't you handling 'talent acquisitions'?" Nikki reminded her.

"If I was flaking out, would I be here right now? They'll be along in a minute." Then she put one leg up on the bleacher. "So what did I miss? How were things with Aunt Vie?"

"She talked some. I think she enjoyed being out," I said.

I downplayed the fun we had. Some of the songs sparked memories in Aunt Vie and she swayed to the beat and even sang the chorus of one of Aretha Franklin's songs, "I Say a Little Prayer." Grandma Sugar, Aunt Essie, and even Mama sang along to it together. Later that night, Nikki found it for me on her phone and I replayed it so much that I practically learned every word.

I flipped to a clean page in my notebook. "Nikki and I are stepping as our talent. Can we count on you showcasing yours? Everybody has something," I said and yanked a pencil out of my hair.

"I'm still deciding," Markie said.

Nikki scoffed. "Really? That many talents, huh?"

"What can I say? I'm a maverick. You'll know soon."

I wrote: Nikki. Georgie. Step. Dance. Duet. Then I wrote Markie's name in all caps and drew huge question marks.

While I doodled, a beat made my feet tap. I glanced up and the pink rhinestones of Nikki's phone glistened as Nikki started playing music. Then she pulled a mini Bluetooth speaker from her purse.

"What! Am I going to finally get to see you dance, Nikki?" Markie said.

"It's your lucky day. My partner and I 'bout to get some practice in before we have to start grooming the extras," Nikki said.

Since I'd been hanging around Markie, I was fairly sure I wouldn't be too nervous in front of her. Not like in front of strangers.

Nikki cranked up the volume to an old Beyoncé song, "Run the World (Girls)."

"You remember this routine, Georgie. Let's do it," Nikki said.

We started back-to-back, maybe a little cheesy, but then I went into a split and Nikki did a Simone Biles flip over me. When we're on our feet, we joined hands and helped each other do windmills. We knew that wasn't really stepping. But we combined it with other dance forms. When it was time to do a more traditional step, Nikki and I froze for a moment, getting in sync. Both our hands were solidly on our hips. Shoulders back. Neck straight, ready to make our hair whip. Well, I had my French braids, but Nikki's braids, even in her upsweep, were whip-ready.

Markie snapped her fingers and waved them in the air. That pumped us up. After a huge gulp of air, Nikki called out from her diaphragm, just like Ms. Jerilyn taught us at the Boys & Girls Club, but Nikki's was always the one with the most fire.

"The B-F-F Steppers are here to slay. The B-F-F Steppers are gonna wreck your day."

Okay, BFF Steppers wasn't the most awe-inspiring or fear-evoking name, but it's what we came up with for just the two of us. Most step teams are about three to fifty people or more.

I was on point, matching every one of Nikki's steps until we did a sharp pivot and there watching us were three kids who'd rolled in like a thundercloud. Nikki kept dancing but try as I might, my legs tangled like wet hair.

The three kids seemed to have stopped the breeze. Or was it that my heart was pumping so fast that I'd raised my body temperature? The last thing I needed was to really pass out in the heat like grown-ups warned us about every hour in Georgia whenever the temperature rose above 90. I needed to remain calm and upright. I couldn't organize a show while sprawled out on the ground.

"Is that how they dance where y'all from?" the older girl asked with an extra dash of salt in her voice. She took a long draw from a Zesto's paper cup, bending the straw.

The girl was taller than Markie and me. She wore dingy shorts and a T-shirt that she'd tied in the front, exposing her outie belly button. The other girl may have been about eight and wore pajamas with double- and triple-stacked ice-cream cones printed all over it and no shoes. On our right was a boy who was straddling a bike with towering straight handlebars and bugle bike horns taped to each bar. His hair was shaved at the sides and the top was reddish twists.

Nikki finished the routine with a salute but hadn't said one word. She stared at the boy like he was the one who had made the shady comment, not the girl. Before it got super weird, she snapped out of it and said, "That's right! It's stepping. Don't y'all step here?"

"Yeah, we do. That's why I was wondering what that was you two were doing," the taller girl said.

"C'mon, Jada. You know that was pretty good," Markie said to the taller girl.

"It was okay," Jada said.

"'Okay' is for second place—that's a first-place routine," Nikki countered.

Jada tugged at the knot in her T-shirt. "Not by the looks of it. Who steps with just two people anyway?" She sucked her teeth and swayed her body to one side, but her feet remained planted. "Who are these wannabe dancers?"

"Wannabe?" Nikki said. "My trophies go higher than you can probably count."

"Calm down, Ciara," Markie quipped. "This is Ms. Essie's grandniece. And this is her BFF, Ricki."

"Don't play with me, Markie, you know it's Nikki. And I got your Ciara comment, too."

Markie introduced the kids as Jada, Latasha, and the boy, Flip. Then Nikki whispered and pinched my arm—he was the "cute boy" from the library.

"Where y'all say y'all from again?" Flip asked.

"Atlanta," I said.

"A-T-L...HotLanta. Up north," Nikki added.

Jada darted her eyes between both her siblings. "She must think we're some country bumpkins." Then she turned back to me and Nikki. "We know about Atlanta. It ain't even close to around here."

"You might have to even get on an airplane," Latasha said. Her eyes soaked in the sky.

"No, you don't," Flip said. "But it sho' ain't near here. That's down Georgia way."

"That's right," I said, like a teacher's pet pointing my clicker to the southeastern part of the United States.

"We're not about copycatting here," Jada said.

Nikki stepped back. "I created that routine myself."

"Really? From what I saw, they're fake Beyoncé moves. That'll make you Fake-yoncé," Jada said.

Now that I was certain I wasn't going to faint in the heat, I had to take charge. Organize. I cleared my throat. "Here's the deal. Nikki's one of the best dancers in Atlanta," I said. Then I turned to Markie. "These are the kids for the show, right?" She nodded. "In that case, we're supposed to form a team to entertain people, raise money. So we should be all about showing our talent and giving constructive criticism. If you can't do that, there's the door."

"Too far with the door," Nikki whispered. "There's the *gate*," Nikki announced.

"She has a point, Jada," Markie said. "You know who it's for. You said you were onboard."

"I know. I know. I just don't like folks that ain't from here acting like they're better than we are."

"You fired off first, sis," Flip said. "Ms. Vie's one of the nicest people you ever want to meet. She's 'bout as nice as Grandma Mirenda used to be. Knows no strangers." He twisted those tall handlebars until the tires ground down in the red dirt.

"That's true," Jada admitted. "Guess we gotta cut her grandniece and BFF here some slack. The routine was pretty good."

I spotted my notebook that had fallen on the ground. I grabbed it and crushed it to my chest. With the faint sound of an ice cream truck in the background, I hoped I could hold their attention. Flip lifted the tail end of his Grambling

T-shirt and dug into his pockets and pulled out a dollar. He gave it to Latasha and she sprinted off.

"So you've seen our acts. What can you two do?" I said.

Flip elbowed Jada. "This sister doesn't have any bones."

Jada punched his shoulder.

"Ooouch," he said.

"No bones? What does that mean?" I said and jotted her name and a question mark. "What 'cha got?"

She glared at her brother. "If I do that, then you know what you gotta do?"

"We'll get to that in a sec," I said. "First, what's this boneless thing about?"

I was on my feet, pacing like a coach in front of a basketball team. Adrenaline pumping.

Jada's words crawled out. "It's kind of boring."

Flip sighed. "It's not."

"If it was boring, I wouldn't have asked you to meet us here," Markie said.

Jada put her phone on the bleachers and stood on a patch of grass. Stretching her arms over her head, she waited a second, then bent all the way back like this kid at Sweet Apple could do with their finger. But bending backward was just the beginning. She planted her elbows on the ground. Markie and I traded glances. I pursed my lips and prayed she didn't hurt herself. Jada held that stance for a few seconds, then she grabbed her ankles.

I had a feeling what she was going to attempt but I wasn't sure. Could she? Would she? Nikki was close to passing out from sheer envy. I held my breath. Jada tightened the grip on her ankles and she slowly allowed her head to peek out between her legs until her chin was level to the ground. Then she even insect-walked a few steps. I put my notebook down and clapped so hard my hands stung. Markie fluttered her hand like it was holding a tambourine. As Jada eased out of her bend, I yanked up my pad and wrote. Jada—Contortionist.

"She can do other moves, too," Markie said.

"Wow! That's impressive," Nikki said. "How long have you been able to flex like that?"

Jada shrugged. "As long as I can remember."

"Jada the Cool Contortionist," I said aloud. "Not the best title, but I'll work on that."

"Did I deliver or what?" Markie said.

"So we got a dance routine and a contortionist. Now it's your turn," Nikki said and pointed cute to Flip, letting her index finger float down like a feather.

"You gotta do it, Flip," Jada said.

"Why? So the whole town can laugh at me?" Flip said. "You remember when I was rapping what they called me."

Latasha was back and unwrapping a strawberry short-cake bar. "Flip the Flop!" she said before shoving the treat in her mouth.

Jada elbowed him. "Do you really care about what people say? You never really wanted to rap. This is what you like," Jada said.

"C'mon, Flip," Markie said. "You know it's for a good cause."

Nikki inched closer to him. "Is it something I can help you with?"

I tapped my notebook, hoping that would bring her back

from crush-town. He pulled at one of his twists. That's when I noticed the diagonal cuts in his eyebrows. Nikki loved that extra dab of swag.

"No, there is nothing you can help with," Latasha said. "He does magic, real magic. I'm his assistant. Huh, Flip. Tell 'em."

"You're my assistant, Tash."

Nikki was back at my side. "Magic, that's what's up."

Flip nodded in Jada's direction, then held his head down and took in a few quick breaths.

I knew that type of anxiety. It's what I felt every time I stood in front of people, especially if I danced. Hiccups that start in your stomach, hands wet and clammy.

Jada stood, pretended to hold a microphone, and said, "Ladies and gentlemen, may I have your attention, please. Introducing Flip the Fantastic and his assistant, Lovely Latasha!" Jada waved her hand like she was that lady from *Wheel of Fortune*.

I still wasn't one hundred percent sure what he was doing. Markie stood looking on like a proud coach.

Flip dug around in his backpack and took out a deck of cards, then whispered to Latasha.

Then he shuffled the cards.

"Will my assistant please step forward?" Flip said. Latasha scurried over to Flip and curtsied. "Now, I need a volunteer from the audience."

Nikki was in front of him in a flash.

"And who do we have here?" Flip said.

"Nikki."

"Well, Nikki," Flip said. He shuffled the cards in front of him again. "Pick a card."

Nikki stared at the cards like she expected them to change colors.

"Study long, you study wrong," Markie said.

Nikki pulled one and held it to her chest.

"Now show the card to the audience," Flip said and turned his back.

Nikki stepped closer to each of us and scanned the card inches from our noses. *Three of Diamonds.*

"She's finished, Magnificent Flip," Latasha said.

"Flip the Fantastic," Jada shouted.

He turned around to face us again. Then he shuffled his cards. Pulled one, and without looking, showed it to Nikki.

"Three of Diamonds," Nikki shouted, probably louder and with more surprise than she realized.

We all clapped. Flip and Latasha took a bow.

"This is going to be fire for the talent show," I said. *Crowd engagement gets more donations*, I remembered reading.

"Told ya," Markie said. "And he has more magic."

I grabbed a pencil and opened my notebook. "Okay, Nikki and Georgie, original Nikki dance routine." I looked up from the notebook, directly at Jada. "Are you good with showing the town your amazing contortionist skills?" Jada nodded. "And you're good, Fantastic Flip?" He gave me a thumbs-up.

"We still need a few people to round out the show but this is a good start. We're all in," I said and stuck my hand out. It was left hanging for a moment until Nikki put her hand on mine. Then Flip, Latasha, Jada, and Markie. Once everyone's hand was in, I shouted, "Bogalusa's got talent on three. One. Two. Three."

"Bogalusa's got talent!"

"Name still sucks," Nikki said.

"Yeah, but as long as the show doesn't, I'm good."

Once the sibs, which is what Markie called them, left, Nikki, Markie, and I sat there talking about the talent show. Still, at any moment, I expected Markie to veer off the topic for a moment and talk about what was in the box, or what I could do next to help. I didn't want to press her. As Daddy liked to say, "The ball was in her court."

I jotted down the date and wrote Saturday in letters that cartwheeled across the page. Instead of saying anything directly about her mama, or Ms. Hannah, I said, "Time to tell me what you're going to do, Markie."

"What do you mean?" she said.

"You're up next. Talent show. Duh," Nikki said.

I whistled a bit. "C'mon, Markie. We all have something. Plus, I already know one of yours: whistling."

Markie rubbed her chin a few times as if she had whiskers. I positioned my pencil next to her name, ready to fill in her talent and cross out the question mark. And in typical Markie fashion, she knew she had our attention and made us wait.

"You know. You're right, Georgie. I can do something. I really want to, matter of fact. But it's not whistling. Ahem. I'm going to sing."

"Like rapping?" I said.

"No, like singing," Markie clarified.

I'd have to be honest and say that she looked more like a rapper than a singer. I knew it was stereotyping and as my social studies teacher would say, "bad business"—not every tall person liked basketball, not every blond person was "clueless," and not even a fraction of Black people, especially boys, who wore hoodies and sagging pants were criminals. And certainly, not every girl without makeup, rainbow nail color, or who didn't wear earrings would rather rap than sing. But I'd have to admit, Mama and I watched that TLC story and Markie's style was more like Lisa "Left Eye" Lopes than one of Tangie's favorites, Andra Day.

"Okay, cool. I'm putting you down for a song at the talent show."

"Yeah, I got you. I just need to get the pipes tuned," Markie said.

Nikki snapped her fingers in excitement. "A singer is money in the bank for a fundraiser. I was hoping we'd have at least one. Didn't expect it to be you, but that's cool. You've been holding out."

"This is perfect. We'll put you on midway and then you can close the show, too. The audience loves singers. Well, don't be shy," I said. "You've seen what we've got. Let's hear something."

Markie cleared her throat. "What you want to hear?"

"Give us a few lines from one of your faves," I said.

I closed my notebook and put my chin on the heel of my hand, giving Markie my full, undivided attention.

Markie stood up in front of the bleachers. "Ahem.

Ahem." She chopped at her throat like I've seen some kids in the Sweet Apple Choir do to warm up.

Then she let us have it.

"Shine bright like a diamond. Shine bright like a diamond. Find light in the beautiful sea, I choose to be happy."

Her words crackled through the air. The sharp edges and unexpected jolts of what was supposed to be a beautiful melody karate kicked us. Pulverized our eardrums.

I couldn't look at Nikki. All I could do was hear the words rattling from Markie's lips, mixing in with the random outdoor noises of cars, kids, and birds, and wish that any of those would drown her out.

When Markie stopped before the second chorus, I was fairly sure that if she was on Mama's old-timey show, *Showtime at the Apollo*, she would be booed off, but she kept going.

I heard Nikki clapping and I started clapping, too. Maybe we'd have to hear her sing something else. Rhianna is hard, especially "Diamonds." That's what the coaches say when someone sings it on any of those reality singing shows.

"I don't know if I'll do that one at the show or not," Markie said with so much confidence I thought maybe it was me. Maybe something was distorting my hearing and I just missed the melodic sound of her voice.

"Or not," Nikki said.

I wasn't quick enough to stop Nikki. Sometimes being "blunt" wasn't always the best way.

"Why?" Markie asked, her eyes wide.

"Because we want to get something newer. You know. Newer," Nikki said.

"What do you think, Georgie?" Markie asked.

"Sure, that makes sense."

"I'll think about it. I'm going to go to the diner for a while. You two coming?"

"In a minute. We'll see you there," I said.

"Cool," she said and threw up a peace sign.

We waited until she'd rounded the corner. Nikki moved closer to me. Her eyes fluttering, both our ears burning.

"Can you believe that?" Nikki whispered like Markie was close by.

"Only because I heard it. She can't sing that song or any other. We want to raise money, not give it back."

"Why didn't you say anything to her?"

"It wasn't the right time. I mean she's trying to help. I'm just supposed to blurt out, 'You can't sing. Stick to whistling'?" Even as I said those words, I hung my head down. I knew I could have said or done more. Truth was that I didn't have the nerve.

"Well, it's clearer than ever that she doesn't have any *real* friends. Who'd let their friend go around thinking she can sing when she can't. If you let her get in front of people and embarrass herself, that's going to be on your conscience."

I could still hear her voice screeching in my ears. "We'll tell her before then."

Nikki put her hand on my shoulder and squeezed it. "Correction. You'll tell her. I can't believe we even have to have this conversation." Then she stood up and pointed her finger at me. "Her arm. That's it, right? Is that the reason you're not honest?"

My eyes shot to the ground. "No, it's not, really."

Everything was piling up. I still thought about her standoff with Mama. And Ms. Hannah putting that mystery box on Markie's lap and the way she stared at it like she wanted to swat it away.

"You can't even look at me. Maybe it's not the only reason, but it's playing a part."

I shrugged. "A little, I guess."

"Not telling her is being a fake friend. Isn't that what you accused Lucinda Hightower of?"

"Yeah," I admitted. I didn't have a defense.

"Well, don't be a hypocrite. You're better than that."

As I listened to Nikki checking the spelling of *hypocrite*, I knew she was right. Telling a friend the truth wasn't always easy but it had to be done.

22

DEAR MAYOR OF BOGALUSA

Late Tuesday morning, I decided that though it was short notice, sometimes short notice is better than no notice at all. Maybe I didn't need a permit, but I'd talked to Tangie and she suggested it to be on the safe side. Luckily, Aunt Essie had a dinosaur of a desktop computer and printer in a spare room and let us use them. That's all I needed to type my letter. Markie had come through with a few more people for the talent show. She still hadn't said anything about the mystery box, though. But I also hadn't asked Mama about the things Markie suspected. Since she hadn't mentioned it to me again, I thought she'd come to her senses.

Before I got started with the letter, I asked Nikki, only because I was desperate, "Don't you think it's strange that Markie hasn't even mentioned what was inside that box?"

"Not really, especially if it was just personal stuff."

"That's true," I said, though I felt like she could at least mention it.

"When she's ready to talk to you about it, she will," Nikki said as she pulled up a chair ready to assist. "But right now, we need to stay focused on the show. Last night was too much fun."

Mama had cleared off the dining room table, and next thing we knew, Aunt Essie and Mama onloaded several coloring books and crayons. Next, Mama dug out a DVD player that was in the closet and she'd ordered DVDs of an old-school show called *Julia*. It starred one of Aunt Vie's favorite actresses, Diahann Carroll, who played the first Black nurse on a weekly series. I'd never heard of it before but Nikki and I kept watching after everyone else had gone to bed.

"Grab your phone and google a business letter." When she found a good one, we got down to business.

"Should I start it with To Whom It May Concern? Or Dear Mayor?"

"Dear Mayor," we said almost in unison.

"Let's go right to the top."

First, I used a comma after "Dear Mayor of Bogalusa," but I deleted that and replaced it with a colon. That was more serious, professional.

Dear Mayor of Bogalusa:

My name is Georgiana Elizabeth Matthews. I am a visitor of your illustrious city this summer. I know that you are busy, but this is of an urgent nature. We are hosting a talent show this Saturday to raise money for the Alzheimer's Foundation and to honor Ms. Elvie Sweetings, the founder of Bogalusa's favorite diner, Sweetings. In her honor we are asking for an emergency permit to gather in McClurie Park to host our event.

"That sounds good, Georgie. The mayor is really going to like 'illustrious.' You sound real grown-up. I'm memorizing that word right now."

"Thanks," I said. "But the big issue is how are we getting this down to city hall. Double-check this again. I'll be right back," I said and left the room.

When I returned, I had Mama in tow. I told her about the letter on the way to the room and showed it to her as soon as she walked in.

"Mama, we want to get this letter down to the mayor." I turned the computer to Mama, and she read my Word document.

"Mmhmm...mmhmm," Mama said as she read.

"And you two wrote this letter yourselves?"

"We googled a template," I said.

Nikki showed Mama her phone with various business letter examples.

"This is soon, Georgie, but it's worth a try."

"We need to print this. Can you drive Nikki and me down there today?"

"Of course," Mama said.

"Mama, I know it's best if you take us since it's dealing with the government, but I want to do all the talking," I said.

"No problem. I'll be there if you need me. But isn't Markie going, too? I mean I know you are working on it with her, but you shouldn't leave her out since it was her idea, right?"

"Yes, she's going," I said, though I hadn't asked her.

"Aunt Essie says she's hearing good buzz about the show in the diner. What a good idea Markie had. And here I was thinking she was just trouble. I hated the way things went between us the other night."

"She seems to think you have it out for her," I let slip out.

"Georgie, I don't 'have it out for her.' Markie Jean has a different life from you and her values may not be the same. But things seem to be going okay now. Let's hope it stays that way."

"All she wants is to be like everyone else. Have a home and people who love her."

"It's never that simple and you don't know her as well as you think."

I thought again about Ms. Hannah's telling us that you can't take back things you say. I wasn't going to repeat Markie's words about Mama hiding something. If she knew anything about Markie's mama, she'd say so. What reason would there be not to?

Mama kissed my forehead.

"So proud of you to help Markie bring this community

together and raise money for Alzheimer's in honor of Auntie. You too, Nikki."

I mumbled, "Thank you."

"And I appreciate how you have refocused your energy. I was a little nervous after the trouble with Peanut Man. But you've shown me what you can do when I don't have you vacuuming the same floor every hour," Mama said and laughed.

"Please share that with my mom when I get back home," Nikki said.

"I'll do that. But first, we need to go pay the mayor a little visit," Mama said.

I pointed to myself. "Remember, Mama, I'll do all the talking."

"You got it," Mama said and left.

As soon as the door closed, Nikki said, "So you're gonna let Sharkie Markie take credit for your idea. That was your chance to come clean."

"Can we just drop that, please?"

"Okay, whatever," Nikki said. "We're gonna make sure it's all that. Then I'm going to tell anybody who'll listen that it was all my idea," she said and laughed so loud, it made me laugh, too.

Nikki and I spent a few minutes more checking the letter. Then Nikki said, "We should find Markie now to make sure she can come with us."

"You don't mind?"

"Even if I mind, doesn't mean it's not the right thing to do," she said like it wasn't a big deal. There was always something that made me remember why we were best friends.

I texted Markie: Where are you?

She replied: Diner.

OMW.

Nikki and I arrived at the diner and grabbed an empty booth, which was okay because no one was waiting. Stacked at the counter were peanuts in mini paper bags and wedges of peanut brittle wrapped in plastic.

Markie waltzed over with two glasses of water on a tray. "What up?" Markie said as soon as she was at our table.

"You want to go to city hall with us?" I asked.

"I'm there. Is your mom going?" Markie asked and placed a glass each in front of us.

"Why?" I snapped, though I didn't mean to. I could feel Nikki's stare.

"Calm down. Just wondering if they'd talk to us without an adult."

I didn't totally buy that. "She's taking us. Around two. We just have to make sure we're looking professional, but without the suits, stockings, and stuff."

"Or dresses," Nikki tossed in and sipped her water.

Markie ignored her. "Have you seen the sibs?"

"No, I haven't seen them," I said.

"If she hasn't, I haven't," Nikki said.

"Well, they are definitely spreading the word. Kids from Central Elementary and Bogalusa High School want to audition. A band and more dancers, from what I've heard."

"Any good singers?" Nikki asked.

I kicked her underneath the booth.

"I bet there are one or two. We'll know when they audition. The more the merrier."

"Remember. Two at Aunt Vie's, don't be late," I said as she went to take an order.

"You're about as subtle as a dog bite, Nikki," I said.

"Well, have you said anything yet about that howling she was doing?"

"I'll know when the time is right."

At least that is what I wanted to believe.

About two hours later, Mama, Nikki, Markie, and I were in Mama's van and headed to city hall, which was located on Arkansas Avenue. I rode in front with Mama. Markie and Nikki rode in that middle row. It took us about a few minutes to see a sign that read, *Welcome to the Business District.* It was odd going into any business district that wasn't so congested with traffic we had to come to a complete halt.

"Business District? Is *this* downtown?" Nikki said.

You could hear in Nikki's voice that she had the Atlanta skyline in her sight.

"Yep," Mama said.

"There's not even one tall building. No big hotels. Nothing?" Nikki went on.

Markie fired back, "Have you even been to a small town before? They're called that for a reason. If we had all that, we'd be an overpopulated city."

I'd printed out two copies of our letter and folded them into envelopes. I addressed them to "The Mayor of Bogalusa."

"Check this out," I said and turned as much as the seat belt would let me. I handed the letter to Markie.

"Did you write this, Ms. Katrina?" Markie said in a syrupy voice.

"That's all Georgie and Nikki's work," Mama said.

"Open it," I said. "You should know what you're representing."

"I can do it for you," Nikki offered.

I felt like a heel for not realizing it might not be the easiest for her to do in a moving car.

"No thanks, I got it." She put the envelope between her knees and opened it. After a few seconds she said, "Pretty good," and slid it back in the envelope and handed it to me. "I'm so glad that you're helping organize this fundraiser, Georgie. I couldn't do it without you," Markie said.

"We were just talking about that earlier, Markie," Mama said.

"And everyone looks so nice. And I really like your earrings, Ms. Katrina."

Mama pinched her ear. "These pearls? Aunt Vie insisted I wear them the other day. Can't seem to take them off."

I wondered if Markie had recognized the earrings as Aunt Vie's. I hadn't even noticed the tiny snowballs that sat on Mama's ears.

"Ms. Katrina?"

"Yes, Markie." I bit my lip waiting for Markie's next words. "I apologize for my outburst at the diner. It just hurts more than I can handle sometimes."

"I understand," Mama said. "Let's put it behind us. You've given us this fundraiser to focus on. I'm proud of you. All three of you."

"Me too," Markie said.

Nikki and I were quiet.

Aunt Essie said that Bogalusa was split into two sections:

the White side and the Black side. It looked like the city hall was on the White side since I didn't see any Black people around. The manicured lawns and canopy-like trees of the area closer to the town hall reminded me more of Atlanta. There was no one around hawking boiled peanuts or vegetables.

Mama parked the car. I checked my teeth and the corners of my eyes in the visor mirror. I reached out my hand to make sure that I wasn't ashy. I took out my travel-sized tube of lotion and rubbed some more on my ankles and heels. Couldn't hurt. Then all I had to do was pace my breathing and not let those butterflies in my stomach get the best of me.

"Thank you for chaperoning us, Ms. Katrina. Doubt they'd even hear us out if we didn't have you with us," Markie said, still cozying up to Mama.

"It looks like a mini White House," Nikki said as we gawked at the huge columns and stark whiteness of the building.

Standing in as our official tour guide, Markie said, "A teacher told us that's exactly the model the architect used for it."

I took a napkin from Mama's glove compartment and dabbed at the sweat on my forehead. Then I made sure that my lips weren't too shiny but not chapped either. Mama turned off the car and we got out. I took a deep breath that was a mixture of dry air and car exhaust.

"If you're too nervous to speak, I got it," Markie offered, wearing the only pair of jeans I've seen her wear without holes, rips, or loops.

"Yeah, nuh-huh. Georgie has it," Nikki said, rocking her flared shorts that looked like a skirt.

Before I moved in front of the car, I smoothed any wrinkles out of my clothing. I was looking "kidfessional"—what Daddy called me when I helped out in his office—decked in my blue-and-white pedal pushers and matching shirt.

Markie, Nikki, and I grouped together and marched up the city hall steps, with Mama trailing behind.

"May I help you, girls?" the guard said. Mama cleared her throat. "Ma'am," he added.

I gripped the letter until it felt as if it had a pulse. But I must have left my voice in the car. Nikki's pointy elbow felt like it went straight to my rib cage, then to my esophagus, and finally shook my words free.

I stood so straight it felt as though I'd grown an inch. "I'm Georgiana Elizabeth Matthews, and I'd like to request an audience with the mayor, please." I held out the letter as if he'd asked to see it.

The guard directed us through the metal detector. "Well, now. This seems mighty important. Not sure if she's available, but she has an open-door policy, so let's get you up to her assistant," he said. After we all passed through the detector, we were cleared to go to her office. By that time, I not only had my voice, but I had remembered exactly why we were there, and my steps were high and steady.

A lady about Mama's age greeted us. Even though she probably thought Mama would do the talking, I introduced myself again, but this time, without a pointed elbow to kick-start me.

"We are here to have a meeting with the mayor, please, and give her this important letter." Then I shook her hand and held out my letter.

"Thank you for coming in today, Ms. Matthews. The mayor isn't available. I'm Mrs. Bridges, the mayor's executive assistant. How may I be of service?"

"Ahem, yes, Mrs. Bridges. We are looking to be granted an emergency permit to gather at McClurie Park. Not too far from Sweetings Diner this Saturday. Do you know Sweetings?"

"Of course. We used to have Ms. Vie cater for us. And McClurie Park is a few blocks from it."

"That's right, ma'am. We know it's short notice, but we need to act fast."

Mrs. Bridges pushed wire-rimmed glasses up on her nose. "May I?" She reached for the letter, opened it, and read it.

She sat down and swirled in her high-back chair, then glanced at me over her glasses. "I'll make sure the mayor gets this. Is there a phone number to contact you?"

"We better use my mama's number," I said.

I glanced back at Mama and she nodded.

After I gave Mrs. Bridges the number, we shook hands, said our goodbyes, and she placed the letter in a wire basket on her desk. As nice as she was, I had a vision of it still sitting there weeks from that second. I took two quick breaths and swallowed what felt like a chunk of ice. "Ahem. Mrs. Bridges. Isn't the town always looking for exciting items to put on the Visit Bogalusa website?"

She pushed up her glasses again. "Indeed we are."

"You should remind the mayor that this would be a perfect photo op for that. And it's ultimately a celebration of the founder of what's surely close to a historic landmark here in

Bogalusa, Sweetings. Most importantly, it's for a good cause, right?"

Nikki, Markie, and Mama were right there with the yeses like my very own backup singers.

"Tell her those statistics you were telling me the other day, Georgie," Nikki said.

"Oh, yes..." I closed my eyes and tried to think of my research. "There's approximately twenty percent of African Americans with Alzheimer's and we make up about twelve percent of the population."

"That's disproportionate," Nikki chimed in.

My voice was cracking a bit, but I wasn't going to cry. "We certainly hope the mayor will join us as we raise money to defeat Alzheimer's. We'd like to bring awareness to this heartbreaking disease. It's the only reason my great-aunt isn't still at the diner every day."

Mrs. Bridges picked up the letter like she'd seen it for the first time.

"You got some valid points there, young lady," Mrs. Bridges said. "I'll make sure someone gets on this as soon as possible."

"Thank you," I said. I stuck out my hand again.

I may have thought to get us to the mayor's office, but it was all of us who sealed the deal. As soon as we stepped out of the office, Nikki and I danced and hugged like we'd won a championship. In my excitement, I hugged Markie, too. It took a second to realize that she wasn't hugging me back. I wasn't going to let it dampen my mood. Everybody doesn't show affection the same. Markie's smile was just as big as ours and we all had something to be happy about.

23

I BELIEVE

The next day the three of us were at McClurie Park, sitting on the bleachers. What Daddy would surely call "the soundtrack" of summer was on repeat—the birds, the squirrels, the ice cream truck, the watermelon man, the mamas who yelled for their kids to go to the store for them or come inside—all on the highest volume possible. And we were right in the middle of all of it planning our fundraiser.

After we talked about trying to build a stage and what food to sell, we talked about other acts.

"Speaking of acts, how many songs you think I should do?" Markie asked.

Oh, about that. This was my chance to tell Markie that maybe singing wasn't her gift, her talent. I know Nikki was expecting me to, but all I could think about were her wanting my mama to like her and her losing Aunt Vie a little more each day.

I ignored Nikki's gaze and dropped my head a little bit.

"She asked you a question, Georgie," Nikki said. "How many songs should she *grace* us with?"

"Maybe three. Each three minutes or so," I said.

Markie nodded. "I'm still thinking about 'Diamonds.'"

"You're not the only one," Nikki mumbled.

Then Markie did a half turn and faced us both directly with as much energy as the sun. Oil glimmered in her hair like dew. "You know what. Why am I tripping? This is for Aunt Vie. I want to make it as special as possible. Plus, this will be my first time singing in front of people. I should go all out. Maybe I sounded too timid before. I wasn't pushing myself. Need to turn it up a notch." After "notch," she pumped her arm like when Serena or Venus Williams wins a tennis match. "We've been spreading the word, so I know the crowd will be colossal," Markie said.

The thought of that excited and petrified me. Tongue-tied, I nodded. Then managed, "We should canvass the town with fliers, too."

"Yes!" she said and pumped her arm again. "That's all the reason for me to turn it up a notch. Maybe I sounded too timid before. I wasn't pushing myself."

"Translation, please," Nikki said, breaking side-eye records for sure.

"One word." Markie looked up to the sky and squinted. "One word."

"And what, may I ask, is that *word*?" Nikki said.

Markie flicked her fingers in front of us like a flash of light. "Whitney."

Nikki planted her palms on the bleachers for support and leaned in.

"Whitney who?"

"Not...not...as in Whitney Houston?" I said. "The one that my mama just calls 'The Voice,' her favorite singer of all time, Whitney Houston?"

"Yep, that's the one. Singers perform her songs a lot on those reality shows, right? She's a little old school, but for an event like this, we need to pull out the classics. Something to get the adults to dig deep in their pockets?" Markie said.

"Good thinking," Nikki admitted.

Markie's voice blazed through my thoughts.

"'I Believe in You and Me' is one of Aunt Vie's favorites. I can't communicate with her like I want to. Maybe through song I can reach her a bit. I've always been self-conscious to get up in front of crowds because of, you know, shorty. But I can't live like that forever."

"No, you can't." Then I thought of how Aunt Vie responded to the music that night at the diner. "Let's hear some of it?" I said.

"Okay, I think there is an instrumental on YouTube. Give me a second and let me warm up." She walked a few paces away from us as she flipped through her phone.

"Have you lost your mind?" Nikki said.

"You don't get it?"

"Obviously not...hmm." She bit her lip. "Expound." The word shot out of her rounded lips like a puff of smoke.

"Markie has a connection to this song. She was nervous before. I bet she can nail this one."

I pointed an ear toward Markie. "The warm-up sounds okay."

Please sound better. Please.

When Markie stood in front of us again, she pushed play. "Ahem." She swayed to the melody.

"I hope 'Ahem' isn't the high point," Nikki mumbled.

Then Markie began. *"I believe in you and me. I believe that we will be."*

It was soft at first. A little unsteady. Seconds later, she was in the middle of it, right in the thick. *"I believe in dreams again."*

Notes that should have been soaring were underwater or belly-crawling along the ground. If possible, this song was worse than "Diamonds." I wanted to stop her, but she stopped herself.

"That's just a sample." Nikki answered her cell phone, though I didn't hear it ring. "A little rusty, I know. But what you think, Georgie? With some practice I can knock it out the park."

Everybody might run out of the park. Ugh.

"Maybe with more practice," I said. The way her eyes searched for a compliment made me want to give one. But I couldn't. Sweet Apple principal, Principal Romain, delivered the quote of the week every Monday. One that I remembered was: "The only way to have a friend is to be a friend."

"Markie, what about the whistling? Remember, you said that you and Aunt Vie loved to whistle."

She bugged her eyes. "All right, what gives with all the whistling talk? You don't want me to sing? Is that it?"

I clinched my notebook in my hands. "No...no, it's not that." Then I thought about the quote. "Okay, it is that. Your singing isn't that good." The words left my mouth dry. I wished I had a bottle of water.

The disappointment in her eyes was immediate. And I felt lower than dirt.

I braced myself for her to rip into me about something. My dancing. My basic clothing. I didn't know what she'd attack. Maybe she'd light in on Mama again. I didn't know. But she stood there and looked around the park. She focused on some kids playing catch for a second.

Her silence made it all the more awkward. I couldn't help but to keep talking. "I didn't know how to tell you before. But I don't want anyone making fun of you or anything."

She nodded quick the way people do when they really want you to know that they get it. They understand. When she spoke, it was the same quiet way she spoke to Aunt Essie when I thought she'd explode. "Do you really think that I'd be concerned about people making fun of my voice? Is that what you think I'd be insecure about after all the things we've talked about?"

"No, I guess not," I said as Nikki walked up.

Markie glanced at Nikki, then back at me. "None of us are professionals, right? This is about honoring Aunt Vie. This is about giving from our hearts and doing the best we can to raise money to donate to fight this cause. If people want to tease me about that. Trust me. My skin is tough. Thought you'd at least know that about me by now."

I was doofus, remixed. "You're right. We all need to get up there and just give it our best."

"Well, I'll get practicing. I want to show I put all the effort I could into it." Then her phone buzzed. "That's Rosella. I need to run an errand for her. I'm hooking up with the sibs later. There's another local band interested."

"Nice," Nikki said.

Markie said goodbye and went on her way.

"Did you catch all that?" I said to Nikki.

"Yeah. It nearly had me bawling. But I just hope she's not setting herself up for a dose of Bogalusa-wide embarrassment. Everybody isn't as nice, kind, and...and...*empathic* as us."

"I think she's got this handled." I wrote Markie—"I Believe in You and Me" in my notebook. I let Nikki's "us" slide.

24

FUTURE ME

That evening, Aunt Vie let Mama wash her hair. Instead of the Bantu Knots, she thought it should be braided.

"Can you do it, Georgie?" Mama asked.

My heart beat so fast I thought I was shaking.

"Yes, ma'am," I said.

"Let me wash her hair and we'll come downstairs. Go in her room and get everything you need. You can braid it in the living room," Mama said. I was nervous I'd upset her. But Mama must have read my mind. "It's okay, Georgie. She had a house call from her doctor. They've adjusted her medication. Don't think she'll startle as easily." I nodded.

About thirty minutes later, she and Aunt Vie were downstairs. Nikki and Peaches helped me set up the living room like a mini beauty salon. While we were waiting, Nikki let Peaches help polish her nails. Nikki could wear polish to school, something I wasn't allowed to do until I was thirteen. I could only wear clear polish, which was the blandest thing ever.

When Mama had Aunt Vie settled in the living room, I held the comb close to her hair but was too jittery to start.

"Just take your time," Mama said.

I didn't want to pull too hard. I was only used to doing my hair, Peaches's, and Mama's. Our hair, especially Peaches's, was so thick that it took two or three tries to get to the scalp. But Aunt Vie's was thinner, delicate.

"You know I'm tender-headed, Essie. Don't yank at my head like I'm your doll baby."

"I won't" is all I could think to say.

She was with us. It didn't matter if she didn't have the names right. She knew she was getting her hair done and she sat still. I couldn't help but wonder if Markie had braided Aunt Vie's hair before. But it didn't make me jealous. I just hoped that she had a memory like this.

Peaches was so excited to see me braiding Aunt Vie's hair, she sat and held the castor oil for me. Each time I parted Aunt Vie's hair, I dabbed the oil on her scalp before I braided. Mama stayed close by and I finished just before Aunt Vie nodded off to sleep.

"Love the way you connected the ends," Nikki said. "Might let you braid mine one of these days." Though we'd tried that before and argued all the way through.

When Grandma Sugar and Aunt Essie came from the diner, we all sat out on the porch and Aunt Essie served up homemade lemon icebox pie with fresh whipped cream. They listened in as Nikki and I discussed the talent show. Along with the businesses Nikki found online, Grandma Sugar and Aunt Essie gave us other shops and churches to contact. They weren't trying to take over, just help, and that was all we needed.

"We're closing the diner during the show. When we open up after, we'll have a limited menu but the business should be worth it," Aunt Essie said. "This is a blessing to my soul."

"Mine too," Grandma Sugar said.

Sitting out on the porch that night was the first time that I thought about the talent show honoring not only Aunt Vie but everyone who loved her. For the rest of the night, we listened to stories of them growing up in Bogalusa and all the famous people who had eaten at Sweetings. They also told us about other famous people out of Bogalusa that we'd never heard of, including a poet Grandma Sugar said won something called the Pulitzer Prize, Yusef Komunya-kaa, and a Major League Baseball player called the Bogalusa Bomber, Charlie Spikes. "Had all the town watching that boring game," Grandma Sugar said and chuckled.

After they'd all gone to bed, Nikki and I stayed up designing posters until sleep took over.

About two the next afternoon, Nikki and I were in the room getting ready to meet Markie and the sibs at the park.

Mama called, "Georgie! You have some express mail."

"It's here!" I shouted, which was fine because Aunt Vie was out on the porch.

"You think that's what it could be?"

"What else?" I said.

Unlike the gentle touch we normally had on the stairs, this time, we both nearly tore them down. The pictures on the walls rattled.

"Hey, take it easy," Mama called.

Even though it was addressed to me, it was c/o Mama.

Once I had the large envelope in hand, I read the address and sure enough it was from the mayor's office. My jumps were short and rapid and like something hot was under my feet.

"We did it! We did it!" Nikki shouted as I tore open the big envelope and took out the second one. Mama bent down and picked up the envelope, not bothering to complain. This one was letter sized. Then I stopped jumping and cleared my throat. I stood in perfect posture like Simone Biles does before she takes flight. I looked at Nikki and then at Mama.

"Well, c'mon. Read it. Read it," Nikki egged on.

I shifted weight from one side to another. *In regard to an emergency permit for a fundraiser to be held at McClurie Park, it is hereby granted.* There was a lot of other legal words but that's all my mind processed. "Granted!" I screamed.

Mama gathered us in for hugs. "So proud of you, Georgie. Your grandma and great-aunts are, too. My baby is a community organizer. This calls for a celebration. Chocolate shakes, root beer floats, or fresh strawberry lemonade?"

"Chocolate shakes," we said in unison.

I swirled my fingers in the air making an imaginary mountain of cream and said, "With extra whip."

"Coming right up," Mama said.

Nikki and I plopped down on the couch.

"Let me see it," Nikki said. I handed it to her and she read it again. "You should frame this. Scrapbook, at least."

"But I didn't do it alone, though. You helped and so did Markie. I wish she was here, too," I said.

"Yeah. She deserves to be. Even if she works my nerves."

"You know when school starts, we can plan another one. This doesn't have to be the last time we fundraise for Alzheimer's."

"Georgie, remember…remember…"

My stomach dipped. *California.*

I hugged Nikki. Not just out of happiness about our permit, but because she was my best friend and she was moving way across the country. Even though Nikki was sitting right next to me, I could feel the distance of California trying to creep in between us.

"Well, maybe when we see each other in the summer, we could do it."

She nodded and I let it go.

Mama appeared with our chocolate shakes.

Nikki and I weren't on the porch for five minutes with Aunt Vie and Grandma Sugar before Markie rang.

"I was just about to call you," I said.

"I need you to get to the library as soon as possible— alone."

She hung up, and I eyed the phone like I expected her to jump out of it.

Nikki and I walked to the kitchen. "What was that all about? You didn't even tell her about the permit."

"She didn't give me a chance. Markie needs us at the library. Actually, she told me to come 'alone.'"

"She is so, *so* full of drama. Oozing drama," Nikki said.

I bit my tongue. "Well, she's going to have to understand that we're a package deal. I'm not leaving you out. Can't risk it with Mama and we'll be far apart soon enough."

I told Mama we were heading to the library, and Nikki and I grabbed fliers to pass out along the way. We waved goodbye to Grandma Sugar and Aunt Vie.

Nikki squirted herself with Sweet Pea body spray as we walked. "Hey, mind if we did split up again, just this once? I'd rather be at the park working with the other kids. You and Markie can come as soon as she tells you whatever it is she wants to tell you. Honestly, I'm hoping she has that box with her so you can stop wondering what's in it. Sheesh."

"Sure you don't mind?" I asked.

"Nope. It's a lot trying to do both. I'll hold this down until you're able to focus one hundred percent, which I hope is soon."

I thanked her, and two minutes later we were going in separate directions.

I rolled up my fliers like a telescope. Everything was coming together. I sighed. It would make it that much better if Markie told me some good news about her mama. I picked up my pace. I couldn't get to Markie fast enough.

As I walked, I waved to the man selling watermelons who was parked in the same location he was when I walked to the library with Peaches.

"Staying out of trouble?" he said. It felt more out of custom than actual curiosity.

"Yes, sir. Thank you," I said. I walked over to him and gave him a flier.

"What are you passing out there," said a frail woman with bedroom slippers with a patch of fuzzy fur on top of them. Every vegetable imaginable was displayed as neat as Mama's favorite store in Atlanta, Publix.

"Fliers for our talent show," I said. "It's honoring my aunt Vie, the owner of Sweetings."

"I know Elvie. Used to supply the collards there when I had a bigger farm. Anything I can do to support, let me know. I'll pass these out to anybody who comes along. And they travel from all over Bogalusa to buy my vegetables."

I left a handful of fliers with her.

When I entered the library, I headed straight for Markie's table. There, just like before, she was surrounded by books. But right next to the books was the box. And its top was loosened.

"Thanks for coming right away," she said without looking up.

"Wow! You opened it?"

She bobbed her head but didn't speak. It was then that I noticed she wasn't just avoiding looking at me, her eyes were fixed on a photo.

"Is that a picture of your mama? Was it in the box?"

"Yeah," she said. This time she raised her head and met my eyes. She glared at me and I reared back. Her eyes were blurry and bloodshot.

"What's wrong?"

"See for yourself."

There was a stout Black lady, standing with her hands

clasped in front of her. Twenty kids stood next to her, some frowning, some smiling. "This was in your box?"

She nodded again. "There were about twelve Black girls in the class."

I glanced up at Markie. I wanted to match her face, her eyes to one of the girls in the picture, someone who I could pick out as her mama. But before I could, eyes that were unmistakable stared back at me.

"This is my mama. Was that in this box?" Then it hit me. And the words came out in a whisper. "Your mom is here, too, isn't she?" I didn't wait for Markie to answer but went back to the picture. There, three girls away from my mama, was a girl with the same bushy eyebrows as Markie. But I couldn't be sure, so I turned the picture over. Irene Whitlock. Trina Townsend.

"Thanks to the librarian, I found these," she said and slapped her hand on a stack of Bogalusa High School Yearbooks. "These have been here all this time, but I guess I didn't want to see another picture of my mama. But when I saw your mama's name on the back of that picture, too..."

Like she was revealing some deep dark secret, Markie said, "Your mom went there, you know."

"We already know that. I think it's the only high school in Bogalusa." My tone was sharper than I intended.

There was a book in front of her. In it was a library bookmark with *Check It Out* on the top half. She flipped the book open.

"Look at this."

I leaned in, almost smashing my face into the book.

"Do you believe me now?" Markie said.

When my eyes focused, looking like the future me was Mama. I'd seen younger pictures of her, but never in school. Never laughing and being silly in Mrs. Thurston's Home Economics Class. There were a bunch of girls, with aprons and every hair in place as they showed off freshly baked pies and cakes. Like always, her complexion was more caramel while mine was chocolate fudge, like Daddy's, but her eyes were my eyes. Aunt Elvie's eyes.

I glanced up at Markie, who was ogling at me the way you do when you're waiting for someone to "get it."

"Okay. That's my mom...*and*..."

"Read this." Markie tapped the page again, then underlined the print with the tip of her pen.

I read it aloud.

"Seniors Katrina Townsend and best friend, Irene Whitlock..." I stopped. Everything else was fuzzy. *Best friend, Irene Whitlock...Best friend, Irene Whitlock.*

"Best friends?"

"Yep."

"I don't understand," I mumbled, thinking I wasn't really speaking the words aloud until someone shushed me. "Why wouldn't my mama tell you that she knew your mama? Why wouldn't she tell me?" I had asked her. She lied.

"Only she knows. But she probably knows why my mom abandoned me. Who knows what else she knows? Like where she is...where my dad is. I told you something was off."

"If she knew any of that, she would have told you."

"You're still defending her?"

"Why are you so stuck on thinking she's keeping

something from you? So what if they were friends in high school. People lose touch...."

"So you and Princess BFF are going to suddenly not be friends anymore?"

"Stuff happens." It was the lamest thing I could have said but it was all I had. I sat in the chair, but it felt like I was spinning. It was like the library turned upside down and all the books were on the floor, piles of them. And everything I knew about my mom was lost underneath the avalanche. I swallowed hard, but unlike the moment in the mayor's office, I still couldn't speak.

Markie clapped the book shut and grabbed her phone. "I'm done with the guessing games. We're getting ready to find out some answers. And we have this picture as evidence."

I studied the cover and "reference only" was stamped on the front.

"You can't check this out."

"Don't need to." Markie took out her phone and showed me where she'd already snapped a picture. "I'm on my way to your mom."

"Now?"

"Right now! Don't you think I've waited long enough?"

"Do whatever you want. My mom can explain it."

"You don't know your mama as well as you think you do," Markie said.

When I tried to think of a comeback, I remembered how I thought Mama was trying to keep me away from Markie. Had I been right then?

We headed toward Aunt Vie's house to see Mama.

I'd already gone down the block before I realized I'd left my fliers.

"Hey, hold up," I said, but she didn't stop. I called Nikki. I couldn't risk her missing the text.

"What's up?"

"I need you at the house. Leave right now."

"Everything okay?"

"Just get there," I said while trying to keep up with Markie.

She agreed and we hung up.

The fast pace we were walking dumped buckets of sun rays on the top of my head. I sweated more than I'd ever sweated in Bogalusa. My mind was running, racing, faster than my legs. I didn't know what confusion had happened, or how Markie would take it, but Mama would clear it up. Each time my sneakers hit the ground, it felt like I was pumping gas into this gigantic tank that held everything I believed and it was about to explode.

25

MARKIE, MAMA, AND ME

When we reached Aunt Vie's gate, I rushed past Markie. There was no way she was going to reach Mama first. I hustled up the stairs. Markie followed. I could see Nikki walking toward us but couldn't wait.

"Whoa, whoa, what's going on here? You two know better than to come stampeding in this house like a herd of cattle," Grandma Sugar said. "Peaches is napping."

We stopped.

"Where's my mama?"

"Believe she's in the kitchen," Grandma Sugar said.

Markie and I raced down the narrow hallway and stood in front of the fridge.

Mama's eyes darted between Markie and me. My eyes

searched Mama's for an answer before we'd asked her any questions.

"You know my mama?" Markie said. It wasn't the forceful way I thought she'd say it. "You know her from school."

Mama's nod was subtle. Even though I was staring at her, I would have missed it with a quick blink.

"She was my best friend," Mama said. "Irene."

No one moved. Every sound in the house amplified. I breathed in waves that crashed and rolled around me.

"Why wouldn't you say something, Ms. Katrina? Why would no one say anything to me?"

Mama didn't move at first. Her shoulders were leaning forward like something was pulling her down.

"Let's have a seat," Mama said.

Mama and Markie walked toward the kitchen table. I didn't budge.

"No. I'm not going anywhere," I said. I wanted the answers now. If Markie had never gotten ahold of that picture, those yearbooks, we wouldn't even be talking about it now.

There was a ringing in my ear like every pot and pan in the kitchen clanged together. The hum of the refrigerator was louder than a trombone.

Mama backed up and leaned against the sink.

Then Markie's words slunk out in a tiny voice that I barely heard over the beating of my heart. "Do you know where my mama is?"

"You'd never know something about Markie's mama and not tell her, right? You must have lost touch with her a long time ago. Is that right? It was before her mama left her."

I could see Nikki in the corner and Grandma Sugar in back of her. I wanted to go to Nikki, but it felt like she was moving farther away.

Mama cleared her throat. Then she clasped her hands in front of her and wrung them. My entire body was in a knot. When Mama was upset that's what she did.

"Markie, I'm so sorry," Mama said. Then she bit down on her lips. "I'm sorry for everything."

I stared at Markie. She hadn't moved. She didn't even ask Mama what she was sorry for.

Now, Mama's tears were streaming.

"I could have done better. All these years I've known that I could have done better."

"Mama, please, what are you saying? What happened?" Nikki was next to me now. She had her arm around my shoulder. Grandma Sugar was next to Markie.

"I'd lost touch with Irene. It'd been years since high school. Many years. Not a call. A letter. Nothing. But out of the blue she called me. She'd gotten my number from Aunt Vie. She was crying. I could barely understand her. When she calmed down, she told me that I was the only one she could trust. That she knew I wouldn't let her down."

My heart was beating so fast it felt like it was shaking the floor.

"What does that mean?" The gentleness in Markie's voice was gone now. Her words were rugged. The sound of them alone broke me in pieces. "She wanted you to take care of me but you didn't want me either?"

"It wasn't like that, Markie. Georgie was a toddler. I was going to night school. And George was a struggling car salesman. She asked me if I could take you. . . .I tried to understand what was happening with her. Was she sick? Was she in trouble? She wouldn't give me any answers."

Grandma Sugar walked over to give Mama some tissues and she rubbed her back. From Grandma Sugar's look, she seemed to be hearing this for the first time, too.

"What happened!" Markie insisted.

"All she wanted to do was arrange to meet me so that I could take you. I told her that I'd call her back. I couldn't decide like that in an instant. I just needed to think things through. And give her a chance to calm down, think rationally. . .I didn't call her back that night. I thought for sure when I called back the next day, she'd answer and we'd talk about it. I'd do what I could to help. The phone just went to voicemail."

Now Mom's crying filled the house. "I don't know how I rationalized it, but I told myself that maybe someone else helped her. Maybe a family member. But when I didn't hear from her again, I started to think the worst. I knew Aunt Vie would look into it for me. But by the time Aunt Vie got involved, Irene had left you with a neighbor and Child & Family Services had taken you. When Aunt Vie finally was able to get you in foster care, I prayed everything would work out."

"Why, Ms. Katrina? Why wouldn't you say something? Do you know where she is now?"

"I don't know. I haven't known for quite some time. . . years."

Markie fired her words at me. "I told you. See, your mama could have helped me. . . ." Then she turned to Mama.

"Why didn't you help her? Wasn't she once your 'best' friend? I wouldn't have been any trouble. I was just a little kid. You probably knew about my arm, right. That's why you didn't want to be bothered with me. Didn't want me messing up your perfect family."

Mama slid the back of her hand across her eyes and stepped closer to Markie.

"Nothing like that, Markie," Mama said and walked toward her.

"Don't. Don't," Markie said and backed away. "If I was made perfect, I wouldn't have been too much trouble then, would I? All of y'all are just the same. You only come around when it's easy. Where were you when Aunt Vie needed you? Now you come and treat me like I'm the troublemaker. Like I'm some bad influence to keep away from your precious *G-baby*."

As Markie talked, she backed toward the kitchen entrance, never taking Mama out of her sight. Then she bolted. Streaked through the living room. The screen door banged against the house so hard I thought it could crumble.

Even if I wanted to, I couldn't go after Markie. It was like everything was frozen. Grandma Sugar was comforting Mama. Then I felt Nikki's arm intertwine with mine and we walked out to the porch and sat on the stairs.

Grandma Sugar came out to the porch several minutes later. "You okay, Georgie?"

"Yes, ma'am," I said. "How is Mama?

"She has a lot of hurt she's been carrying around. Knocks you off your feet when it tries to come out all at once."

I stood up. "Mama needs to talk to Markie, Grandma. Don't you think?"

"I do, baby," Grandma Sugar said. She came over and kissed my cheek. "You know that's my daughter in there. So I'm telling you this from a mama's point of view, that Katrina hurts that she let Markie down and put an extra burden on Aunt Vie. Along with all of that, though, she thinks that she's let you down, too."

I was quiet. A part of me felt that she had.

"Give it time, Georgie. No one is asking you to come to terms with this all at once."

"I need to find Markie. I hate to think of her somewhere alone." Then I looked at Nikki.

"If you didn't ask to go find her, I was about to."

To have a friend, you have to be a friend. I thought it but I didn't say it. That would have made the moment way too emotional and boy, we'd had a load of that.

"Slow down, girls," the vegetable lady called. She added an umbrella to her chair since I'd seen her earlier. "You two don't have to get anywhere that's worth you having a heatstroke."

"Yes, ma'am," we said but only slowed until we rounded the corner.

We kept up our racewalking speed until we reached the library. I bent over and grabbed my knees, trying to catch my breath so I wouldn't enter into the library like a panting wolf.

"You okay?" Nikki said.

"I'm good. You're handling the heat better than I am."

As soon as we walked into the library, the librarian said,

"Back so soon." Her smile worthy of a blue ribbon. I forced a smile but not a word. I quick-stepped to Markie's table.

Please be here, Markie, please. But the table was empty. All the books cleared like the hour before never happened. I just stood next to it. Then I went to retrieve the yearbook again, so that I could show Nikki. I found the picture and we both just stared at it for a while. Mama and Irene looked like they were inseparable, the way their arms linked and their smiles were almost one.

Mama's hair was in a huge, neat Afro and Irene's was in what I'd heard called a "mushroom." I couldn't help thinking of all the secrets they shared.

"Nikki, you don't think this will happen to us, do you?"

She just shook her head so quickly, I knew that it had to be on her mind, too. Neither one of us really wanted to talk about it. We've seen best friends not survive changing homerooms and lunch tables, and she was moving more than two thousand miles away.

Before we left the library, I stopped and asked the librarian, "Have you seen the girl that I've come in here with?"

"Oh, Markie. Not since you were in here earlier. If she's not at the diner, she's usually here. I'd just check back."

"Thank you," I said.

"Oh, wait a second. One of you left these," she said and handed me our fliers.

"Thank you," I said.

"Markie already posted it on our bulletin board. And I have a short note on our website. I've kept a few here at the desk. She inquired about us attending with our bookmobile last week."

"She did?" Nikki said before I could.

"When I saw this date on the flier, I checked and either I or another librarian should be able to be there and loan books to kids."

"Sweet!" Nikki said with enthusiasm I couldn't muster.

"Thank you," I said.

"No problem. We're always looking for ways to connect with the community and Markie speaks so highly of you and your great-aunt. You're Georgie, right?" When two kids walked up with stacks of books, she excused herself.

"Didn't picture Markie as a bookworm," Nikki said.

"Yeah, neither did I, at first. I was hoping she'd come rushing in while we were talking."

"That would have been too easy, I guess," Nikki said. "Now what?"

I hesitated before I told her where we needed to go next.

26

SPIRIT FARMS

"Try calling her again," Nikki said as we were on our way to the diner. I dialed Markie's number and it went to voicemail.

We stood on the side of the diner and looked in the front window. No Markie.

"She might be back in the kitchen," I said. I had to go inside.

As soon as we did, Aunt Essie walked up and hugged me and said, "So sorry for all this, Georgie."

"You didn't know?" I asked.

Aunt Essie shook her head. "No, ma'am, I didn't."

I looked around and one of Aunt Vie's friends I'd met before was helping out.

"Is Markie here?" I asked.

"Nope, she didn't work today. If you two don't find her shortly, go on home. She probably just wants some time to herself. We'll get a fresh start at it tomorrow."

"Yes, ma'am," I answered and Nikki and I left.

"The show is only two days away. We need to find her now."

"So where do you think we should check next?" Nikki asked. "You think she's at the park?" I raised my eyebrows. "The outskirts? You think she's out to Ms. Hannah's."

"Besides the library and diner, that's the only other place that makes sense."

"You think it's worth it?"

"I do," I said.

"Yeah, me too," and took out her phone. "How many miles did you say?"

"About three."

"Okay, if we walk at a steady pace in this heat, not too fast, we should be able to do three miles in about forty minutes. You know the address?" I shook my head.

"I remember how to get there," I said with a little more confidence than I should have.

The first moment I realized we were lost was when I didn't see Nettie's. Once I thought to ask Nikki to google it, her signal was too weak.

"Does any of this look familiar, Georgie?" Nikki asked.

But that was the problem: it all was familiar. Nothing but road, trees, and telephone poles.

"There should be a store coming up soon. Remember, the one Markie and I stopped at?" I said.

"With the parrot," Nikki said.

I slowed my pace a little because, if we were lost, I didn't want us to get too tired. "Yep, that's the one," I said. I wanted to give it a little more time before I confessed that maybe we should have seen that store by now.

Nikki craned her head around. "I can't believe anyone would walk out here at night. It would be scary even to drive."

I couldn't help remembering some of the bad stuff I'd learned about the town and got a little jittery. What if someone yelled a bad name out the window?

A car zoomed by us. I swallowed so hard it felt like I gave myself the hiccups. And with Nikki with me, if we were lost my guilt was times ten. Just at the height of thinking about the unsavory side of Bogalusa, a car was creeping up behind me slow and it was closer to the side of the road, along the shoulder.

"A car. . .a car is behind us," Nikki said.

Seconds later we heard, "Grandniece? Is that you?"

I recognized the voice—Peanut Man.

I breathed out and relaxed for the first time since I'd started thinking those scary thoughts. "What are you two doing out this way? And you're not even heading toward town. Where's Markie Jean?" he said as he put the car in park and searched off to the sides like she'd emerge from the bushes. Guess he hadn't ever seen me without her.

"I'm on my way to Ms. Hannah's to meet Markie." I knew he had a hotline to the diner, so I sounded confident. I could say that Grandma Sugar and Aunt Essie both knew we were looking for Markie, but they didn't mean this far and I knew it. "This is my best friend, Nikki, she's visiting from Atlanta."

"How you do," he said and nodded to Nikki, tugging at the edge of his cap.

"Well, you missed the fork back there that would have led you to it. Unless you planning on cutting across Mae's watermelon farm, you can't rightfully get to it this way," he said.

"How far is it if I go back?" I dug my nails into my palm and bit my lip.

"Good ten to fifteen minutes or more." He reached over and opened the door. "If you two are destined to get there before it gets late, hop in. I've done some work up there. Take you right up to the door."

I'd told Nikki how Peanut Man took me to Aunt Vie's to make sure Markie and I stayed off the property. As soon as we were in Peanut Man's truck, he pulled off and the taste of dust was on my tongue. The pleather seats were so hot, I rocked like I was on a seesaw. I looked up at the sky that was still bright. I said a quick prayer that we'd find Markie before a layer of evening settled on us.

This morning I'd woken up making fliers for the talent show and now I was clopping along the road with Peanut Man and Nikki. And what I thought I knew about my own mama was twisted around, and that hurt most of all. Then I thought about Markie. If Mama not being honest with me hurt this much, I just couldn't imagine how I'd feel if I thought she didn't want me.

I closed my eyes and prayed that Markie was at Ms.

Hannah's. It was like I could feel Aunt Vie's presence helping us find Markie.

As we traveled Peanut Man schooled us on the nutritional value of all things peanut.

"Now everybody can't be around the peanut. I understand that. It's one of eight common food allergens, you know. I've seen a man's tongue swell up to near 'bout the size of a catfish just from one peanut. Neither of you are, right?"

"No, sir," we said, seconds apart.

"I have a cousin who is allergic, though," Nikki added.

Peanut Man took a swig of water. "I picked up a man and his son one day. And we didn't know that just the peanut dust would trigger the boy." Peanut Man flipped down his visor. "Lawd, I tell you if I didn't have one of these EpiPen on me I don't think that child would have made it."

"There it is," I said aloud when I spotted Nettie's store.

"Oh, Nettie. She opens the store a little more these days. But she still spends most of her time in New Orleans at the Audubon Zoo. She's a real zoologist and she does some kinda bird rescue, too."

He went up about another five minutes and we were at the entrance to Spirit Farms. "Here is good," I said.

"Well, not in my book. Ms. Hannah don't like much traffic on her property cause of the horses, but I'd feel a little better about this whole situation if I took you up to the front door." As we approached, the way the ground crackled underneath his tires was eerie.

"Seems larger than when I was here the first time,"

I said, hoping that Markie didn't decide to hide out somewhere on the property.

"There was a time when you could lose more than time coming up on Guidry Farms without a proper invite."

I hated to correct him, but it didn't seem like he'd mind. I said it as softly as I could. "Excuse me, Peanut Man, but isn't it called Spirit Farms?"

He chuckled. "That's telling my age. And you're right. Guidry Farms was before Ms. Hannah and her mother, God rest her soul, took it over years ago. We call a few of them the "Good Guidrys." Some folks in Bogalusa believe there is no such a thing. We believe Black people have met their end on this farm. No proof, though. Ms. Hannah changed it to Spirit Farms to honor that."

I tensed up a little, but I knew this was a chance to learn more about Ms. Hannah. "Oh, that's why Aunt Essie and my grandma don't favor them much."

"Some can put water under the bridge, but sometimes it hits too close to home," he said. Close to home. I knew that I'd gotten about as much out of Peanut Man as I could, which was more than I knew before. But even if I wanted more information, my thoughts had shifted to Ms. Hannah's porch.

Nikki's fist hit my leg. "You see what I see?"

"Sure do," I said.

There, like a mirage, was Ms. Hannah standing next to Bessie, whose rein was tied at the post. Ms. Hannah's hair was braided the time I'd seen her before, but now it was loose and wavy. And sitting on the porch steps, watching us drive up, was Markie.

Ms. Hannah turned and waved at us as we pulled up. Markie stood and leaned against the bannister.

We thanked Peanut Man again and got out. "Y'all sure there's no problem with getting back home, right?"

"I got them covered," Ms. Hannah said.

Peanut Man tipped his hat and drove off.

I didn't even know what to say to Markie. Did I apologize for Mama? Since Nikki and I had been looking for her, I forgot to think about what to say or do if we found her.

"We're glad you're okay, Markie," Nikki said.

She just hunched her shoulders, not looking at either of us.

"You must be Nikki," Ms. Hannah said.

"Yes, ma'am. That's a beautiful horse."

I was thankful for every word out of Nikki's mouth. It was like she was speaking for me while I gathered my thoughts.

"You knew about my mama and Markie's mama. Why didn't you say anything?" I asked. My voice was light as I tried to get the words out.

She glanced up. "It's getting late. Why don't we all go inside for a bit?" We all nodded.

She led us into the house. I took a deep breath and looked around for the source of the scent that calmed me.

"That's sage you're smelling. Wards off any negativity that tries to settle in on old Ms. Hannah. I'm not having none of it, you hear me?" She shouted that up to the ceiling. "Can I get you three something to drink?"

Nikki and I said, "Water," and Markie said, "No, thank you."

"Have a seat, please," Ms. Hannah said.

Considering the rickety porch, I didn't expect to see a comfy sectional and a big screen TV inside. Light shone in from several huge, back windows revealing miles of land.

I hoped that Markie would sit with us but she didn't. Nikki and I sat at the glass-top kitchen table, and Markie slid a chair from the table and pushed it against the kitchen wall.

When Ms. Hannah placed a glass of water on the table, I drank mine in just a few gulps. Then Ms. Hannah put the kettle on for tea and turned to face us while it heated. I couldn't stop crisscrossing my legs. My entire body felt like a long piece of string with knots in it that I couldn't untie.

"Georgie, I know you asked me why I didn't say something about your mama and Irene being friends, all I can say is that it wasn't my place. I had to let that information come from your mama. As soon as I saw you and Markie together, I knew there was no coincidence that you two bonded. Now, that may fall on the side of the worst reasons a person could have, but it is mine. And it's exactly what I told Markie Jean."

Markie's foot beating against the chair sounded like Bessie trotting in the middle of the kitchen. "Aunt Vie knew, too. She never told me. How could she make Aunt Vie keep that a secret for so long? That wasn't fair. Ms. Katrina could have stepped in a long time ago to help me find my mama."

I clenched my teeth the way you do when you're trying to stop yourself from crying. I wanted to defend my mama and was mad at her at the same time. My emotions were so split I thought I'd break in two.

Ms. Hannah readied her teacup. "Remember what we talked about, Markie? We weren't in their shoes then, right?"

Markie nodded.

"Vie hoped that if she was the foster parent, when Irene came back for Markie, she'd easily find her. But years went on and Vie began to realize that she wasn't coming back." The teakettle whistle pierced the air. Ms. Hannah lifted it and turned off the stove. As she set it down, I heard her sniffling. Then she turned to Markie. "Not knowing your mama is an open wound. None of us know exactly how to heal it. There is no doubt that mistakes were made. It didn't go the way any of us planned. Vie did her best. But Markie, she stayed close to you some way or another."

Ms. Hannah poured her tea. Both Nikki and I dabbed at our eyes. Since she was sitting with her head down, I couldn't see Markie's face.

After taking a few sips of tea, Ms. Hannah said, "On top of all this, we don't need folks worrying about you three. Let's get you all back into town."

"Markie." I couldn't believe I was speaking to her because I hadn't come up with the perfect thing to say yet. I stood up and so did Nikki. "Will you come back to Aunt Vie's? I know my mama wants to talk to you. And maybe you need to talk to her, too?"

"Might help both of you," Nikki said.

Every word Nikki spoke was like a hug. I was just glad she was there.

Markie shrugged. "Yeah, okay. If she wants to talk to me or not, I want to see Aunt Vie."

Ms. Hannah walked us out to the porch. "Wait right here," she said and then patted Bessie on the nose and mounted her. "I'll be back in a jiffy." She trotted around to the side of the house.

"Think she has a carriage back there or something," Nikki said.

"Glad she's giving us a ride. It would be a long walk back," I said. "A Koolickle would be nice, though, if it were earlier." When Markie didn't say anything, I turned to Nikki. "It's a dill pickle dipped in Kool-Aid."

Nikki swiped her hand across the air. "Think I'll pass."

Moments later, two headlights beamed from the right side of the house along with the purr of an engine.

My eyes adjusted to what was in front of me: a platinum Mustang. Ms. Hannah rolled down a window. "Jump in!"

Markie took the front seat and Nikki and I got in the back.

Once we were buckled up, we were heading out the gates. That's all it took for Peanut Man's words to start circling in my head. "Ms. Hannah?"

"Yes, baby," she said.

"Is it true?" I took in a deep breath. "Is it true that your family was mean to Black people? Maybe hurt some and that's why my aunt Essie and Grandma won't let Aunt Vie come here?"

The rocks underneath the car sounded like popcorn kernels popping. "I have brothers. Three half brothers. Two are decent people. The other was accused of shooting a young man home from college. O'Neal. I think of him often. He was working at Sweetings. Lots of evidence against one of my brothers, but he hasn't been charged. Doesn't matter that my mother and I broke ties with the racist people in our family long ago. Aunt Vie trusted me. They can't see me without seeing them, I guess."

"Do...do you think you could talk to my grandma and Aunt Essie? Aunt Vie is the only one who can't say exactly what she wants to right now. Someone has to speak for her. Shouldn't that be you?"

"I wish it was as easy for grown-ups to work through issues as it was for you young folks. But it's not," she said. "We let stuff eat us up inside for too long."

I could see Markie raise her head and look at Ms. Hannah. "You think this is easy for us to work through? We didn't even cause these problems. They all were dumped on us and we're doing the best we can."

"I didn't mean it that way," Ms. Hannah said but didn't take her eyes off the road.

"We...we are going to have a talent show to raise money for Alzheimer's. It's a fundraiser and it's happening Saturday. The three of us are all organizing it in honor of Aunt Vie. Maybe if you come there. That would help make things better," I offered.

"With all this going on, you three still managing to do something good for Vie."

"Yes, ma'am. Maybe kids could ride Bessie? Bet people would donate money to do that."

"Young lady, you are truly your great-aunt's niece," she said and laughed. "In the midst of trouble, you still hold on to something that could help others. Should have seen her during Hurricane Katrina." She rubbed that steering wheel like it was Bessie's coat. Ms. Hannah chuckled again.

"Turned Sweetings into a station to get water if yours was out. Made gumbo by the ton to feed people," she said.

"That sounds like Aunt Vie," Markie said.

"She didn't say she would come," Nikki whispered to me. But I knew that all I could do was tell her about it. Her decision was out of my hands.

27

IT'S ME

About one block away from the house, I could see Aunt Vie's house aglow. Every light was on in the windows, and on the porch, those mosquito-repellant torches burned. Aunt Essie sat in the rocker. Mama and Grandma Sugar stood on the sidewalk. When the three of us exited the car, Mama was the only one to come around to talk to Ms. Hannah. But it was keep-the-engine-running conversation. Daddy and Mama had those all the time. Neither Aunt Essie nor Grandma Sugar waved to her or said, "Come sit awhile." And it hurt my heart that the one person who'd say those words to her couldn't.

"I told Mama that you'd be back soon," Peaches said.

"See, Mama, I told you." Then she whispered, "I was only a little bit scared." I hugged her and kept her close.

Grandma Sugar ushered all of us inside the gate and directed her words at me. "You're just lucky that Peanut Man stopped by and told us he'd delivered you two safely to Ms. Hannah's and that she'd said she'd bring you home. That's the only reason we weren't worried sick. Goodness knows we didn't need that on top of everything else."

Mama came over to Markie and me. "I know you two have questions, especially you, Markie. Some I can answer, some I can't. Can you call your guardian and let her know I'll bring you home a little later, if that's okay?"

"Yes, ma'am," Markie said, without any resistance. Mama looked away and I kept my eyes on Markie. She didn't reach for her phone once.

Before Mama could talk to us, Ms. Hannah's car, which was still in front of the house, went silent. The engine was off and she opened her door.

"Thanks again for getting the girls home safely, Ms. Hannah. Did you need something?" Mama asked.

"Need to talk to Essie and Lilly. And a chair if you can spare an extra one out here, please."

Neither one of them had the pleasant look they gave to customers at Sweetings. "I'll get the chair," I offered. As soon as I'd set it on the porch, I signaled to Nikki and Markie to go back in the house.

When we were in and everyone else was outside, I said, "Come with me, upstairs."

"What are you getting ready to do?" Nikki asked.

"Get Aunt Vie," Markie said, with more pep than she'd had in a while.

Once in Aunt Vie's room, I could hear voices from the yard. Nikki moved the TV tray from in front of her. "Aunt Vie, Ms. Hannah is downstairs. Ms. Hannah," Markie said.

Aunt Vie repeated, "Hannah."

I held my hand out and she reached for it. Markie grabbed her lightweight robe. And we eased her into it. We led her downstairs without any problem. Nikki was the first one out the door. She held it while Markie and I escorted Aunt Vie.

Ms. Hannah wasted no time. She reached over to Aunt Vie and took both her hands in hers, brought them to her lips, and kissed them. "Sorry I haven't been to visit like I should. I'm sorry." The heart necklace Ms. Hannah wore shimmered on her neck from the porch light.

"Hannah?" Aunt Vie said.

"It's me…it's me…." Ms. Hannah said.

I didn't know if Aunt Vie was just repeating Hannah or if she really knew it was her. Either way, it didn't matter at the moment.

When Markie, Mama, Nikki, and I were all in the living room, I was just thankful that Markie was open to talking to Mama. Nikki offered to go upstairs with Peaches but I wanted Nikki to stay and Mama agreed.

Mama and I sat on the sofa. Markie and Nikki took the armchairs.

"Markie, there is no one conversation that I can have

that will totally explain my actions. One moment I think I made the best decision, the next second, I know I took the easy way out. I didn't even tell my mama because I knew that she would have convinced me not to put that burden on Aunt Vie."

"Why couldn't you just tell me the truth, Ms. Katrina?" Markie said.

"Some of it was shame. Guilt. It hit especially hard when I knew you and Georgie were getting along. Every second it reminded me of how much I let Irene down. Over the years, Aunt Vie did so much to try to take my guilt away. And it was clear that she loved you, but I should have faced this long before now. This guilt is something I need to start dealing with."

"I guess that's why you didn't tell me either, huh?" I said.

Mama nodded. "I know you're rushing to grow up, Georgie. But you're still my child." She started wringing her hands. "And as my child, how could I tell you what a big mistake I made? I didn't tell anybody, even your daddy. I just prayed that Irene was okay and that I hadn't ruined Markie's life. When it wasn't denial, it was regret."

"Would you like some water, Aunt Katrina?" Nikki asked.

"Yes, please," Mama said.

We were quiet for a moment, trying to process everything. Nikki came back with three glasses and napkins for coasters. "Here you go," she said and handed one to Mama, as well as Markie and me.

"And you and my mom were really best friends in high school?" Markie asked.

Mama nodded. "Thick as thieves, as they say. But Markie, this happened so long after high school. Your mama didn't really have any people from Bogalusa. And I'm ashamed to say how little I knew about her family life. Soon after graduation, she and her aunt moved to Jackson, Mississippi. But she lived in New Orleans and Baton Rouge, too."

"Ms. Katrina, do you mind if I talk to you? Just us." Then she glanced at Nikki and me. "I don't want to be rude, but there's just some personal things I need to know."

I started the bobblehead doll nod. I was happy that Markie wasn't shutting Mama out. Neither of them needed more of that. "We understand," I said. "We need to talk about a few last-minute things for the talent show." Markie and Mama walked out into the kitchen.

The voices on the front porch were steady as Aunt Vie's rocker that was tapping against the house. Peaches came down and joined us in the living room as Nikki and I talked about what needed to be done for the show.

"I want to read a poem, G-baby," Peaches announced. "If everybody is doing something to raise money, I want to do something, too."

"Sounds good, Peaches. We need to find one for you to memorize," I said.

"Grandma Sugar already helped me find one. It's a surprise," she said. "I'm going back upstairs to practice."

When Peaches went upstairs, instead of Nikki and I planning, we just sprawled on the couch.

"What a day," I said.

"You can say that again," Nikki said.

"What a day," I repeated and kicked off my shoes. We

both laughed a bit, which was our first real laugh in a while. For a moment, it was just enough to hear the voices on the porch and Peaches screaming the words to "Hey Black Child" upstairs.

I just hoped that Mama and Markie's conversation was going okay.

After we rested for a minute, I pulled my notebook out and we checked the various lists we'd made.

"I need to ask you a serious question, Georgie," Nikki said. "A few things have happened that could have canceled this show."

"That's true," I said.

"Lots of kids are counting on this and, from what I know about fundraisers, this one will get people giving. I need you to think *really* hard. Is there anything you can think of that could come back to bite us now? *Anything?*"

"No, there isn't," I said.

"Look at me, Georgie." I obliged. "Are you sure?"

"Yes," I said because I couldn't think of anything at all and it wasn't worth worrying Nikki, but I had to cross my fingers.

28

IN MY DREAMS

It was Friday and we weren't close to ready.

"He's here," Aunt Essie shouted. "My husband the traveling man is finally home." I rushed down. And Uncle Dean didn't disappoint. He had flowers and candy for everybody, especially Aunt Essie. They kissed and Aunt Essie blushed.

"I'd know this beauty anywhere," he said when he saw me. He presented me with pink carnations. "Your great-uncle would pick you up and swing you around, but I got to keep what little life I got in this back," he said. Then he turned to Nikki. "And who might this be?"

"This is my best friend, Nikki," I said.

Uncle gave her a single carnation. "Pleased to meet you."

"Is Uncle finally home?" Mama shouted from the kitchen. A basket plopped to the floor and she rushed in.

"Long time, girl," he said to Mama and handed her a bouquet. "If you stay away this long again, I'm driving that trailer out there looking for you."

"Won't happen again, Uncle," Mama said, sounding like a little girl.

"You know your great-niece got big plans for a talent show. You need to get settled and see where you can lend a hand," Aunt Essie said.

"I've seen some signs for it driving in. Put me to work," Uncle Dean said.

Two hours later, he was with us and the sibs at McClurie Park. Markie was babysitting for Rosella.

"We're creating an outdoor theater right in front of the bleachers. I sketched it out," I told him. It was "rudimentary," which is what Daddy called the sketches he drew for his third dealership he envisioned.

"Let me take a look," Uncle Dean said. He studied it, turning it at different angles. "What you got here is a stage, right?"

"Yeah, but we can just use the ground. It's even. We're going to rake it and make sure there's no stones or anything."

"What time is your show tomorrow?"

"Six p.m."

He reached into the pocket of his pants and pulled out a watch. The gold chain glistened from a belt loop. I knew it was something I wanted to get Daddy for Christmas. Uncle Dean turned to Flip. "You available to help me build this stage?"

It seemed like Flip stood at attention to the directness in Uncle Dean's voice. "Yes, sir," he said.

"I'm going to get my pickup and stack it with pallets from the mill. I know they got plenty to lend to such a good cause," Uncle Dean said.

Jada and Nikki were at the other end of the park practicing. I sat on the ground next to Latasha and watched. They'd added even more to their number. The new deal was that we'd do our routine and Nikki'd do a separate one with Jada. I watched them for a while and wondered if I should just bow out of the dancing and focus on the emceeing. But I didn't want to let Nikki down.

"Hey," I said, as if I hadn't been watching them for a few minutes. "Guess what?" Nobody said a word until the end of the song. They didn't end back-to-back—that was our thing, as boring as it seemed now—but Nikki and Jada ended with Nikki backflipping over Jada, who was already in one of the most coveted of splits—the side split. They shined.

If only in my dreams.

"Uncle Dean and Flip are going to get some material now. Says it will be smooth and strong enough to hold up to any dance routine. They'll be back in about an hour."

Nikki and I ran through our routine again. After about thirty minutes, we went up to the diner for some cool air and lemonade, then we headed back to the park.

"Just in time," Uncle Dean said as he and Flip arranged the pallets in the center of the park. "There are some gloves on the bleachers, grab a pair." Uncle Dean handed me a hammer and a pair of safety goggles. "Don't want any of that stray wood hitting you in the eye."

With my goggles, gloves, and hammer, I was ready.

"Nikki, take some pictures," I said.

"On it," she said and grabbed her phone. Something about that moment made everything so real. We were constructing a stage. And somehow, the adults were helping and not taking over.

The hammering had a beat of its own. Before we knew it, other people had joined in to help, too.

"Peanuts on the house," Peanut Man said right before he started helping Uncle Dean.

After another hour of hammering and aligning planks, Nikki and I left and walked back to the diner. From a distance, the hammering and sawing had a rhythm that sounded like a giant waking up and walking around.

Nikki and I were skipping, jumping, and as playful as puppies while we were walking toward the diner.

"Hey, guess who asked me was I coming back next summer?"

"Let me guess...Flip," I said.

"He is totally crushing on me," she said. "I mean *totally*."

"What did you tell him?"

"I said, 'Of course. My best friend will be here visiting her great-aunts.'" Then she kicked her leg up and touched the tip of her sneaker. "The way I figured it, one week with you in Snellville, one week here." She did a Herkie jump. I tried to emulate her without the height. More like a baby Herkie.

"Not bad. Not bad," she said. Then she hugged my neck. "Wait till he really sees me on the stage. He's going to crush *extra* hard."

"C'mon, he's kinda cute and all, but we've got to stay focused," I said.

She lifted her eyebrows as high as her jump. "You're not the only one who can multitask. Think I might give him my number. What do you think?"

"Did your parents say it was okay?"

"They're moving me all the way to California. Do they expect me not to keep in touch with friends, even if the friends are boys?"

"Whatever you say," I said.

Then she slowed her steps. "I have to ask you something and you need to be *honest*, honest."

"What's up?"

"Jada is a better dancer than I am, isn't she? I mean. You've seen all the stuff she can do. And she's never been to any kind of camp. No coaching. Nada."

I thought back to all my years knowing Nikki, and I don't think she'd ever asked me that question before. Not even Lucinda Hightower had that power.

"Nikki, can I give you one of Principal Romain's quotes? And honestly, it's one that I need to follow more myself. I even wrote this one in my notebook. 'Cause I had to remember it when it comes to you."

"Really? What is it?"

I pursed my lips. A little embarrassed to say it. "'Comparison is the thief of joy,'" I said. "I can't remember who said it, but Principal Romain posted that a couple times, remember?"

"Nah. But you had to use that about me?" I nodded. "Oh, about the dancing, huh?"

"Instead of comparing myself to you, I just want to concentrate on how you're so good, you make me want to be better. Does seeing Jada make you want to be better?"

"Meaning you're not going to answer me."

"All I'll say is this: you're both good. Phenomenal," I said.

"Oh, good word," Nikki said and repeated it into her phone. Then she hit me with a fifteen-second version of her latest choreography.

I stopped walking.

"Oh, want me to run it back?"

"No time for the routine now, Nikki, look." Defying Mama's no pointing rule, I extended my forearm and pointed my finger toward the diner as steady as a bird dog.

Nikki studied me instead of where I was pointing and said, "What's gotten into you?" Then she saw what I was pointing to. A police car. In front of the diner.

"Dang," she said. Then, as if she was inside my mind, her next words were, "Think it has something to do with the talent show?"

There was no way they could stop it now. I tried to believe that as I walked to the diner. Maybe they needed to check our permit and someone directed them to the diner instead of Aunt Vie's. I wanted to run through all the scenarios before we got there so I wouldn't be caught off guard. Nikki grabbed my hand and hurried me along.

But then she stopped at the corner and wouldn't budge. "Wait, Georgie. Remember what I asked you?" She bugged her eyes. "Is there anything that you and Markie did that could wreck everything?"

This time, I put some *real* thought into it. "No. I don't think so. Let's not freak out before we find out," I said and clasped my hands behind my back to keep them from shaking.

"Don't *think* so? You should know so. I asked you if anything would come back and bite us, remember? The show is tomorrow. Your mama wouldn't care if your uncle was building us the Superdome. She'd shut it down if you and Markie are in some type of trouble."

"It is a diner, you know. We serve food. The best in town." I accidently bit my tongue on that last word as terror swept across my body.

She kept her arms folded the rest of the way while I let mine swing, creating my own Bogalusa breeze as worry free as possible. A half a minute later, we were in front of the diner, and any smidgen of hope that the police weren't there on business was doused. Through the diner window we saw two officers, Mama, Aunt Essie, and Markie. One officer was writing something on a notepad. In a flash, I squeezed my eyes shut and wished he was sitting down and Markie was taking his order.

29

CAGED BIRD

For the first time, when I entered Sweetings, no song played on the jukebox. The voice of the note-taking officer ricocheted off every picture in the place, then the word "stolen" thumped me on the forehead.

"Georgie, get over here right now," Mama said.

"Yes, ma'am," I said as innocently as I could.

"These officers are here asking after you and Markie Jean." Mama maneuvered me next to Markie, placing one of her hands on each of our shoulders. "Now, please state again your business here, Officers."

"We are following up on a report from a local business owner. She states that she believes that girls associated with this diner may have stolen a valuable item from her."

"And why would she think that?" Mama said.

"She heard the girls say 'Sweetings.' And even heard them call each other by name." The officer looked at his pad. "Georgia, Georgie...and Markie. The shop owner's name is Nettie Collins."

Aunt Essie pulled at her apron strings. "Owns Nettie's Market a few miles from here. Peanut Man didn't say anything about stopping in there before he took you to Hannah's. Did you three go in there with her?"

"Georgie? What do you know about any of this?" Mama said.

I was silent.

The officer spoke directly to Markie. "Would you happen to be Markie Jean? You fit the description rather closely."

"I'd be crazy to steal something. Not like I don't have a distinguishable appearance," she said.

"Respectfully, Officers, no one here is her legal guardian. You'll have to address her another time."

"Well, we're just following up, as a personal favor. She hasn't yet filed a formal complaint."

"You said it was valuable, but you didn't say what it was," Mama said.

"A bracelet. A genuine ruby bracelet, according to the owner," the officer said. A swoosh of wind hit me in the face and blew me back to that moment when Nettie opened that first aid kit that had that gun and the ruby bracelet. I shivered back into the moment only to find Nikki glaring at me. I stared at Markie. Markie was looking at her phone like we were all boring her and she had somewhere to be.

"Until a formal complaint is filed, Officers, let me show you out," Mama said, and she and Aunt Essie walked them to the door.

The huddle was quick. "Did either of you take it?" Nikki said.

"Of course not," I said.

Markie didn't say anything at all.

Mama stomped back toward us, casting a shadow like she was ten feet tall.

"Nikki, you stay here. Georgie and Markie Jean, let's go in the office right now and have a talk."

"Sorry," I mouthed to Nikki.

"Spill it, you two!" Mama said. Markie stayed quiet and so did I. Then Mama addressed me. "Georgie, the police were here. *The police.* I know the conversations we've had with you for sure. Markie Jean, I can tell that you know how serious this is. What if she files formal charges? Do you really want to deal with that? So I'm going to ask you both one more time: did either of you take that bracelet?"

I started singing like a caged bird. "I saw it in the box, but I didn't take it. Some kids came when we were leaving. Maybe they took it. We don't know. Maybe she didn't put the box away and someone stole it." Mama held up her hand and my lips clapped down on the next word I was about to say.

"Markie Jean, I'm going to ask you this, one time and one time only. With everything I have, I believe Georgie when she said she didn't take it. Now, I'm going to give you that same level of trust."

"Is it trust or is it guilt?"

Mama glanced up and squeezed her eyes shut for a second before answering. "Markie Jean, I can't say I don't deserve that. You have a ways to go to trust me, if you ever do. But if this store owner believes you or Georgie stole from her...this is a different kind of trouble.

"Markie Jean, I'm going to ask you one more time. Whatever you tell me will stand and we will proceed accordingly. Did you take that bracelet?"

Markie pursed her lips. She was gonna plead the Fifth. Everything was falling apart.

Lifting Markie's chin to face her, Mama said, "Tell me the truth, please." Mama found that gentleness that only she has.

Markie yanked her chin from Mama's hand. "I took it."

What she said dazed me.

Mama grabbed her purse. "Where is it?"

After a heavy sigh, Markie said, "Home. Where it belongs."

The office door opened and Aunt Essie peeked in. "Everything going okay?"

"I've got it handled, Auntie," Mama said. Then she said to Markie, "Let's go. I'm taking you to your guardian now. We'll get the bracelet and take it back to its owner."

As we were leaving the office, Markie said, "It's already back to its owner."

Mama hung her head. "What are you talking about? You just said it was home."

Markie stepped back some. "It's back with Aunt Vie. It's her bracelet. I'd know it anywhere. I took it from Nettie and gave it back to Aunt Vie."

"Markie Jean, I'm trying to be patient. But I need to make this right before it gets worse," Mama said.

Markie straightened the cuff on her rolled-up sleeve. Then she took a deep breath. "I had come to visit Aunt Vie a while ago. She wasn't working as many hours at the diner, and she wasn't even driving anymore. She wanted to go to town. So we just walked. It wasn't a big deal. On the way there, she wanted to stop at Goldie's Pawn Shop. I didn't know if she needed the money or not. I just didn't know."

Aunt Essie put both hands on her hips. "I remember Vie saying something about Goldie's, too. This was about two years ago."

"Aunt Vie told me not to say anything. How could I not do what she said? I had a feeling something odd was happening, but I was scared. I didn't want anyone to know. Then everything seemed okay with Aunt Vie. We went back to get it and it was gone."

"Markie Jean, I believe everything you're saying. But if Nettie bought it from Goldie's, it's her property now. We have to give it back."

Markie was turning her sneakers to the side. "But Aunt Vie didn't mean to sell it. I wasn't able to help her. It's my fault that it's gone. I wasn't even able to take care of her. I should have figured out what was happening." Then Markie faced Aunt Essie. "I should have told you we were walking into town. I tried to buy it back before he sold it. I tried," she said.

Aunt Essie came over and put her arm around Markie, which was the first time I'd seen her do that.

"Exactly where did you leave it?" Mama said.

"The last time I saw Aunt Vie, I slipped it into her pocket."

"So it's there?"

"Yes, ma'am."

"Let's get the bracelet and take it back to Nettie's. If she wants to sell it back, great; if not, hopefully we can just explain the situation and return it to her. And she won't ever file a formal complaint."

"Think she'll understand, Mama?" I said.

Mama hiked her purse on her shoulder. "There is only one way to find out."

I hadn't imagined—this time—that Markie was lying. That her elaborate tale about stealing the bracelet to return it to its rightful owner was nothing more than a masterfully told tale. But Mama and Grandma Sugar double searched all the pockets of Aunt Vie's housecoats for the bracelet that Markie said she'd returned. When they both turned up zilch, I had to consider the possibility.

"And you slid it right into the pocket of the housedress she had on the night Ms. Hannah was here," Mama said after the failed search.

"Yes, ma'am," Markie replied.

Grandma Sugar was involved, too. She and Peaches even looked around the yard.

"Well, I did what I said. If nobody believes me, what's new?"

"You stop that," Grandma Sugar said. "Aunt Essie wouldn't have you working at the diner if she didn't trust you."

"She only does it cause Aunt Vie asked her to."

"We both know that Aunt Essie don't do nothing she don't want to do."

Mama's shoulders drooped. "Let's go take another look."

"Can I go, too?" Markie said.

As Mama opened the screen door, I called in another wish. *Please, please, let Mama find that bracelet.*

When we got to Aunt Vie's room, she was watching TV and nodding.

"Hello, Auntie," but she didn't respond.

Markie was behind me, but she brushed past me and Mama and wrapped her arms around Aunt Vie.

"What's wrong, child? What's wrong, child?" she repeated.

But that's all Aunt Vie said. Markie straightened up and seemed to remember why we were up there.

Mama was searching the floor and rechecking the clothes Aunt Vie had recently worn.

"Did you check her hiding place?" Markie asked.

"I did," Mama said. "I knew it was a long shot, but Aunt Vie used to hide things under her mattress." I lifted it. Nothing.

As Mama straightened the mattress, Markie said, "There's another place," and tipped her head toward the walk-in closet. "Her favorite chef's coat. It's red. Ms. Hannah had it custom-made for her for Christmas one year. It's the one she had on in the picture, Georgie, remember? The one I showed you."

"I remember," I said.

Markie nodded.

Mama walked in the closet and found the red chef's coat in the rear and brought it out. It was in dry-cleaning plastic and neatly pressed.

When Mama held it up, Aunt Vie said, "Time to go to the diner?"

"Not right now, Aunt Vie," I said. "You're going to a talent show soon." She nodded.

Then Mama lifted up the plastic and plunged her hand into one deep pocket. *Please be there. Please be there.* Nothing. But when she reached her hand inside the second pocket, she closed her eyes.

I jumped. "It's there, Mama? Isn't it?"

Mama's eyes opened and her hand emerged with the sparkling bracelet.

I hadn't noticed that Grandma Sugar had come upstairs until her voice rang out, "I'll be. Looka there."

Mama held the bracelet in her hand.

"Told ya," Markie said. "That's her hiding place. She didn't want to lose it again. Ms. Hannah had that made because Aunt Vie liked pockets."

"Something else is in here," Mama said and reached in again and pulled out a necklace. Mama held it up.

I gasped. "Oooo. Half a heart. That's just like Ms. Hannah's, Mama. She should have it on," I said.

We all had our attention on Aunt Vie now.

"Aunt Vie is always fighting to let us know she's here," Mama said and looked at Grandma Sugar. "The girls and I need to go talk to Markie's guardian."

"Still?" Markie said.

"Sorry, Markie Jean, but we do," Mama said. "She's your

guardian and needs to know about something like this. And I'm sure she'd be happy to know we're returning it. What's her name?"

"Rosella," Markie mumbled. "Why people always think that everybody cares about everything when they don't?"

Mama didn't answer. Markie went over and squeezed Aunt Vie's hand. But she never took her eyes off *People's Court*.

My phone dinged. A text from Nikki. "Found it?" she texted.

"Yes. Taking it back."

"Cool. Get here soon. Talent is crazy good."

I just couldn't wait to put this behind us so Markie and I could jump back in the middle of things.

The ride to Markie's foster home was quick and quiet. Although Mama had found the bracelet, we were back to where we were before that, which wasn't the best place. Mama wanted Markie to sit up front with her. I don't know if she thought that Markie would make a run for it, but I didn't mind keeping an eye on her from the back seat. Bogalusa boomed with afternoon activities. I caught a glimpse of Scooter coming from the store. I almost expected Mama to honk like she knew him, too.

I was nervous thinking about how Rosella would respond to Mama stopping by, but to calm myself, I visualized McClurie Park. Nikki and the sibs were there. And Uncle Dean was building a stage. We'd made all that happen. When Mama pulled up to Rosella's, I just had to remember the good stuff as Mama knocked on her door.

"And who are you, the new caseworker? Where is the one we had just a few weeks ago?" Rosella said to Mama. Then she directed her questions to Markie, "Did you lose your key?" Markie shook her head.

"I'm not a caseworker. Markie Jean works down at Sweetings. It's my family's place. I'm Katrina," Mama said.

"*Katrina?* Humph. Would still be living my life in New Orleans if not for that nightmare. Trying to make my way back after all these years."

"It changed the lives of so many," Mama said. "You're Rosella, right?"

She nodded.

"Can I come in?" Mama said.

"Mind if we talk out here? I wasn't expecting company. Haven't had much help around here lately," she said.

"Markie Jean took something that didn't belong to her. I just wanted you to know that we've recovered it and are making things right."

"Okay, glad to hear it. So why the house call?"

"Just thought you'd want to know."

Rosella had a tiny nose ring that looked like a speck of gold glitter. "Markie. Unless you want to find yourself at some group home, don't take what doesn't belong to you," then she looked at Mama. "I haven't had any problems with her like that before. She's basically a good kid. Are we done here?"

Mama stepped back. "We are."

"In this house before dark, Markie. If not, you better call and let me know where you are," Rosella said.

Markie nodded but didn't speak. Maybe Rosella realized

how mean the threat of the group home was. If she said it in front of us, who knows how often she said it to Markie, who didn't react to it. But maybe Markie was crumbling on the inside.

As the door clicked, Mama squeezed her eyes shut and reopened them. "Let's go return the bracelet," Mama said.

Nettie's open light wasn't on when Mama eased up on the store. There was a car parked out front, which gave me some hope. "We're all getting out," Mama said. I'd already unbuckled my seat belt. Mama and I were out of the car before Markie made a move. We waited in front of the car as Markie finally eased out. As soon as she did, Mama opened the door. The store smelled like maple syrup.

"Nettie?" Mama asked.

"All day, every day. 'Bout to close but take your time. Never rush a visitor." She was stacking shelves with bird food. Then she looked at us. "So you two are back, huh?"

Mama set her purse on the counter, right next to the Koolickles and pickled pig lips. "Think we have something that belongs to you."

"What you got to say for yourselves?" she said after nodding to Mama.

Markie held her head up and spoke out like she does at the diner. "Georgie didn't have anything to do with it."

Mama bought us something to drink while Markie told Nettie what happened, starting all the way back to Goldie's Pawnshop. Afterward, Nettie and Mama worked out a price and Mama wrote her a check for the bracelet.

Nettie looked at us. "I knew you two were good kids.

Didn't know what was going on but knew it was something. Who'd take a bracelet and not snatch the cash? Had to be more than two hundred dollars in the box." She wagged her finger at Markie. "Main thing is that I wanted you to confess to it. I called in a favor from an officer friend of mine. I hope I scared you straight," she said and pointed to Markie. "You grabbed it quick as the dickens, though. Almost didn't see you."

Markie bugged her eyes. "You saw me?"

"I work with birds mostly," she said and laughed. "I got an eagle's eye."

"Just glad you gave her a chance," Mama said.

"If a small town can't give nothing else, it can give out chances," she said.

"Markie, do you have anything else to say?" Mama said.

"Sorry I stole the bracelet back. I'm happy that Aunt Vie gets to keep it, though."

"I am, too," Nettie said.

Thinking back to when Nikki and I rode with Peanut Man, I asked, "Are you a real zoologist?"

"Yep, first Black one around these parts. I'm an ornithologist who dabbles in entomology."

Markie rocked back on her heels. "That's the study of birds and insects."

Mama and I both looked at Markie like we couldn't believe she could have possibly known what it meant, then I thought about our conversation at the park. I may have shared my bird video with her, but she obviously knew way more about birds than I did.

"That's right. Impressive," Nettie said. Mama nodded. "You two stay out of trouble."

"We will," Markie and I said.

I eyed the store again. "Where's your parrot?"

"Back in her habitat for a while," Nettie said.

I opened my purse and pulled out a flier. I unfolded it and handed it to her.

"Can you please bring your parrot to our talent show?" I took a moment and told her the reason. "People would love to hear your parrot talk," I said.

"Sounds like a good cause. If I get back from New Orleans early enough tomorrow. We're there."

We all thanked her again. On our way out, Mama put her hands on both of our shoulders and Markie didn't shrug it away.

Nettie waved to us as we were leaving. Mama blew her horn and Markie and I both waved until she went back inside. I was just so happy that Nettie saw the good in us instead of the bad.

Soon as we were on our way home, I said, "Mama, please drop us back off at the park to meet up with Nikki and the rest of the kids. There's still tons to do."

If I knew Nikki, she was keeping things moving, but it was time the three of us were there, as Daddy would say, "dotting the i's and crossing the t's."

30

LIGHTS, CAMERA, ACTION

"Are you up?" Nikki asked the morning of the show. She'd slept in her pink satin hair bonnet this time. With the beige blanket wrapped around her, she looked like a strawberry ice cream cone.

"Yeah. Been up for an hour or two."

"Nerves?"

Last night, once we were ready for bed, I spent time practicing speaking to the crowd with Nikki as my audience. At one point, I went into the bathroom and practiced talking to the crowd in the mirror when I needed a break from Nikki's critiques. Didn't matter how much I practiced, I couldn't shake the emcee jitters.

"Yeah. Um. Do you think that we can cancel our dance? That way I can concentrate on running the show."

"Why not both? I know we haven't practiced much, but we can do that routine in our sleep."

"I want this to be perfect."

"You sound like Jada. She's working me harder than a coach. I thought I was a perfectionist. Sheesh. She's sorta zapping the fun out of it."

"What?! Didn't think you'd ever feel that way."

"Me neither. Her dad works construction in Mississippi. And the mom works at the mill. But both are trying to make it tomorrow. Flip is just as excited. It'll be the first time his dad sees his magic act. Flip said he was reading about the history of Black magicians and illusionists when I saw him in the library that day."

"Cool beans."

Nikki took off her cap and shook her braids a bit. "I know the show is all about raising money for Alzheimer's, but you are helping other people, too."

"We're both helping and need to get up and get going. Or 'rise and shine' like my stepdad likes to say."

"It's really happening today. Can you believe it?" Nikki said.

And that's when the excitement really kicked in and we grabbed each other and hopped around the room.

Nikki stopped jumping for a second. "When my parents hear about this *and* I hit them with all my new vocab, laptop is in the bag." We danced to celebrate.

There was a knock on the door and I expected it to fling open. Nikki and I glanced at each other.

"Come in," I said. The door opened and there stood Mama. Behind her was Markie.

She walked in and Mama closed the door.

"Figured since we had a lot to do, I'd get here early."

I got my notebook out to walk us all through a few things. After our meeting, Nikki and I would shower, eat, and the three of us would walk to the park. Then...*Lights, camera, action.*

Around ten o'clock, I stood next to the bleachers, stressing to one of the rappers, B. Lusa, that no performances could contain profanity. "We'd have to cut off the microphone," I emphasized. He told me he understood and I put a check-mark next to his name. I knew someone was behind me and thought it was another performer. When I turned around, it was my stepdad, Frank, and Mama. And behind both of them, with waist-length braids, was Tangie.

"Heard Bogalusa was the place to be," Tangie said.

I couldn't yet respond for hugging her. "I'm so happy to see you. And wow, look at your hair!" Tangie leaned forward and motioned for me to touch.

"A little long for my taste," Frank said. "But I hear it's the style." Frank strode up and gave me his light shoulder punch the way Daddy kisses me on the cheek—quick and unexpected.

I ran my hand along the ends of her hair that tickled my palm. "You look like that poster of Janet Jackson and Tupac in that poetry movie. Beautiful," I said.

"That's *Poetic Justice* and that movie is *way* older than me," Tangie said.

"Watch it now," Mama said and laughed. Frank laughed, too.

Tangie's braids were thick and got skinnier at the waist. "They're box braids. My bestie did them. Took about eight hours."

I touched my hair and wondered when I'd be able to choose whatever style I wanted. I loved my twists, but when I started middle school, it might be time for a change.

"Hey, Tangie and Mr. Frank," Nikki said, sweat rolling from her forehead.

"You've been working hard," Tangie said and put her arm around Nikki's shoulder.

"This show is going to be *lit*," Frank said, sounding a little like Daddy when he tries to use a cool word. He let his fingers beat on his air drum. "Let me go get my hands dirty," Frank said and hustled over to Uncle Dean. There was now a full stage in the middle of McClurie Park. Along with the stage, Uncle Dean and Peanut Man constructed benches that extended around the stage.

I dug my sandals in the dirt. "Nikki's moving to California."

"All right! A bestie that lives cross-country. How cool is that," Tangie said. "It doesn't seem so now, but it will." Jada called Nikki and she excused herself and left.

"Think you can do something for the show?" I said to Tangie.

"Yeah...watch. That's all you and your crew. I'll be cheering you on. You know your mama gives my dad the play-by-play and he's told me some of it. I'm proud of you, Georgie."

"Thank you," I said.

I didn't want to tell her how scared I was. When she hugged me, she said, "Do your best. That's all anyone can ever ask. We already see your heart in this."

Seconds later, Markie appeared. She said that Rosella had offered to braid her hair. And she'd outdid herself with a zigzag pattern and her Afro puff. Markie had on jeans and a crisp white blouse. And on her wrist was Aunt Vie's bracelet.

"Look what Ms. Essie let me wear for good luck," she said and held up her wrist.

"That's enough good luck for all of us," I said and introduced her to Tangie. Markie was the first to extend her hand for Tangie to shake.

That made me smile.

Hours flew by like minutes. At four in the afternoon the town started coming out. We'd designated a few Sweeting's regulars to watch the table where we'd set up the steel tubs marked "Donations." We were able to get hundreds of pamphlets about Alzheimer's from the Bogalusa Senior Center, including care of patients, as well as additional ways to help with the research. Pastor Douglass, from Aunt Vie and Aunt Essie's church, Mt. Caramel, stopped by with the donated microphones and amplifiers. Just the thought of a microphone made my palms sweat.

I gathered the major players for a meeting about an hour before the show: Nikki, Jada, Flip, Markie, and Latasha stood in a tight circle waiting for me to speak. "Thanks to each of you for helping make this happen." My voice was shaking and I already started to question how I'd speak in front of a few hundred people. "Today we all have a chance to do something we love to make someone we love proud of us. And to raise money for a disease that steals memories that people make. Anyone else want to say something?"

"Today, it's showtime," Nikki said.

"I feel in spirit that Aunt Vie knows what we're trying to do," I said.

"I believe it, too," Markie said.

I stuck my hand out and Markie's was the first one on top of mine, then Nikki's.

"We got this," I said, and all our hands reached toward the sky like we were throwing confetti.

"It's time," Mama said when the crowd swelled to about two hundred or more. When Frank handed me the microphone, I squeezed it so hard that my knuckles hurt. The local zydeco band volunteered to set up next to the stage so they could play in between acts. The leader of the band said that he'd known Aunt Vie since he was a boy. He gave me a thumbs-up.

Like Coach Jerilyn taught us, I took a deep breath and let my voice flow out like how Nikki would with a cheer. "Hello, Bogalusa! Thank you for coming out to our Bogalusa Talent Show Alzheimer's Fundraiser, also known as Bogalusa's Got Talent." What I didn't expect is applause after that. People were eager to cheer me on. And though a lot of the people were a blur due to my nerves, there was Nikki right in the front giving me her encouraging finger snaps.

"Perhaps every person here has been touched by the

kindness of my great-aunt Vie. And maybe we've all heard about Alzheimer's and didn't think there was a way to help. This talent show is our way." My voice cracked a little. "Take your time, baby," someone said. It didn't matter who it was. The words hugged me. I took another deep breath before continuing. "All the money we raise from the talent show today will go..." I looked around the crowd and there next to Mama was Aunt Vie. She had on her red chef's coat. "It will go to Alzheimer's research." The applause erupted again. And once they quieted, I heard, "That's my girl," from the corner of the stage and there was Daddy. I didn't know he was coming. Peaches had the best seat ever, on top of his shoulders.

He signaled if it was okay if they came closer. I nodded. When they approached, he kissed my cheek and spoke into the microphone. "As the proud father of these two young ladies, and someone who loves Aunt Vie, Matthews Motors will match what this talent show raises today."

My heart soared. Peaches waved to the crowd and people laughed and cheered. Everything was happening at a dizzying pace, but I knew I had to keep moving. I held on to the microphone like an anchor.

My feet puttered with excitement. "Thank you, Daddy...I mean, Mr. Matthews."

Another voice rang out, "I don't sell peanuts for nothing," Peanut Man said. "I'll match it, too."

Then Reverend Douglass called out, "Aunt Vie's church home will match."

I started jumping right there on the stage. The money was coming in. I just needed to make sure that the show earned it.

I was just about to speak again when the neigh of a horse drew the crowd's attention. Everyone turned toward the park's entrance. Ms. Hannah, holding on to Bessie's rhinestone-studded reins, walked toward the stage. But stopped. I was thankful for the cordless microphones. I signaled to the volunteer audio lady to get a microphone to Ms. Hannah. Static crackled before Ms. Hannah's voice was clear.

"I know most people in this town know the evils associated with the Guidry name. From talking to Aunt Vie's sisters, I've recognized that I haven't done enough to speak out against those evils and work to right what I can." Soon as she said that, a few people in the audience shouted, "Justice for O'Neal." Ms. Hannah continued. "As someone who dearly loves Vie, my first obligation is to support this fundraiser fight against Alzheimer's. At Spirit Farms, I rent out my stables to other horse owners. All I've earned over the past six months is in this satchel." She unhooked the satchel from Bessie. "Every penny is going to these efforts. And I'm offering rides on Bessie here to those who make donations today."

The applause was like a thunderstorm. I was so happy that Aunt Vie was there under the sound of Ms. Hannah's voice. Aunt Vie was clapping and there was nothing that could convince me that she didn't feel Ms. Hannah's presence.

"Whoa! Thank you, Ms. Hannah...and Bessie," I said. Kids were already circling around them. "Now, Bogalusa, let's get this show underway!" The microphone pulsated in my hands. "Our first act is going to amaze you. I hope you're ready for uh…amazement. Uhm. Without further ado. Here is the Magnificent Flip and his lovely assistant, Latasha." *Fantastic Flip*. Right before his music queued, I said the right name.

Jada fluffed the tulle of Latasha's skirt so she was spotlight ready. Latasha bowed as soon as she took the stage and her sequin leotard glistened. A lady stood up and started snapping pictures. The man next to her was still in work clothes and there were two bouquets of carnations next to him.

Flip had on his top hat and his long black cape with red satin lining. He swirled the cape before completing magic tricks like finding coins behind someone's ear and making smoke rise from his top hat.

His showstopper, that I didn't even know about, was when he pulled a real-life rabbit from his hat. If Nikki knew that was happening, she'd kept it a secret. The oohs and aahs from the crowd circled around like a gust of wind.

All throughout his performance, people were making their way to drop money into the bins. It was transformed from a talent show to a true festival. There was the mobile library setup letting kids check out books. The grown-ups had worked behind the scenes and got the city to bring out a few Porta Potties and put up temporary lighting in the park.

Markie bobbed over to me and said, "We're not even at the first act and we've raised more than five hundred dollars, not including Ms. Hannah's funds." The excitement in her voice matched mine.

Butterflies were swirling in my stomach. "Just want everything to continue to go well," I said.

As Flip and Latasha took their bows, I had to search my notepad to see what we'd scheduled next. My stomach felt like the inside of a washing machine as I walked back to the stage. With all the good news and a great turnout, I knew the jitters could take over anytime.

I waved to Daddy, who hustled over. Peaches was at his side now.

Our hug surrounded me with his favorite Drakkar scent. "Thanks for coming, Daddy. Is Millicent here, too?"

"She's at the diner. They're closing up and will be here in a bit."

"I'm excited to see her," I said as I searched the crowd again.

Peaches sparked up. "What about me? Can I do my poem now?"

"Sure you're up for it?" I said.

"Yep! I saw a girl on YouTube do it and she was just a baby."

As Flip and his family posed for pictures, the accordion, or as Aunt Essie calls it, "the squeeze box," and drums of the zydeco music entertained the crowd.

Mama saw us approach the stage and got her phone ready and so did Frank and Tangie.

"Thank you, Flip the Fantastic and his lovely assistant, Latasha...please give them some more applauds"—*ugh... you should have said another round of applause*—"Thanks to everyone who has donated so far. Are you having a good time?" I pointed the microphone toward the crowd like I'd seen singers do. "Everyone, I'm so pleased to introduce our next act. She is one of the people I love most in the world. Here is Patrice Ranee Matthews, aka my baby sister, Peaches. She's reading a poem by Useni Eugene Perkins, 'Hey Black Child.'"

I couldn't believe the confidence Peaches had when she let go of Daddy's hand and grabbed hold of the microphone. The best I can describe it was like the time we watched her zoom along the sidewalk after her training wheels were off.

With both hands on the microphone and her shoulders back, she said, "My grandma said that this was Aunt Vie's favorite poem and she'd want me to know it by heart." Then she closed her eyes.

"Hey Black child, do you know who you are…"

Even when the microphone squealed, Peaches didn't lose her nerve. The band had come in with a rhythm in sync with her words and I was glad Daddy was video-taping because Mama was mouthing words with her and forgot about pictures.

As soon as Peaches finished, I hugged her and said, "You were wonderful," then she took another bow and instead of leaving the stage, I held her hand and that gave me even more confidence. Tangie was in a quick huddle with Nikki and Jada as soon as they finished. Nikki pumped her right arm, which meant "let's do it."

"Hello again, let's keep things rolling. Next up is my best friend, Nikki, and one of my newest friends, Jada. They represent the Atlanta Bogalusa Connection. Let's hear it for the ABC Dancers."

"Go, Nikki, go!" Peaches shouted. Nikki and Jada were a cross between dancers and gymnasts, so much so that we decided to combine Jada's contortionist skills into their routine. Nikki and Jada had combined bounce and trap music, and you couldn't tell they hadn't been dancing together for years. All throughout their performance, I was prouder than I'd ever been of my best friend. Once they finished, sweat sparkled on their faces as they grabbed hands and took a bow.

The crowd was so fired up by the dancing and music that I let the deejay play a few more mixes before we changed the tempo. So many people were congratulating Nikki and Jada that I couldn't even get to them. I finally felt it was time to take the stage again. Now I was nervous for a different reason: it was time for me to announce Markie.

"Can you believe that those two didn't know each other a week ago? That's what can happen when you work together." I wanted to say something else, but ended it there. "To keep the show moving on..." *You used that already.* "Next up is a person who taught me more about confidence, honesty, and appreciating who I am and what I have. Here is Markie, singing 'I Believe.'" For this song, I wanted to sit out in the audience, so I took Markie's seat, which was next to Mama and Aunt Vie, and waited.

Markie stepped forth as the deejay started the music. Two bars into the song. The screeching of her voice made the audience giggle as if it was a gag. No one booed.

"Ahem. Can you start the music over, please? I'm a lot nervous, not a little....Oh...wait...I just need to say that this is dedicated to Aunt Vie. And I also want to say to Ms. Katrina and everyone that Georgie thought of this fundraiser on her own. I shouldn't have tried to take credit for it. Please give her another round of applause." The band added a little extra zing to her words.

Mama reached across and squeezed my hand. Aunt Vie seemed focused on something beyond the stage, and I had to remember that as long as she was comfortable with staying in this crowd, that was all we could truly hope for. Now, Markie gave the deejay a thumbs-up. Aunt Vie's bracelet glistened like fireflies circling her wrist.

I squeezed my eyes tight, like I was summoning every singing fairy godmother in the universe. It wasn't about her voice anymore but rather if she'd have courage enough to sing. Nikki sidled up next to me, kneeling on the ground. Jada was close by.

"C'mon, Markie, you got it. You got this!" I shouted as Nikki and Jada shouted out encouragement as well.

When the music started this time, Markie sang into the microphone, but the static of the speaker crackled. Markie dropped the microphone to her side and belted out a note that was maybe only a little less shrill than the one she sang to us that first time. Then she eased the microphone back in front of her, belting out a song from her heart because that's what she had to give. Maybe some giggled or snickered but the majority of us heard the love there.

"I believe in you and me" flowed out of Markie's lips. The tone was flat, the key was off, but the way she stood there and owned every note made the notes take flight. Her voice evened out and the crowd cheered. The way Aunt Vie perked up and focused on the stage it was as if it was the most beautiful sound she'd ever heard.

31

WE'RE HER MEMORIES

As we listened to Markie sing, the crowd was as quiet as they'd been all night. The notes were clearer and more melodic than we'd heard in practice but the crowd was still with her even when her voice cracked. But as the song went on, Markie's voice grew stronger.

"Sing, girl!" someone shouted. Two older women waved white handkerchiefs in the air. "Now that's love," one of them said. If anyone expected her to sound like Whitney, she didn't. But now I realized what she was telling me all along, she sounded like Markie and there was beauty and courage in each note.

Aunt Vie was next to me. Her knees shaking. Then I felt

the pressure of her hand against my knee as she attempted to stand. Mama supported one side and I had the other.

Markie saw her standing and left the stage and eased toward us. Markie took the microphone from in front of her and held it out to Aunt Vie. First, there was mumbling. And Markie's voice returned to the microphone. Aunt Vie was still standing. We were just there to steady her. And she reached toward Markie, who put the microphone back in front of her.

"When all the chips are down I will always be around." Aunt Vie's voice chugged along with Markie's. Everyone was on their feet adding their own off-key rendition. Phones popped up around us like umbrellas. The only one who wasn't crying was Aunt Vie. She sang another verse, then she reached out and touched Markie's face. I held my breath. "Thank you, Markie....Thank you, Georgie...on my mind."

"Mama, did you hear her? Did you?" Mama nodded, though I didn't know if she did or not. Aunt Vie squeezed my hand tighter.

Hoping that we'd have more time with her, I pleaded, "Keep singing, Markie. Keep singing, please, please." Markie didn't lose her flow but walked back on the stage. Now her voice was soaring. Aunt Vie wasn't even looking at the stage anymore. Mama's hand was on my back. It wasn't until that moment that I knew that those few seconds were all that we'd been waiting for forever this summer. And I didn't know, no one did, if it would ever happen again.

Most of our performances went off without a hitch. Although, we did have to cut the microphone off for a comedian who had been advised against profanity. Once the variety portion of our show was winding down, the Reverend Douglass stood onstage to say a few words.

"A few of us here were barely teens when we marched with the late A.Z. Young from Bogalusa to Baton Rouge demanding rights. Bob Hicks and Charles Sims and all of the Deacons for Defense risked their lives for young people because they knew then what we know now, young people move this country forward. Who's championing climate change, natural resource depletion? Young people. And who's marching through every city in this country, reminding the world that Black Lives Matter? Students. Young people. And right here, right now, a disease that robs us of what we hold dear—our memories, our independence—needs us to be proactive against it, fight back. God bless our youth. Enough from me. Georgie Matthews, please come back up and say a few words."

The microphone was something I welcomed in my hands now. Everyone quieted. "I just want to thank everyone again for coming out. I didn't really understand Alzheimer's before Aunt Vie. Maybe people think that Alzheimer's is an "old people's" disease, but it robs younger people of so much, too. It takes the stories and history that we need from our...our...elders. Thank you, Bogalusa, for all your help this evening in battling this disease. Thanks for all the money we've raised. And please keep supporting Sweetings."

"Bogalusa Got Talent. Bogalusa Got Talent," I heard repeated and there was Nettie and her parrot in the crowd. I waved.

As I wrapped up, there was Aunt Essie signaling that she wanted to speak. "Everyone, my great-aunt Essie," I said. Uncle Dean stood close to the stage, clapping.

"My sister, Elvie, is Sweetings." She glanced out to Grandma Sugar. "Elvie's the reason it's a landmark. We don't just serve food, we serve memories, comfort, peace of mind. A community is made up of people and their memories. Every meal we had together made this community stronger. Hurricane Katrina stole memories from Bogalusa and lives from Louisiana as a whole. And pray as we might, we can't get them back." She sniffled and cleared her throat. "Now Alzheimer's comes for us one by one and takes from us. But I'm renewed by these young people here this evening, with my great-niece Georgie leading the way, reminding us that we can fight back against anything that comes for us and those we love." The crowd applauded and cheered. "Before I go. I have a young lady who wants to come up and ask a favor."

The crowd was milling and watching the stage. I had no idea what was happening. And then Nikki popped up.

"I know it's getting late but could everyone give a bunch of applause for my best friend, our organizer, and our emcee, Georgie. . . .And, Georgie, could you do this just for me?" That's all she needed to say, and Tangie took the microphone as Nikki turned to the side and folded her arms. The momentum I felt grew with Beyoncé's "Run the World (Girls)" blaring through the speakers. I couldn't believe that after everything, we'd still have our moment together. I would have never thought to do it. To make it even more special, Mama, Millicent, Frank, and Daddy were all gathered around Aunt Vie.

Nikki and I didn't dance the best we ever had, but even she didn't care. I wasn't nervous and it was the most fun ever, especially when Peaches, Latasha, Jada, Tangie, and anyone who wanted to surround the stage joined us. As the music played and we danced on beat and off, there was no doubt we'd all remember that moment forever.

The next morning, Daddy and Millicent said goodbye before the big breakfast that Grandma Sugar, Aunt Essie, and Mama prepared so that they could head back to Atlanta. I didn't get to spend much time with Millicent, but I promised to make it up when I was back home.

Markie got permission to stay at Aunt Vie's that night, so we were all at the diner together, except for Tangie, who wanted to sleep in. After such a late night, Aunt Vie wasn't in the mood to come to the diner that early either.

Markie, Nikki, and I were sitting at the table and I looked over at Mama and Frank and thought about Nikki telling me that I was good at planning things. That gave me the courage to plan something else, something that I couldn't believe I hadn't thought of until that moment.

I excused myself from the table and marched over to them. They glanced up from their coffee cups, then Mama removed her purse from a chair so I could sit down.

"Our advisor at the Alzheimer Association is going to be so pleased."

"Is it really more than five thousand?" I asked.

"Closer to six," Mama said. "After I do the final tally, it's just a matter of putting the money in my account and wiring it."

I was so happy about the money we raised and the good

it would do. All the joy of last night rushed back to me in a second. But there was still something missing. I took a deep breath, then said, "When are we leaving...."

Mama raked her hair. "We were just talking about that. Now that Uncle Dean is back and Ms. Hannah will be more involved, and Aunt Essie has decided to bring on a full-time manager, I think we can go home in a couple days. I might come visit next month after you and Peaches get settled in school, but just to tie up a few things."

"Think Aunt Vie will go live out at Spirit Farms?" I said.

"From what I gathered last night, Ms. Hannah invited us all out there for dinner and Mama and Aunt Essie agreed."

"Wow...that's a big step," I said. Then I took a deep breath. "And what about Markie?" As soon as I mentioned her name, what was in my heart shot out my lips. "I don't want to leave her, Mama. I want her to come with us. If she doesn't have Aunt Vie to take care of her, she needs us. She won't say it. But she does."

Mama didn't speak. She dropped her head and sipped her coffee. When I saw her start to wring her hands, my heart dropped. "I don't think I can make this right."

Frank lifted Mama's chin. "It's about now, Katrina. Doing the best you can for her now." Then Frank turned to me. "You and your mama think a lot alike," Frank said and put his hands over Mama's to calm her.

"What does that mean?" I said.

"I thought about it long before we got here this summer, Georgie. But you and your courage and Markie in her determination help me know it was what Aunt Vie would have wanted, too."

Then Frank said, "I need to put my handyman skills to use and work on converting half of that den downstairs into another bedroom with its own bath?"

My hands clenched the edges of the chair. "For Markie?"

"Good guess. But, in fact, for Tangie," Frank said.

"We'd talked to her about giving Markie her room. And she'd have an even bigger room with her own bathroom downstairs." Frank chuckled. "That cinched it."

Mama sighed and looked up. "But this is us considering the possibilities. It's not that easy and it's not only our decision."

"It's Markie's, too." I said her name louder than I meant to. She and Peaches came over and Nikki was right behind them.

Mama nodded. "Yes, it's Markie's, too."

Markie kept a little distance and said, "What's going on? Did I do something?"

"Markie, come closer, please," Mama said.

At that moment I saw the sadness in Markie's eyes.

"I knew it was coming sooner or later. Y'all are leaving."

"We are planning to leave soon," Mama said.

Everything was happening so fast, but I wanted it to happen even faster. "That's not it," I said.

After taking a sip of her coffee, Mama said, "I'm so sorry I haven't paid attention to how much missing Aunt Vie was affecting you. I can't promise you we'll ever find Irene or that when we do, she'll want to be found. Same for your dad."

Mama didn't wring her hands, but she did clasp them in front of her like it gave her strength.

Then Mama looked at Markie. "I know this would be a major change for you, but Markie, would you consider coming home with us?"

Markie eyed Mama for a few seconds but didn't respond.

"Did you hear her, Markie? You can come with us. Wouldn't you like that?" I said.

Peaches, who had stopped sipping her orange juice, said, "You told me that you'll be sad when we leave. You just said it. Now you don't have to be sad."

"That means I could see both of you when I visit. That'll be cool," Nikki added.

Markie shoved her hand in her pocket. Then she took deep breaths. Her left foot tapped on the floor like it was pressing a brake. She pursed her lips for a few seconds.

Markie's glance shifted to me, then back to Mama. "To *Atlanta*?" Markie mumbled.

"Yes. Home with us in Atlanta," Mama said.

"But what if you change your mind? What if I make you mad...? What if you make me mad? Where would I go?"

"This lady won't change her mind. And if you do something you're not supposed to, you'll be on punishment like these two," Frank said. "I'm sure you will get mad at us, but there's plenty of space in the house for you to find some time to yourself until we can talk about it. And a huge backyard."

Peaches moved in closer like her words would be the clincher. "With a pool!" She said it with so much excitement we all chuckled, except for Markie.

"It's only a few weeks left of summer. I guess Jada or Flip could fill in for me here. They both are going to talk to Ms. Essie about working. But Rosella...she won't be too happy about it, at least not right now. She needs me to babysit a lot in the summer."

"Markie, we're talking about forever. We'll have to obtain guardianship first, but I've been looking into it. If you're open to it, we'd want to make it permanent."

I thought back to our conversation in the library. "A forever home, Markie, just like Simone Biles." I was ready to jump higher than the birds, but Markie didn't say anything. She just stared at us.

She nodded. "Oh...that's not what I thought was up. Not even close. Do I have to answer right now?"

"Of course not," Mama said.

Markie patted her pocket. "My phone. I think my phone is in the kitchen. I was supposed to check in with Rosella this morning."

"Sure, go ahead," Mama said.

She walked backward a few steps and then headed to the kitchen.

"Wait up!" I said, then waved to Nikki. "Let's go help her look." I walked shoulder to shoulder with Markie, Nikki followed.

Once we were behind the partition she said, "Thought I was going to take off, huh?"

"We have a little reason to believe that," Nikki said.

Markie sighed. "Atlanta is so big. I've seen it on TV. If my mom didn't keep me, why would your mom? I'm not perfect like you."

"Stop saying that. Nobody is and no moment has to be," I said. "You helped me see that."

Markie's expression didn't change. I didn't know what to say to her. Being a friend was all I could promise. Like I learned from the divorce, only time and actions made the hurt *hurt* a little less.

Before she grabbed her bag, I hugged her. When she pulled away, I held on. Just as I was about to let go, she hugged me back. Then she squeezed me tighter.

"I know Aunt Vie wants you and me to be friends forever. You have more memories of her you can share with us. And we're all making new ones every day. My mama made a big mistake and Aunt Vie stepped in and did what she could. But you and I both know, Markie, that Aunt Vie would want you with us. I know you feel that, too."

She didn't nod, didn't speak.

We stood next to each other. If she went out the door, I wouldn't try to stop her again. She stepped away from me and my heart fell down to my stomach. Right before she reached the door, she grabbed the backpack on the counter and hitched it on her shoulder.

"Atlanta, huh?" she said

I nodded. "Well, Snellville, actually."

She ran her hand along Aunt Vie's bracelet.

A moment later, the three of us walked back into the dining area. Everyone gathered around us.

"Can I really come live with y'all, Ms. Katrina?" Markie said.

"Do you want to, Markie?"

"Yes, ma'am."

Markie was as scared as we all were. As scared as Nikki with the fear of moving to an unfamiliar place. As scared as I am at the thought of my best friend moving thousands of miles away and my new school full of faces that I've never seen. As scared as Aunt Vie must have been when she couldn't remember the names of common items in her home, diner, and then of the people she's loved all her life.

We all walked back together to Aunt Vie's. That paper mill was just as stinky as ever and the heat was burrowing down like it was sure to reach well over one hundred degrees before noon. As we walked, talked, and laughed, no one complained.

The closer we got to the house, I couldn't wait for Markie to tell Aunt Vie that Mama had invited her to come stay with us like her mama had wanted her to years ago. But if that had happened there's a chance that Aunt Vie and Markie wouldn't have the bond they share. And maybe Peaches would have never come along. I'll never have the memories of Aunt Vie that Markie has and that's okay. I have the ones that we've created this summer and summers to come. Those will last forever, like memories should.

As the three of us walked to see Aunt Vie, I thought of how we worked together to fight that bully that snatches memories away. It didn't matter what the upcoming days would bring, I was certain, as certain as I'd ever been, that there was almost nothing that we couldn't do when we put our minds to it and gave it our best.

AUTHOR'S NOTE

To young readers and caretakers whose loved one is changing because of the effects of Alzheimer's disease, remember that their memory of you remains in their hearts. Thousands of young people share this sense of uncertainty and loss all over the world. Even though there is currently no cure for Alzheimer's, advances are being made. That is encouraging for all of us.

Like many, I have loved ones courageously fighting this battle. We continue to cherish memories and create more whenever possible. When I would sit with my grandmother, she'd ask me, "Do you hear the children singing?" Except for our breathing and her words, the room was quiet. But each time she asked, I said, "Yes." Later, I wrote about that moment and shared it, then others shared memories, too.

Ultimately, Alzheimer's will not win. Through each of us, our families' and friends' memories will last forever.

For more information and ways that you, your friends, your community, and your school can help combat Alzheimer's disease, please contact:

alz.org

usagainstalzheimers.org

ACKNOWLEDGMENTS

The publication of a second book is an answered prayer. It is a joy to share *Forever This Summer* with the world, especially with characters set in my fictionalized hometown, Bogalusa, Louisiana. I hope the town takes in stride any creative license I took. It is all out of love for my birthplace. Thanks to my cousin Debra Ann Sampson for her Bogalusa insights, and to the Sampson family, those living and the ancestors, especially my great-uncle McClurie Sampson Sr., whose legacy continues to be an inspiration. And my great-aunt Elvie, who I don't have many memories of, but her food was some of the best I've ever tasted. As a note, the names of real-life family members in *Forever This Summer* don't represent the actual person but my appreciation of the name and the spirit of it.

To say the least, 2020 was topsy-turvy. But my landing at Little, Brown for Young Readers was an unexpected blessing. I thank each member of my LBYR family for your support, especially my editor Liz Kossnar and her assistant, Hannah Milton. Special thanks to Victoria Stapleton, Christie Michel, Alvina Ling, Megan Tingley, and all those working behind the scenes. Thank you, John Rudolph, Dystel, Goderich & Bourret, for all your time and guidance. And I look forward to many future works with my agent Tanya McKinnon and Carol Taylor, editorial director, of McKinnon Literary Agency. And to the talented illustrator Vashti Harrison, thanks for your gorgeous artwork.

Love Like Sky's Acknowledgments thanks many friends and family members. Though I cannot reiterate all of their names, I hope each knows that my appreciation is forever, especially my aunts, uncles, and cousins. I'd be remiss if I didn't mention my cousin Dale Shepard, whose name I previously jumbled, and my cousin Wendell Harris, who I didn't mention. Both errors were mistakes of the head, not the heart.

There is rarely a week that I don't talk to at least two of the following confidants. Thank each of you for filling my life with laughter and love: Jerilyn P. Harris, Patricia Elder, Laverne Dutkowsy, Valerie McGrady Blake, Eric Hodge, Angela Ray, Niami Thompson, Erica McNealy, and Lily Shepard Carter. And a special thanks to my biggest social media cheerleader, Aunt Jeanette Thomas. And my parents, Winston and Daisy Raby, whose support is immeasurable, as well as my grandparents, who watch over us.

My siblings are treasures. Jerilyn P. Harris, Randall J. Raby, Winston Raby, and Isiah Raby, your love and support means everything. To our heavenly brother, Samuel C. Griffin, you are loved and missed every day. And so that they can know all their dreams are within reach, much love to my nieces and nephews: Nikkol and Khaylin Harris; Cameron, Isaiah, Leah, and David Raby; Daylan Raby; and Melody, Mia, and Malakai Walker.

Thanks to Tokeya C. Graham, who champions *Love Like Sky* and was one of the first readers of *Forever This Summer*; Ruth E. Thaler-Carter, for being a second pair of eyes on anything I send her way. Thanks to Andre Langston, David Bryant, and the Wake-Up Club of 103.9 WDKX for their ongoing support. WDKX was the music in my world before I was a writer. I appreciate We Need Diverse Books for assisting me and many other authors in time of need. Dr. Scot Brown, Marita Golden, Cathy Booker, Ciera Robinson, Linda Sue Park, Dr. Jewell Parker Rhodes, Terry Kennedy (UNC-Greensboro MFA Program), Angie Thomas, Paula Chase, Laura Pegram, Janice Rickerman, Curtis Rivers, Marva Gardner, Martha Bridges, Virginia Perkins, The Avenue Blackbox Theatre, Rochester Black Authors Expo, Women's Foundation of Genesee Valley, Rochester Area Children Writers and Illustrators, WXXI, #5amwritersclub, and Facebook Family for motivation and support.

Thanks and love to my friends and family in Atlanta, Georgia, throughout Texas, Florida, Mississippi, and Rochester, NY. And Zion Hill Missionary Baptist Church, who continues to keep us in prayer.

As always, special thanks to all the teachers, librarians, and readers who work selflessly to get books in the hands of young readers and encourage writers, myself included, to keep writing.

And to each young reader, thank you for reading my work. I look forward to hearing from you.

© Sarah Salvilla

LESLIE C. YOUNGBLOOD

received an MFA from the University of North Carolina at Greensboro. A former assistant professor of creative writing at Lincoln University in Missouri, she has lectured at Mississippi State University, UNC-Greensboro, and the University of Ghana at Legon. She's been awarded a host of writing honors, including a 2014 Yaddo's Elizabeth Ames Residency, the Lorian Hemingway Short Story Prize, a Hurston/Wright Fellowship, and the Room of Her Own Foundation's 2009 Orlando Short Story Prize. In 2010 she won the Go On Girl! Book Club Aspiring Writer Award. Born in Bogalusa, Louisiana, and raised in Rochester, she's fortunate to have a family of natural storytellers and a circle of supportive family and friends. She is the author of *Love Like Sky* and *Forever This Summer*.